JINX IN THE HINTERLANDS

JINX IN THE HINTERLANDS

ACADEMY OF NECESSARY MAGIC™ BOOK SIX

MARTHA CARR
MICHAEL ANDERLE

DISRUPTIVE IMAGINATION®

Copyright © 2021 LMBPN Publishing
Cover Art by Jake @ J Caleb Design
http://jcalebdesign.com / jcalebdesign@gmail.com
Cover copyright © LMBPN Publishing
A Michael Anderle Production

LMBPN Publishing
PMB 196, 2540 South Maryland Pkwy
Las Vegas, NV 89109

Version 1.02, August 2022
eBook ISBN: 978-1-64971-866-2
Print ISBN: 978-1-64971-867-9

THE JINX IN THE HINTERLANDS TEAM

JIT Readers
Dave Hicks
Zacc Pelter
Dorothy Lloyd
Diane L. Smith
James Dyer

If I missed anyone, please let me know!

Editor

Skyhunter Editing Team

From Martha

To everyone who still believes in magic and all the possibilities that holds.
To all the readers who make this entire ride so much fun.
To Louie, Jackie, and so many wonderful friends who remind me all the time of what really matters and how wonderful life can be in any given moment.

From Michael

To Family, Friends and
Those Who Love
To Read.
May We All Enjoy Grace
To Live The Life We Are
Called.

CHAPTER ONE

Amanda Coulier couldn't believe this was where she was spending her winter break. And not in a good way.

With a low growl, she finished shoving the heavy green metal cabinet across the greenhouse floor. The wheels shrieked and wobbled beneath the movement, threatening to spill the entire unit over if she wasn't careful with how she directed her anger. It didn't stop her from slapping the side of the cabinet in irritation, which let out a hollow *bong* and quivered under her hand.

She said I'd be ready to hunt monsters by Christmas. That was a week ago. How the hell does Caniss think looking after a few stupid plants is more important than catching that thing?

The shifter girl's mood had only worsened over break the closer she got to starting her second semester of junior year. Because of course, nobody from the Coalition or the Canissphere bothered to tell her anything at all while she waited forever, doing absolutely nothing.

She'd been checking her fancy lab-issued phone every single day. More than once.

"And here I am…" Amanda grunted as she lifted the trapdoor to her secret cellar beneath the Academy's very own greenhouse.

The lid jerked up and banged against the wall. "Babysitting some stupid freaking plants…" She stared down into the dirt-lined hole illuminated by the UV lights she'd rigged inside and puffed out a sigh. Then she hopped down into the cellar with a thump as her sneakers hit the packed dirt floor. "That they already got from me a month ago."

She took a moment to survey the contents of her greatest hiding spot since the greenhouse had more or less become hers freshman year. Her three Fatethistle plants glowed with internal purple light along one wall, where she'd had to smoosh them a lot closer to the wall and each other than she'd wanted. Because now the rest of the space was taken by the four other potted plants Dr. I-Know-Everything-And-You're-An-Idiot Caniss had instructed her to grow on her own time last Halloween.

Sticking her hands on her hips, Amanda glared at the potted Dreadhock, Feral Headhorn, Hangman's Ivy, and Pixie's Breath, all of them with apparently highly potent healing properties. Maybe only for shifters. Perhaps for magicals everywhere. She hadn't been able to find these specific plants in the *Magical's Guide to Magical Greenery*, and all she had to go on was Dr. Caniss' word.

Not like it means anything anyway at this point. All she does is boss people around. Grow the plants, Amanda. Figure it out, Amanda. Keep this giant secret from everyone you know because the consequences are too extreme, and we'll maybe call you to possibly be useful even though you can do more than most of my stupid shifter scientists put together, Amanda.

She rolled her eyes and kicked a loose pebble across the dirt floor, where it lodged beneath the pot of the Dreadhock. "Not my fault if they can't figure out their fancy magical-plant-science whatever isn't gonna heal Jenkins. The mermaid told me, anyway."

Technically, the not-mermaid housed in the Canissphere's underground lake had *shown* Amanda what was happening. Some weird cross-species telepathy that only worked when she ran around as her ghost-wolf instead of as a girl. Or a real wolf.

"They're wasting everyone's time. Especially mine." Amanda dropped to her knees in front of the potted plants to check the soil and the thin tubes of the timed irrigation system. She'd set it up with the leftovers from having done the same thing in the greenhouse's troughs above. Those were all school-sanctioned, of course. She couldn't even tell Principal Glasket or her teachers, let alone her friends, what she was doing down here in *her* private cellar for the oh-so-superior Coalition of Shifters.

Everything looked good so far, considering how quickly she'd grown these four plants in the first place.

Looks like Johnny's accelerant really does work on more than explosive bolt tips and Fatethistle plants.

A soft, quick knock on the greenhouse door ripped her away from her frustration and her focus on the plants.

Crap.

She lurched to her feet, thumped her head against the cellar's low ceiling, and growled as she clapped a hand to her now-throbbing head.

The knock came again.

Oh, come on. It's winter break, and I'm allowed to be in here whenever I want. Can't Glasket leave me alone for two weeks so I can grow secret and illegal plants in private?

She spun and hoisted herself halfway out of the hole.

"Coulier?" It wasn't Glasket. It was Jackson.

Heaving a sigh of relief and rolling her eyes, she pulled herself out of the cellar the rest of the way.

"Hey. I can hear you moving around in there, by the way," Jackson called again, his silhouette darkening against the frosted glass window in the greenhouse door. The doorknob jiggled, but of course, she'd locked it.

Amanda always had to keep it locked now.

"Be there in a sec." Dusting off the legs of her jeans, she kicked

3

the trapdoor back down into place with a heavy *thump*. Then she stomped around to the other side of the cabinet and shoved her weight against the thing to roll it with agonizing slowness back into place. The wheels rumbled and squealed with a shrill pitch that made her teeth hurt.

"What..." Jackson pressed his face to the frosted window and cupped his hands around his eyes, but even that wouldn't let him see anything inside the greenhouse. "What are you *doing* in there?"

"Gardening!" Huffing out a sigh, Amanda glanced at the underside of the cabinet to be sure she'd fully covered the trapdoor, then hurried across the greenhouse. When she unlocked the door and opened it, Jackson reeled backward and jerked his hands back down at his sides, his eyes wide and his lips peeled back in a mad grin. She snorted. "Who told you that face makes you look innocent?"

"What?" The wizard's expression remained unchanged.

"Well, I hope your face doesn't get stuck like that."

He blinked at her, then let out a self-conscious chuckle and rubbed the back of his neck. "You like my face?"

"Compared to the one where you look like you're about to murder everyone and laugh over their corpses? Yeah." She left the door open and turned, nodding for him to step into the greenhouse. "It's not like I couldn't see you trying to see through the window."

"Aw, come on, Coulier." Jackson jumped forward to hurry after her. "You can't blame me for wanting to know what you're doing in here. What was all that noise about, huh?"

"I told you." Amanda stopped at the workbench at the end of the center trough and flipped absently through the pages of *Magical's Guide to Magical Greenery* laid out on the wood. "Gardening. It's a greenhouse."

"So you're growing plants that sound like they weigh five hundred pounds?"

She smirked and barely shook her head. "I'm busy. You know, keeping everything from dying."

Wish I was busy hunting down the monster that stole the not-mermaids' power-cell thing instead.

"Sure, yeah. I get that." Jackson scuffed the soles of his shoes across the tile floors and shoved his hands into his pockets as he gazed around the greenhouse. "Looks like you got it handled."

"Yeah. Thanks." Amanda shot him a sidelong glance as he took two steps along the side of the first trough, then turned to head back toward her. "Did you, like, need something? Or…"

"Food." He shrugged. "Figured I'd come let you know we're all at dinner. Unless you're hiding some kinda feast in here. In which case, I'm totally down to help you get rid of the evidence."

"I don't keep food in the—wait." She looked sharply up at him. "You mean lunch."

"Nope." He popped his lips and gave her that goofy grin again. "Dinner."

"No… I just got here."

"No, you've been in here all day, Coulier. Or at least since you ran away from breakfast." Jackson narrowed his eyes. "You feeling okay?"

Amanda wished she had a watch right about now. The only thing on her to tell her the time was the insanely thin cell phone from Dr. Caniss, and it wasn't like she could casually pull that out to take a look.

Not like he doesn't already know it exists, but still.

"It's seriously dinner right now?"

"Seriously." Jackson glanced over his shoulder, then stepped closer. "You can tell me if something else is going on in here. I mean, hey, if you love growing plants so much that you're cool with skipping lunch and have no idea what time is, that's cool. But, you know…"

She stared at him. "But what?"

"You can tell me about the other stuff. If you want. No biggie."

His gaze circled the greenhouse, darted back toward her face, then repeated before he shrugged again.

Amanda drew a deep breath and nodded. "Thanks. I appreciate it. Really. But you saw how pissed-off Fiona was when she thought I was, like, spilling Coalition secrets to you behind the dorms."

"Uh-huh…"

"If anyone found out I actually *was* spilling secrets, I don't think that would go over very—" She jolted when the shifter-tech cell phone buzzed obnoxiously in her back pocket.

"Whoa." Jackson stepped back to look her up and down. "Yeah, you should totally come to get some food. You look like you're about to pass out."

"What?"

He whipped both hands up in surrender and chuckled. "Or attack me. Either way."

The phone kept buzzing, and she knew if she didn't answer it, they'd have a repeat of last semester with Fiona popping in to scream in her face whenever she wanted. Grimacing at the thought, Amanda pulled the phone from her back pocket, saw the unknown number on her screen, then glanced at the open greenhouse door. "Could you…"

"Totally." Jackson hurried across the room, and Amanda answered the call before lifting the phone to her ear.

The greenhouse door shut softly, and when she turned to make sure the coast was clear, she'd almost forgotten she was supposed to be answering an "important call."

Jackson nodded at her, dusted off his hands, then shot her two thumbs-up.

I meant could he close the door with him on the other side of it. Guess I'll be more specific next time.

"Amanda?" Rick's gruff, frustrated voice whipped her attention back to the nonexistent conversation.

"Sorry. Hey. What's up?" She turned her back to Jackson to at least *feel* like she had some privacy.

"You want the good news or the bad news first?"

"Uh…" Scrunching up her face, she tried to picture the huge, muscular shifter scientist who'd helped her set up for her telepathic chat with the not-mermaid giving her good news at all. Somehow, she couldn't imagine him smiling. "Bad news, I guess?"

"The antidote is a bust."

"What?"

Rick cleared his throat. "The medicinal combination of shifter-specific healing medicines and the alchemized essences of the plants you've been—"

"Yeah, yeah. I know what it is. I just… I mean, you guys sounded so sure about the whole thing. It didn't work?"

"No. Jenkins is still out."

Right. Of course, he was. Because it wasn't poisoning that Jenkins needed an antidote for to cure him magically. He'd been put under by the not-mermaids. Sleeping with their blood in his veins, or so she'd been told. Only the mutated mermaids could reverse something like that, and now Dr. Caniss' team of brainiacs was finally figuring out that they'd been wrong.

They would've been right if they'd believed me about it in the first place.

Despite the unfortunate predicament the unconscious Jenkins still found himself in, a small smile bloomed on Amanda's lips as she turned slowly around. "Okay. So let me guess. The good news is that we're finally going out to hunt the—hey!" She snapped her fingers in Jackson's direction, and he looked sharply up at her. "Don't touch that."

The wizard spread his arms and backed away from the trough, where he'd come this close to touching the Underweaver. "Why, does it bite or something?" he whispered.

She scowled at him and waved him farther away. "To hunt down the monster, right?"

Rick drew a deep breath on the other end of the line. "No."

"Seriously?"

"We have one more option, and that's why I'm calling you."

"Okay, I know you *think* there are options, but I saw everything super clearly when the—"

"There's a package on its way to you right now. New seeds. We need you to do the same for this species that you've done with the others. Accelerated timeline, understand?"

Amanda wrinkled her nose. "Yeah, but—"

"Within the next two weeks would be preferable. Faster than that, if you can."

"Faster than *two weeks*?" At her disbelieving screech, Jackson jumped and spun to face her with wide eyes. She ignored him. "Okay, first of all, I don't even know if what I used can *go* that fast. And second, I don't even—"

"You're the girl who cut the Fatethistle's maturation time from two years down to just a few months," Rick growled. "Don't try to convince us you can't do it. You'll figure out a way, and we'll be in touch. Happy New Year."

"Wait, you don't…" The line had already gone dead, and Amanda glared across the greenhouse. "Oh, boy."

"Everything okay?" Jackson shuffled forward as though he didn't know whether to approach and comfort her or get the hell out of there in case she exploded.

"Not really." Swallowing, she slipped the super-thin phone into her back pocket again and puffed out her cheeks with a noisy exhale. "This isn't at all what I thought it was gonna be."

"Working for the Coalition?"

"Yeah. They want me to grow another plant in record time. I have no idea how I'm supposed to do that in the first place, but I wouldn't have to if they'd listen to me."

Jackson nodded sagely. "Because they want you to grow the wrong one. I get it. You're smarter than pretty much everyone in our class, Coulier. You'd think a bunch of shifters would've figured that out by now too, right?"

She huffed out a laugh. "I'm not smarter than everyone in our class."

"I mean, you might as well be. You're smarter than *me*, anyway."

Shaking her head, Amanda checked over the rest of the plants she had to nurture and grow both for the Coalition and for the Academy's teachers to use in their classes. "It doesn't matter how smart I am. Everyone at the lab sees me as a kid, which automatically means they know more than me. Even when *I* was the one who had to go down into the lake and…"

"And what?" A sly smile broke across Jackson's lips. "A *lake*?"

"I can't talk about it. Sorry. Hey, I gotta make one more call, though. You should go to dinner with everyone else. I'll be there when I finish."

"Nah, I'm good."

Amanda scoffed and eyed him sideways. "It wasn't, like, a question."

"Wasn't, like, a command either. Right?"

"Not technically, I guess." She looked him up and down and couldn't hide a small smile.

What's he trying to pull with this? I hurt him during a stupid Bag the Bounty attack. He catches me on the Coalition phone, and now what? He's trying to be my partner in juvenile crime?

Jackson gave her a closed-lipped smile and stayed where he was.

"Okay, well, at least go watch the door. Let me know if anyone's coming."

"No one's coming, Coulier. You're in here all the time."

"Yeah, and I didn't expect *you* to knock on the door, so…" She nodded across the room, and with an exaggerated sigh, the wizard shuffled toward the door to play lookout.

9

Kinda nice to have some help, I guess. As long as he doesn't try to touch any more of my plants.

She quickly pulled her phone out again and dialed one of the very few phone numbers she knew by heart.

The line rang three times and picked up halfway through the fourth. "If you're tryin' to sell me somethin', I ain't interested."

Amanda snorted. "Hey…Johnny. It's me."

"Huh?" Something metallic clacked around through the line. Then the phone rustled like her guardian was smashing it up against something. "How the hell'd you change your number without me knowin' 'bout it?"

"No, this is my…other one." She eyed Jackson, who dutifully stood against the door and tried to squint through the frosted glass. He didn't know about the first phone she'd snuck onto campus as contraband.

"From the Coalition?"

"Yeah. I didn't have the other one with me."

Johnny sniffed. "You save my number in this one?"

"What? No. I needed—"

"Good. Make sure you delete the call history after this. I got nothin' against your new boss, kid, but I ain't fixin' to have my damn phone ringin' off the hook every time they need somethin'."

Amanda frowned. "Why would they call *you*?" When he didn't immediately reply, she could so easily imagine the blank stare that came over Johnny Walker's face anytime he realized someone else's point made more sense than his. "You know what? Never mind. I'll delete the call. I just…need a favor."

"Huh. Another one."

She rolled her eyes. "Yeah…"

"Can't give you an answer one way or the other if you don't tell me what for, kid."

"Right. Do you…" She grimaced and lowered her voice. "Do you have any more of that accelerant? By any chance?"

The line fell silent, then the bounty hunter's rare chuckle

filled her ear. "I already gave you more'n I wanted to part with when you came home for Thanksgivin'."

"I know. But I—"

"You tellin' me you used up that whole batch already? In a month."

She sighed and tried not to let her temper get the better of her. "I *had* to, Johnny. The Coalition needed this stuff to make their healing potion or whatever."

"Well, did it work?"

"Um…not really."

"Not—" He scoffed. "I tell you what, kid. You're blowin' through my stash faster'n the hounds go through an open pantry."

Amanda fought back a laugh at the image and tried to keep sounding remorseful. "I know, but I wouldn't ask if I didn't need it."

"More, you mean."

"Yeah, Johnny. I need more. So…can you help me out?"

He sniffed, cleared his throat, and the squeal of the cabin's screened-in porch door came before the telltale *clack* she'd come to know and love. "Nope."

"What? Why not?"

"'Cause I ain't got any, kid. Gave you the last of what I had."

"Oh. Okay." Amanda slowly paced along the ends of the troughs. "Well, can you get some more for me?"

Man. If anyone else heard this conversation, they'd probably think I'm on drugs or something. I swear if Jackson says anything about it…

"Naw. I ain't trekkin' on out to Marco Island to get you more of the stuff you ain't even supposed to know exists, by the way." Johnny snorted. "Much as I'd get a kick outta addin' to your tab, kid."

"Hey, I have no problem paying you back for it. I'll clean the airboat. Polish Margo. Whatever you want. I really need this, okay?"

"Someone's life on the line or somethin'?"

She rolled her eyes. "Yeah, actually. And they want me to get them this next ingredient for their antidote that probably won't even—"

"Then why the hell don't those scientist friends of yours ship their asses out here and get it their damn selves, huh?"

It took a minute for the answer to fully sink in, and Amanda almost burst out laughing. "Um… Probably because you're the only one with the connection. Like with pretty much everything else."

Johnny sighed, and the rough scratch of his fingers through his wiry beard made it all too easy to picture him doing that. "All right. I tell you what, kid. Here's the first lesson they ain't teachin' y'all in bounty-hunter school, so pay attention. You want a thing done; you gotta do it yourself. Cut out the middleman. That's me. So I'm gettin' you in touch with the guy who can get you what you need, and you take it from there."

"Really?" That was all it took to get her to perk up.

"Really. I'll text you his info. You handle the rest. And write it down or somethin', then make sure you—"

"Yeah, yeah, I know. I'll delete the text too."

He grunted. "Good. Don't do anythin' stupid, you hear me?"

"Me?" Amanda grinned. "Come on, Johnny…"

"Uh-huh. Y'all havin' a party up there tomorrow or what?"

"Probably. I don't know. Are you?"

"Party at my place?" Johnny snorted into the phone as the hounds bayed somewhere off in the distance. "I got the hounds and Lisa with me, kid. All the party I need. We'll just—"

"Okay, definitely TMI."

"What?"

"Nothing. Tell her I said hi. And thanks."

"For what?"

"The *contact*, Johnny."

"Aw, hell. Don't thank me yet, kid. And don't forget to delete—"

"Yep. I'll do it. I gotta go. Bye." Amanda ended the call with a quick stab at the screen and puffed out a sigh.

I do not need to hear about him and Lisa partying. Maybe it's a good thing I stayed here over break.

Jackson leaned away from the greenhouse door and gave her a sidelong glance. "Get it figured out?"

"Kinda." She buried the phone in her back pocket again and headed across the room. "When in doubt, call Johnny Walker, right?"

The wizard snorted. "You know, I still haven't met the guy, but somehow I get the feeling he wouldn't exactly be all that happy to get calls from a bunch of kids at bounty-hunter school."

Amanda opened the door and laughed. "It's a figure of speech, Jackson."

"Is it *really*? 'Cause I thought a figure of speech had to be, you know, commonly used by at least more than one person."

"Okay, well, maybe I'm starting a new one." She made a face at him, then locked up the greenhouse before joining him down the hall. The main building was completely silent and empty, especially with no teachers in their offices and no students bustling around until the semester officially started.

That silence made the ferocious growl ripping through Amanda's stomach that much louder. She and Jackson both stopped at the sound, and he looked her up and down before bursting out laughing. "Oh, *man*, Coulier! For a minute there, I thought we were about to be attacked or something."

She slapped a hand against her stomach. "We still might be."

"Okay, now I *really* hope there's still food left on the tables."

CHAPTER TWO

Unfortunately for both of them, by the time they made it to the outdoor cafeteria, dinner was almost over, and most of the food on the banquet tables had been picked clean. Not to mention it was cold now.

"Aw, *man...*" Jackson dragged his hands down both of his cheeks and groaned. "Why? Why does everyone have to be stuff their faces so much, huh?"

Amanda grabbed two paper plates and handed him one. "I did say you could go without me."

"Yeah, but that's beside the point, Coulier. I wanted to stay."

"Okay. Well, on the bright side, there's still *some* food left."

The wizard lifted the ladle out of the gravy dish beside the mashed potatoes. The cooled and now congealed slime of what was usually excellent gravy took forever to drip off the utensil before glopping back into the dish. Jackson stared at her. "Yeah. Some food, all right."

Trying not to laugh, Amanda piled the remains of the rotisserie chicken and green beans onto her plate, then scooped a pile of cold mashed potatoes as well but stayed away from the gravy. "What do those rolls feel like?"

He picked one up and instantly dropped it back into the nearly empty basket. "Rocks."

"Want some chicken?"

"No. Forget it. I won't even enjoy it now, anyway." Jackson turned with hunched shoulders and moped to the picnic table where the rest of their friends sat over the last of their meals.

All that talk about me *needing to eat, and he won't even touch perfectly good food. I guess somebody feels left out.*

When she finished plating what she could from dinner, she poured herself a glass of iced tea and headed toward her usual table.

"Wow. *Finally.*" Summer slapped the tabletop and grinned. "You decided to grace the lowlifes and peons with your superior presence, huh?"

"You know me." Amanda took a seat on the bench next to Grace and dropped her plate on the table. "I'm better than the rest of you, and we all know it."

Alex scoffed and shook his head, eyeing a dejected-looking Jackson.

"What took you so long?" Grace asked.

"The plants." Amanda ripped off a huge chunk of cold chicken between her teeth and stared at her plate.

And I can't even tell them how screwed I am if I can't get more accelerant from Johnny's contact. This sucks.

Summer nodded as though she understood what her friend was going through. "I get it, shifter girl. Those plants can be a real pain in the ass sometimes, right? I mean, you gotta feed each flower by hand, brush their spiny leaves, bathe them, read them a bedtime story... Super time-consuming."

Amanda chucked a stripped chicken bone at the witch, who ducked it with a laugh before flipping Amanda the bird.

"Gross." Grace failed at holding back a small laugh. "So you spent *all* day...what? Checking plants?"

"Yep." In went a forkful of green beans and Amanda still wouldn't have tasted them even if they were hot. "There are a *lot*."

"Come on." Summer downed the rest of her drink and slammed the plastic cup down on the table. "You didn't spend, like, ten hours in there playing magical gardener."

"No, I really did. I guess it's easy to lose track of time when I don't have anywhere else to be."

Like out there with a team hunting down the mutated monster we should've been looking for the second I told them what it looked like and where we'd most likely find it.

"Oh, we had somewhere else to be," Jackson grumbled and stabbed a finger down onto the table. "Right here. Eating."

Alex barked out a laugh. "Dude, is *that* what's wrong with you?"

The wizard looked up at his friend with a piercing glare.

"Damn, shifter girl." Summer snickered. "Looks like you got some competition in the 'bottomless pit for a stomach' category."

Amanda washed down her last bite and looked from one friend to the next. Alex and Summer shared a poorly concealed joking look, Grace stared blankly at Jackson, and the wizard folded his arms on the table before dropping his head onto them. "Um… I'm pretty sure the kitchen pixies won't mind making a little extra if you missed out on dinner."

"Missed out?" Grace wadded up her napkin and chucked it at Jackson's head. "Why would you tell her that?"

He whipped his head up and flinched away from the napkin tumbling to the ground. "I didn't."

"This guy." Alex pulled a spare cookie from the pocket of his sweatshirt and crunched it. "Amanda's got a real excuse, dude. Seeing as you're not a shifter, you should probably get checked for tapeworms."

"That's disgusting." Fully out of napkin projectiles to toss at the Wood Elf, Grace scowled at him instead and gestured toward Amanda. "One of us still eating."

"I don't have worms," Jackson muttered.

Amanda lowered her fork to her plate and looked around the circle of her friends. "I'm missing something."

"Ha!" Summer pointed at the wizard. "Yeah, like the giant plate of food he already ate before he booked it out of here like someone was trying to kill him."

The shifter girl's mouth fell open, and she stared at Jackson. His gaze roamed everywhere but at her. "And I even offered you some of my *chicken*."

He mumbled something none of them could hear.

Summer put a hand to her ear. "Sorry, what was that? Sounds like the shame mumble—"

"I wasn't gonna take your chicken, Coulier, okay?" Jackson spread his arms. "I wanted my own."

"Again," Alex clarified.

"Yeah, again! I swear, every year, it's like they're *trying* to feed us less and less. I could've gone back for seconds *and* thirds if I wanted."

"I'm super glad you didn't," Amanda said through a mouthful of mashed potatoes. "So there's that."

Alex and Summer burst out laughing. Grace shook her head and gathered up the trash on the table as the last few groups of students still sitting around the outdoor cafeteria made their way toward whatever else they had planned tonight.

Jackson gritted his teeth and looked like he would explode. Then he puffed out a sigh like a deflated balloon and hunched over his folded arms on the table again. "Maybe I should get checked for tapeworms."

"Stop!" Grace shouted.

Amanda almost spewed mashed potatoes all over the table but clapped her hand down over her mouth before it happened. Then she swallowed painfully and burst out laughing.

"Yeah, okay. Laugh all you want." Jackson pointed at her. "I'm gonna take you up on your offer now."

"Wait, for what?"

"Extra snacks."

"Hey, I didn't offer to get you extra food." She pointed her fork at him. "I said the pixies would probably be cool with it."

"So let's go, then. I mean, when you're done eating."

Amanda scooped up another bite and shot him a playful frown. "Go ask them yourself. They don't bite or anything."

Summer snickered. "Not *that* much, anyway."

The buzz of Amanda's Coalition phone going off in her pocket again almost made her leap up from the bench.

That better be Johnny. I don't think I can handle anything else from the Canissphere right now.

"You okay?" Grace leaned away from her and looked her up and down. "You look like you're gonna be sick."

"Yeah… Maybe." Clearing her throat, Amanda stood from the table and grabbed her cup and mostly eaten plate of food. "I think I'm gonna go lie down or something."

"See?" The blonde witch shot Alex a pert look. "Bad idea to talk about tapeworms when someone's eating."

"Aw, come on." Summer laughed and spread her arms. "You think *that's* gonna gross her out? When have you ever seen her get all squeamish about anything?"

Grace pointed at Amanda heading toward the trash can. "Just now."

"You okay, shifter girl?"

"Totally fine," Amanda called back, raising a hand toward her friends. "Nothing to do with the worms. I'm super tired. See you guys tomorrow." Then she jogged away from the outdoor cafeteria toward the girls' dorm building.

"Huh. Super tired." Summer raised an eyebrow at Jackson. "What were you guys doing in that greenhouse, exactly?"

The wizard straightened and stared back at her, his usual deep flush rising up the sides of his neck. "Talking."

"Right…"

"No, seriously. Just talking. I mean, maybe she's pissed that I almost touched some of the plants in there, but—"

"Dude." Alex shot him a crooked smile. "Did you seriously learn *nothing* from the whole 'too many people touching too many flowers' issue freshman year?"

"Yeah, you're one to talk." Jackson pointed at him. "Confessing your undying love by accident didn't stop you from drooling all over Zimmer every time you see her."

Grace clapped a hand to her mouth and let out a short, squeaking laugh.

Alex stared at the wizard without any expression whatsoever, then shrugged. "Maybe it changed."

"Uh-huh. Right." Summer socked him in the arm. "Keep telling yourself that, Woody."

He turned to look at her, and his gaze flickered up to her rainbow-dyed hair she hadn't changed since last semester. A tiny smile twitched in one corner of his mouth. "Who knows?"

"Okay, cut that shit out. It's creepy." She scoffed and looked at Jackson and Grace as she stuck a thumb out toward the Wood Elf beside her. "Can you believe this guy?"

"Um…" Grace pressed her lips together, her eyes wide.

"I know, right?" The rainbow-haired witch cleared her throat and stood to gather up her dinner trash. "I got shit to do. So have fun…doing whatever. Later, suckers."

She headed quickly toward the trashcan, dumped off her plate, and tossed the plastic cup into the bus bin, then stalked off toward the central field, flipping up the hood of her black hoodie before shoving her hands in its pockets.

Alex watched her until she disappeared around the corner of the kitchens.

Grace finally shut her mouth and grinned. "What was that?"

The Wood Elf shrugged. "She seems pretty normal to me."

"Uh-huh. But *you* don't."

Jackson frowned, spun on the bench to gawk at where

Summer had already vanished, then turned back toward his friends with wide eyes. "Oh. Oh, *shit*."

Grace pressed her lips together and looked back and forth between the guys.

"Whoa." He laughed and slapped his hands down on the table. "Dude, you're even more obvious than *I* am."

The blonde witch shook her head. "No. Definitely not."

"What? Oh, come on."

Alex snorted and stood from the table.

CHAPTER THREE

Amanda couldn't get to her dorm room fast enough. When she finally slammed the door shut behind her and leaned back against it, she felt safe enough to pull the Coalition cell phone from her pocket again.

It was, in fact, a text from Johnny with the name of his contact and a phone number. Below that, he'd added a final line.

Answers 24/7. DELETE THIS!

With a snort, she scribbled the number down on a piece of paper, then deleted the entire text as her guardian demanded. Then she puffed out a heavy sigh and dialed the number.

He better be right about the twenty-four-seven answering.

The line rang five times, then picked up with a *click.*

"Hello."

"Hi, is this—"

"Thank you for calling Wallace Fine Jewelers. You've reached us after our normal business hours. Please leave a message with your name and number, and we'll get back to you in twenty-four hours."

"Oh, come on." She rolled her eyes and only had a brief moment to consider whether leaving a message was a good idea before the beep at the end of the message filled her ear. "Um…hi. I'm calling for Wallace. Johnny gave me this number and said he answered all the time, but I guess that's not happening today. Johnny Walker, I mean."

Wow. Worst voicemail ever.

Amanda cleared her throat. "Anyway, I need some help with—"

Another click came over the line, followed by a quick rustle before a nasal voice asked, "Did I hear you say Johnny Walker?"

"Uh…hello?"

"Yes, you have an actual living being on the other end of the line. Who is this?"

"My name's Amanda. Are you Wallace?"

"This is my private number. Emergencies only. You'll have to come down to the shop to speak with our team in person."

"Wait. Sorry. I'm sorry." Amanda wrinkled her nose and shook her head. This already wasn't going well. "I can't come down to your store right now, but—"

"Well, why the hell not?"

"Because I'm at *school*."

Crap. That was the wrong thing to say.

Wallace paused on the other end of the line. "College, right?"

"High school."

"Great. Now I *know* something's wrong. Johnny Walker giving out my number to teenagers? Sorry, kid. Gotta have some kind of license to do business with me."

"I'm not some kid," she said, trying not to shout and until her voice crushed itself into a low growl. "I'm *his* kid. Johnny's…ward."

The guy paused for so long that she wondered if he'd hung up. Then he sucked in a sharp breath. "Johnny Walker's kid."

"Yeah."

"You the shifter girl?"

Amanda rolled her eyes. "Yeah."

"Well, why didn't you say so in the first place?" Wallace's voice was all happiness and cheer now. "Amanda, right? What can I do for you?"

"You'll help me now?"

"Of course. You're family!"

Forcing back a laugh, she paced across her room and sat on the bed. "Okay. Great. So you made Johnny some magical accelerant he uses on his weapons. Silver-white. Yellow, sometimes."

"Depending on whose magic is fueling it, yeah. Is that why you're calling?"

"Yes." A massive sigh of relief escaped her. "I need to get more of that for a...project. Johnny already knows and approves, so it's not like I'm doing anything in secret."

Mostly.

"Hey, no problem. He gave you my number, and I'm not in the habit of asking too many questions when that dwarf's involved. No problem selling to a high-school kid, either. As long as you can pay for it."

Crap. Money. There goes my entire allowance for the semester.

"Right." Amanda grimaced. "How much is it, exactly?"

"Twenty-five hundred."

"Dollars?"

Wallace chuckled. "I don't take payment in three-ring school binders."

"Okay, well, I don't need, like, a whole suitcase of them or anything. Just one vial the same size as what Johnny puts in those bolt-tips."

"Yep." The guy's amusement was clear in his voice. "Twenty-five hundred."

Amanda's gut turned over on itself. "For *one* tiny little...thing?"

"One tiny little thing packing a hell of a punch, girl."

Oh, man. I've used up like fifteen thousand dollars worth of Johnny's supplies. I'll be working it off at home for the rest of my life.

"Kid? You still there?"

"Yeah. I'm here."

"I can have that whipped up for you tonight to pick up tomorrow morning. At our main location in Everglades City, obviously. You do have a way to get down here, don't you?"

She puffed out a sigh, her shoulders slumping. "Probably. I just…didn't know it cost *that* much."

"Worth every penny. I promise."

"Yeah, I know."

Where the heck am I gonna get twenty-five hundred dollars? Johnny won't give it to me. He said to cut out the middleman…

"Hey, is there any chance you might be willing to, like, put this on a payment plan or something?"

"Sorry, kid. Call me back when you're ready. I'm not going anywhere." The guy hung up after that without giving her a chance to say anything else.

Great. I need all that money yesterday and no way to get it. Johnny's out. The Canissphere isn't gonna shell out that much for a single vial, especially when I didn't have to buy them last time.

Amanda scrolled through the laughably short list of numbers saved in her Coalition phone and stopped at Fiona Damascus' name.

Worth a shot.

She made the call, but the line rang endlessly, and her mentor still hadn't decided to set up a voicemail system. Fiona rarely answered phone calls anyway.

So now how was she supposed to get this done?

If I can't get that accelerant to grow the last stupid plant they don't actually need, they'll drop me just like that. I already know the Coalition doesn't mess around. Dr. Caniss especially.

With a frustrated growl, Amanda leapt from her bed and headed for the dresser to stow the Coalition phone in the bottom drawer beneath her duffel bag. The drawer slammed shut. She straightened fully and frowned at the plain brown package tied with white string and resting suspiciously on the top of the dresser.

She glanced around her room, which made her feel stupid and overly paranoid, then snatched up the package and slowly opened it. If the thing had been dangerous or deadly, she would have smelled something off about it. The string and brown paper fell to the floor as she pulled out a small wooden box that rattled when she gently wiggled it. A small sheet of paper came with instructions for how to grow the seeds, but it didn't even include a species name or any warning against what might or might not have been severely deadly magical qualities. Other than that, there was nothing else. Not even a note.

Apparently, someone had thought stamping the official letter-head of Dr. Melody Caniss on the bottom of the box would get the message across clearly enough.

Obviously, it did.

Rick said a package was on its way. That was ridiculously fast. How did it even get in my room?

After another curious glance around her room, Amanda buried the box of mystery seeds in her bottom drawer as well, then grabbed a towel, a fresh change of clothes, and her shower bag from the closet. She could wash the day off herself and come up with a plan at the same time. And she needed a plan.

She hurried into the hall, not bothering to make sure her door closed all the way because she was the only student who felt like being in the dorms right after dinner the night before New Year's Eve. And the other girls on this floor knew by now not to mess with the shifter girl's stuff.

The shower was marginally helpful. Amanda was clean, at least, when she stalked back toward her room, but the bright idea she'd been hoping for wasn't that much of an epiphany. More like a last resort.

She dropped her wet towel and shower bag in the corner of the closet, then grabbed her Coalition phone one more time.

Cut out the middleman. Thanks a lot, Johnny.

Before she could redial Wallace's number, the hairs on the back of her neck prickled with apprehension. Amanda straightened where she sat on the edge of the bed and looked slowly around. A few sniffs of the air pulled up nothing but her scent and the inherent new-concrete smell of a dorm building that was only two-and-a-half years old.

Feels like somebody's in here. I'm paranoid because I'm using this secret phone that would get me into even more trouble than using the one Johnny gave me.

She brushed off the weird feeling of being watched and made the call.

This time, Wallace picked up immediately. "That was fast."

"Yeah. Listen, I can't pay for the accelerant—"

"Then I can't sell it to you, kid. Sorry."

"Well, what if you...you know. Sent me a recipe."

Wallace snorted. "I'm the owner of a jewelry store and an alchemical technician, Amanda. Not a bakery."

"No, I mean to make the stuff on my own."

"You're kidding, right?"

Amanda wrinkled her nose. "I'm not. I need this stuff, okay? It's important. And I can pay you for it later, you know? Like, when I can get the money."

"You're asking a magician to give away his tricks for free. To a teenager."

This is going so badly...

Scanning her room for the source of whatever still made her feel like she was being watched and studied, she shifted on the bed and swallowed. "I can promise you a *lot* of sales for you in the future if you can help me out."

The guy hummed. "I'm not interested in taking a commission. Not when I have no idea how effective your product would be without supervising the production of it. It's too risky to—"

"Wait, no. No, I'm not trying to *sell* it." A laugh of disbelief escaped her. "I'm talking about *referrals*. I know a lot of magicals who will want to buy stuff like this directly from you. This would be for my personal use. I promise."

"Uh-huh. Personal use for a teenage kid."

"Please, Wallace."

"What kind of magicals are you running around with who you'd send to somebody like me?"

"Um…magicals like Johnny. Kinda. Listen, I have this internship, and I have no problem giving them your name and number so they can do business with you directly. After this one time."

Wallace paused. "What kind of internship?"

"At a hidden lab in the middle of the Rocky Mountains run by a bunch of shifter scientists who *definitely* can't do any magic, let alone alchemize it without somebody to handle it for them." Amanda bared her teeth in expectation as she waited for the guy to mull all this over.

That has to be good enough for him, right?

He sighed. "All right."

"Wait, really?"

"Yeah. But only because you're Johnny's kid." Wallace chuckled. "I'll send you the materials list and instructions. You know how to follow those at least, right?"

"Totally. Easy."

"Well, text me your email address, and you'll get what you need in the next few minutes."

"Thank you so much, Wallace. You have no idea how much this helps me out right now."

"Uh-huh. Wait 'til you see the list. Tell Johnny I said hi. Haven't seen him in a few months."

"I will. Again, thank you."

"Enjoy your night, Amanda. Nice talking to you."

When he hung up, he was a lot more polite about it this time and at least said goodbye.

Amanda heaved a massive sigh and flopped backward onto her bed. As she stared at the holes in the segmented ceiling panels above her, another laugh of disbelief burst from her lips. "That worked."

She spent the next ten minutes constantly refreshing her email inbox pulled up on her Coalition phone, then Wallace's email finally arrived. Trying not to break the ridiculously thin phone in her excitement, she stabbed open the email and read the short, terse-sounding content above the attached file.

Most alchemical supply shops will have these. You might have to get creative for a few. Use steel or glass appliances only. DO NOT mix ingredients in plastic.

When you have what you need, delete this email.

Amanda snorted.

Yeah, I get it. Johnny and his network don't like leaving paper trails. Even virtual ones. Fine.

She opened the attachment and found a list of seven alchemical reagents needed to create the accelerant, plus a list of appliances to make the stuff. Most things on the list she recognized from having taken five semesters of Alchemy with Mrs. Zimmer. The rest should have been easy enough to get if the supply stores had them.

Below the first list was a second with itemized prices for each ingredient.

All of Amanda's previously bubbling excitement deflated when she saw the total price tag tallied up so very conveniently at the bottom.

"Oh, come on," she snarled at her phone. "A thousand dollars to make it myself? *And* I'll have to buy equipment too, 'cause I'm not a freaking magical lab!" With an exasperated grunt, she tossed her phone onto the mattress beside her and closed her eyes. "Jeeze, it's probably cheaper to have Wallace make it in the first place."

A muffled snicker filled her room. At least, it sure *sounded* like someone was trying not to laugh at her.

Amanda pushed herself off her back and scanned her room with wide eyes.

Either the stress of wasting so much time with all this stupid work for Caniss made me totally insane, or there's someone—

The air shimmered right in front of her bed, and Summer Flannerty appeared out of thin air, grinning like a lunatic.

Amanda's immediate reaction wasn't to scramble away from the witch a foot in front of her but to lash out and shove Summer away instead. "Are you *kidding* me right now?"

Summer laughed. "Not even a little, shifter girl. Guess this means I finally mastered invisibility *and* getting rid of my smell."

"What are you doing in my room? How did you even get *in* here?"

With a shrug, Summer pointed at the door. "You left your door open. Anyone could've walked right in here and found all your secrets. You're lucky it was only me."

"Summer, you can't..." Frowning, Amanda leaned forward and sniffed the air between them. "Wow. You really did cover everything up."

"Thanks to Big Red and her big mouth, right? Baking soda saves the day."

Amanda shook her head and muttered, "It really does eliminate odors."

"Yeah, you know, they say that on the box, but I didn't think it would get rid of *everything*." Summer smirked. "You're gonna spend all semester on your toes, shifter girl. Because now you'll never know when I might be stepping up behind you, ready to pounce."

"Please. I still knew *someone* was watching me."

I'm not crazy. I guess that's one *good thing to take from this.*

"Right. Whatever you gotta tell yourself, shifter girl." Summer scoffed and plopped down on the edge of the bed beside her friend. "We both know how clueless you were. This is so awesome."

Taking a heavy breath, Amanda glanced at her phone and almost panicked over the need to hide it before realizing Summer had seen and heard everything since she'd come back from her shower. "You can't tell anyone about this. Not even Grace and the guys. Got it?"

"Sure. No problem." Summer turned her head and grinned. "Which is why *you're* gonna tell them."

"What? No. *You* weren't even supposed to be in here."

"I know, right? So cool. But listen, unless you got an extra couple g's floating around, and it didn't sound like you do, then you gotta tell them what's up. Or you can write this off as one epic fail for the shifter girl." The witch shrugged with an exaggerated grimace. "Doesn't look all that great on the shifter girl's perfect reputation, you know?"

"What perfect reputation?" Amanda snorted. "We both got detention freshman year. Both semesters."

"But you never hit a dead end, right? Not like this one anyway."

"Okay, thanks for the advice. Now please show yourself out so I can think about how I'm supposed to get all this done in the next two weeks. And no, I can't tell you exactly what *this* is. I can't tell anybody."

Summer stared at her, her eyes widening further by the second. "After everything, you still can't see *the* most obvious fix, can you?"

"What, do *you* have a few thousand dollars to spare?"

"Please." The witch thumped her chest, then spread her arms. "I'm way more valuable than cash, shifter girl."

"That doesn't explain why I have to tell you or our friends anything."

"Wow. You're seriously dumb right now." Summer jumped off the bed and spun. "You don't need *money*. You need a *team*."

"You sound like a lunatic."

The witch's harsh laughter filled the room. "Maybe. But it's still free, and *you* get to make whatever you're trying to make for...whatever reason. Win-win."

"For who?"

"You and me. We've done it before, right?"

Amanda shook her head. "I have no idea what you're talking about."

"I have to spell it out for you? Fine. We'll help you *steal* all the supplies, and you won't—"

"Summer, what's *wrong* with you?" Amanda leapt off the bed and hurried across the room toward her door. She opened it a crack to check the hall, but her shifter hearing didn't pick up the slightest sound on this floor—not even on the other two below them. The dorms were apparently still empty.

And if somebody had heard that, this would've been a whole lot harder.

She spun toward her friend and scowled. "You can't yell stuff like that in a dorm."

Summer folded her arms and waggled her eyebrows. "Nobody heard me, right? And you *know* this is the best way to get...whatever."

"Maybe." Swallowing thickly, Amanda scanned the carpeted floor and couldn't figure out a better option. That didn't mean it was a good one. "What's in it for you?"

"Are you kidding?" Summer laughed again. "I get to grab a bunch of off-limits crap without getting caught. And hey, maybe even watch a few explosions while you try to do what some random magical dude charges twenty-five hundred bucks to do himself."

"No explosions."

"I said *watch*. Relax, shifter girl. I thought this was important."

Amanda gritted her teeth and stared down her grinning friend.

She's right. This sucks.

"Then it's you and me. We don't need to tell anyone else. We can't."

"Stop fighting this and listen. We need a team. I can't grab all that shit on my own. I can't even say half the words on that list. If we're trying to pull off something as big as this, the two of us won't cut it. Trust me."

Despite how crazy it was that she was even considering this, Amanda huffed out a wry chuckle. "When we're talking about stealing alchemy supplies and *not* blowing things up, Summer, you can't blame me for not trusting you a hundred percent."

The witch shrugged. "Fair. But I know what I'm talking about. For real. Look, we have my perfected illusion, your list, a couple of bozo dudes who can shove all the supplies into a bag or whatever, and Blondie can…I don't know. Play lookout or something. You and I can't do all those things on our own and make it *fast*. I mean, unless you're super into taking our sweet time and getting caught before we can bag more than, like, two things—"

"Okay, fine. Fine." Rolling her eyes, Amanda gestured toward her door again. "I'll ask them."

"Excellent."

"If they say no because they probably will, I need to figure out a backup plan. And it won't be breaking into the supply rooms with just you and me."

"Nah, come on, shifter girl." Summer slapped the back of her hand against Amanda's shoulder. "When have we ever needed a backup plan?"

"Ha. Yeah. And how many times have we been caught?"

"We won't be. I got this. Just watch." Grinning again like she'd received some kind of award, Summer strutted toward the door and stopped. "Perks of staying at this stupid school all year, right? Thank God you have problems. I've been bored out of my *mind*."

"Oh, *I* have problems?"

Laughing, Summer whipped open the door and disappeared into the hall.

Amanda had to make sure the door was completely closed again this time before she let herself think about what she'd agreed to.

They were going to break into Zimmer's off-limits supply room to make a highly volatile magical accelerant so she could grow the Coalition of Shifters a useless plant in under two weeks. Only for Caniss and her team to realize how ineffective their medical attempts would be for Jenkins because he wasn't poisoned. The mutated mermaids were only holding him hostage until someone hunted down the monster with their power source.

Amanda would never get to *go* on that hunt at all like she'd been gearing up to do if she didn't do exactly what the shifter doctor ordered.

I do sound insane. Awesome. Guess that's part of the bounty-hunter training they don't give us here too, right? Find a way to make it work even if you have to break a few rules. Sure sounds like Johnny, all right.

CHAPTER FOUR

The next morning at breakfast, Amanda had no idea how she was supposed to start the conversation she wasn't supposed to have with the rest of her friends. It seriously affected her mood.

Summer took it as her cue.

"So." The rainbow-haired witch thumped her elbows onto the picnic table, propped her chin in her hands, and swept her gaze from Grace to Jackson to Alex. "You guys got plans tonight?"

Amanda stared at her plate and shoveled more eggs into her mouth. Then she'd have an excuse not to say anything.

Why does she have to bring this up now? They're gonna think I put her up to this.

Grace frowned at the other witch and tilted her head in suspicion. "I mean, it's New Year's Eve, so…"

"Oh, yeah? What happens on New Year's Eve, Blondie?"

Jackson grinned. "A party."

"Big one," Alex added, nodding as he crunched down on a strip of bacon.

"Kinda like the one you threw at the beginning of last semester." The wizard shot her a playful grimace. "Except, you know, with *more* fireworks."

"And less magical middle fingers thrown up in the air," Grace added.

"Unfortunately." Alex shrugged when Summer shot him a confused look.

After eyeing each of them again with a raised eyebrow, Summer smacked Amanda's arm. "See? Even better, shifter girl. Big party, big distraction."

"Wait a minute." Grace leaned forward and folded her arms on the table. "Distraction from *what*, exactly?"

"Yeah..." Jackson wagged a finger at them. "Sounds a lot like you guys are planning something."

Amanda swallowed another mouthful of eggs and for a moment thought they'd get stuck forever in her throat.

This is not *how I wanted to bring all this up.*

Her friends' gazes prickled her skin, and all she could do was wrinkle her nose.

"Seriously, Amanda." Grace lowered her voice, which was all business now. "If that's true, you guys better tell us right now what it is. You can't bring it up and not expect us to get suspicious."

Alex snorted. "If they weren't gonna tell us, Summer wouldn't have brought it up."

"Really?" The blonde witch scowled at him. "That's exactly the kind of thing she'd do."

"Aw, thanks, Blondie." Summer grinned.

"It wasn't a compliment." Despite her growing suspicion, Grace let out a short laugh anyway. "Of course, that's why you think it's a compliment."

"Yeah, you should know by now."

After playfully rolling her eyes at the other witch, Grace returned her attention to Amanda. "What's going on tonight?"

"Nothing yet," Amanda muttered, then buried her face in her cup of orange juice and drained the rest of it. Her stomach didn't agree with the treatment, and she grimaced.

Her friends all looked at each other, then Jackson spread his arms. "Come on, Coulier. You can tell us. I mean, hey, if we haven't spilled the beans on any of your secrets yet, it's not like we're gonna start now."

The look he gave her made Amanda think he knew exactly what this was about.

"Go on, shifter girl." Summer elbowed her in the ribs. "Say the thing."

"You brought this up the wrong way. You know that?"

"Yeah, well, *you* weren't gonna do it. Sitting here all mopey like you found out Santa Claus isn't real."

"You said *I* had to be the one to ask them."

"Yeah, and now you can." Summer gestured across the table at their friends. "They're all lined up and ready to go. I only warmed them up."

"Summer…"

"I'm serious. If you don't do it, *I* will—"

"Just tell us what the hell is going on!" Grace shouted.

The droning murmur of just under fifty students eating breakfast momentarily faded as everyone stopped talking to look at Grace Porter—the witch who didn't lose her calm, especially over breakfast.

Grace blinked furiously and ignored the stares aimed her way. Eventually, the conversation picked up again.

Amanda bit her lip. *At least it wasn't the whole school. Just all the other juniors and seniors living here 'cause they have nowhere else to go.*

"Hey!" Summer pointed at Tommy Brunsen, who'd stood and leaned forward over his picnic table with a wide grin, trying to figure out what the sudden outburst was all about. "None of your business, Clown Boy. Sit your ass down."

Tommy shot her a crooked smile and frowned. "Clown Boy?"

"Yeah, and now it's gonna stick. Move your creepy eyes somewhere else." Summer waved him away, but Tommy didn't sit until the other junior boys at his table laughed and started chanting, "Clown Boy."

"Don't worry, Blondie." Summer rolled her eyes. "They'll get over it."

"Fine. But *I* might not if one of you doesn't start talking." Grace raised her eyebrows at Amanda. "Like right now—"

"I need your help, okay?" Amanda finally blurted. "All of your help. That's what this is."

"Okay, but to do *what?*"

When the shifter girl glanced at Summer, she got nothing but a grin and an exaggerated sweep of the hand to keep talking.

This is gonna suck so much.

She drew a deep breath and puffed it all out again through loose lips. "Okay, look. I wasn't supposed to say anything about it, but this is pretty much my only option now. For real, you can't tell *anybody* else about it this. I wasn't supposed to tell anyone either. By order of the Coalition and all that."

"Wait, so how come Summer knows?" Grace asked.

"Because *Summer* snuck into my room last night and listened in on my conversation."

Alex snorted. "How'd she pull that off?"

Summer clicked her tongue and shot him the guns with both hands. "Baking soda illusion."

Jackson barked a laugh. "You finally went full-on insane, didn't you?"

"That's what *you* think—"

"Okay, stop." Grace glared at them. "Amanda's about to say something obviously important, and if you guys don't cut it out, I'm gonna have to shut you up myself. Got it?"

"Whoa." Jackson gave her a crooked smile. "I'm impressed."

"Yeah, me too, Blondie. Looks like I'm starting to rub off on you, huh?"

The blonde witch ignored them both and stared expectantly

at Amanda. "I guess now your options are to spill everything or watch me beat up our friends."

Amanda forced back a laugh and had to take a moment to recover from that surprise.

They have been spending more time together. So when is Grace gonna start rubbing off on Summer?

"Okay. Just…" Amanda glanced around at the other juniors and seniors, who'd all gone back to their meals like everything was normal again. "I could get into a lot of trouble if this gets out. Like, at all. Nobody can know you know."

"Not like we have anyone to tell," Alex muttered.

So Amanda laid it all out for them because she had to—why she'd been whisked away during the Halloween party last semester. About seeing the mutated mermaids at the Canissphere and talking to one of them, what the creature had told her, and what she had to do so they'd bring the unfortunate shifter scientist back out of his magically induced coma. Her skin prickled with growing anger when she told her friends about how little Dr. Caniss had trusted her when Amanda tried to explain a team of shifter scientists couldn't make an antidote for their colleague because it didn't work that way.

Then she finally got to the part about needing an extra dose or two of the magical accelerant, her call with Wallace, and why she was currently between a rock and a hard place despite having the entire list of ingredients and the necessary equipment to make the volatile concoction herself.

"I can show you guys the list," she finished. "I'm pretty sure all these things are here at the school. In Zimmer's storeroom—"

"You need a team." Alex nodded sagely. "Sure. Yeah. We'll help you steal it."

"Wait, what?"

"Yeah, *what?*" Grace peered past Jackson—who stared at Amanda with his mouth hanging open—and glared at the Wood Elf. "No, we won't."

Alex shrugged. "I'm in."

Summer laughed and pointed at him. "I knew there was a reason I liked you, Woody."

"You do?"

She blinked quickly, then leaned back and rolled her eyes. "Yeah. I mean, more than any of these other losers."

"She didn't say anything about *stealing*." Grace scoffed and shook her head. "You can't jump to conclusions like that."

"Grace." Amanda grimaced when the girl turned to look at her. "I'm kind of asking you guys to help me."

"Yeah, but you haven't told us what—"

"To break into Zimmer's storeroom and help me get these ingredients without getting caught."

Grace froze. "Are you crazy?"

"Probably, yeah. Look, I can't even tell Glasket about this. That was pretty clear when I left the lab, and she won't *give* me all this stuff without an explanation."

"Amanda—"

"I don't think you were listening, Blondie." Summer spread her arms. "There's a monster on the loose, and shifter girl over here won't be let off her leash to go bring it down until she gets this done. We do this, and we're basically heroes with her, okay?"

"I'm not a hero," Amanda muttered.

"Is that really what's going on?" Grace asked. "That everything gets hung up without this last plant you're supposed to grow in record time?"

The shifter girl swallowed and nodded. "Pretty much, yeah. Look, I'm not trying to lie to you guys, and I wouldn't have even brought it up if I had no other option."

Summer snorted. "Or if I hadn't been here to get the ball rolling."

Grace chewed on her bottom lip and stared at the table. "I don't know. Maybe you should at least *try* talking to Glasket about it first."

"If she says no, I'll still have to get those supplies. Then she'll know *exactly* who took them, and I'll be kicked out of here before I have a chance to explain."

"Yeah, good point."

"Oh, shit." Jackson straightened quickly in his seat, his eyes wide with realization. "We have to do this. Man, I didn't even *think* about it."

Everyone stared at him as he ruffled his shaggy blond hair and waited for the wizard to share his epiphany.

"Dude." Alex thumped him in the shoulder. "What're you—"

"It's the only thing we have now," Jackson added and looked straight up at Amanda. "So we'll do it, and you can call it a birthday present from all of us, okay?"

"Jackson, why would you volunteer us all to—" Grace stopped, her eyes growing wide, then shrank into herself when the realization hit her too. "Oh, no. Amanda, I'm so sorry. Your birthday was *yesterday*, and we completely missed it."

The tension racing through Amanda's muscles released all at once. "*That's* what you were so worried about? It's fine. Don't even worry about it."

"Why didn't you say anything?"

"Oh, I don't know, Grace. Probably because I got more phone calls from the Coalition with another impossible job that's still completely useless but has to get done anyway." Amanda shrugged. "I didn't even remember."

"You forgot your birthday." Jackson shook his head, then quickly leaned toward Grace. "We *have* to do it now."

The blonde witch rolled her eyes.

"Come on, Blondie." Summer grinned at her. "You know your clean little conscience won't let you sleep at night if you don't give your best shifter friend a giant birthday bash."

"I'm her only shifter friend," Amanda muttered.

"That makes you even *more* special, okay?" Summer snorted. "For real, Blondie. You can't say no to this."

"I definitely can." Grace licked her lips and looked way too nervous about the whole thing. "Especially if we don't have a plan."

"Oh, come on. You think we'd go into this without a plan?" Summer's smile faded when no one else around the table looked particularly convinced. "Okay, fine. Sometimes there isn't one. But this is different. I'm invisible."

Jackson looked her up and down and shook his head. "Nope."

"Just wait, Romeo." She grinned at him. "You'll never see me coming."

"Guys, I get it if you don't wanna help me," Amanda added. "I don't know if I'd wanna help me either if I were you. But Summer's illusion is really good. Like, obnoxiously good."

"Thank you very much."

"I have the entire list. Plus two weeks to grow this plant or get kicked out of the Coalition before I'm even officially a part of it, so…"

"I already said *I'm* in." Alex shrugged and shoveled more bacon into his mouth.

"Yeah. Me too." Jackson nodded. "I mean, we'll be missing the *entire* party tonight. That I was looking forward to."

"We'll make our own party, Romeo." Summer pointed at him. "Just wait."

"Grace?"

The blonde witch shook her head a fraction of an inch, then looked up at Amanda. "Well, I guess we can't technically get detention if we're not technically in school yet, right?"

"Hell yeah!" Summer pounded the table with both fists and stood to offer Grace a high five. "That's what I'm talking about!"

Grace leaned away and shook her head. "Don't do that."

"Why not? It's a present for our shifter girl and *your* debut appearance with the Delinquent Society!"

"Not if you keep talking about it like that," the blonde witch warned.

"It's not a *bad* thing—"

Amanda grabbed the back of Summer's hoodie, gave it a quick tug, and forced the witch back onto the bench beside her. "Don't push it."

Summer snickered. "This is gonna be awesome."

CHAPTER FIVE

It took them the entire day to come up with a plan that everyone could agree on. For the first time, Amanda realized how rare and cool it was to have so many different opposing personalities helping her out on this little extracurricular project.

Summer and Alex kept cracking jokes at each other that only they understood. Jackson was excited to do whatever Amanda said, and she had to stop making suggestions so he wouldn't try to implement all of them at once. Grace tried to keep them all on task despite how nervous she was.

"I can't believe this," Grace muttered as they finished going over the crudely drawn map and the steps they could finally all agree to as a group. "I'm sitting here *premeditating* this whole thing with you guys."

"We appreciate it," Summer said.

"Whatever. We should go over it one more time, so everyone knows what we're—"

"Forget it, Blondie. I'm starving." Summer stood from where they'd huddled over a notebook at the edge of the training field. "Dinner comes first. Then I'll see you suckers at the party." She grinned and spun away, hurrying toward the outdoor cafeteria.

"Dinner." Amanda nodded. "Sounds good to me."

"I could eat." Alex pushed himself to his feet and brushed loose grass off his sweatshirt. "A lot."

"Yeah, you don't have to tell me twice." Jackson thumped his friend in the shoulder, then they both took off after Summer. "This is gonna be epic."

"How?" Grace stared at Amanda. "How can they actually think about food right now? We're about to break at least four school rules that I know of. *Willingly.*"

"You should probably eat something too. You know, so do you don't pass out or anything while we're doing this."

The blonde witch scoffed. "I don't pass out."

"Still."

"Fine." Grace got to her feet steadily enough, but her face paled quite a bit as they headed for the outdoor cafeteria to eat dinner with the rest of the junior class and act like everything was perfectly normal.

Grace didn't do a very good job of hiding how ridiculously nervous she was, but no one else at the Academy of Necessary Magic cared. It was New Year's Eve. The other juniors and seniors who lived on campus year-round were way too excited about the party they were about to throw to pay attention to one witch looking like she was going to puke. Glasket and their teachers were almost as blinded by the celebration.

The kitchen pixies put out an incredible spread, going overboard because there were just shy of fifty students and less than a dozen staff and faculty to feed. Before most of them had finished eating their meal, Glasket got up to make an announcement in front of everyone who called the Academy home.

"This is weird," Amanda muttered. "Does she do this every New Year's?"

"Well, she *tries*," Jackson muttered.

"I know we're not officially in school for the spring semester yet," Glasket pronounced, "so I won't bother you today with any announcements I'll have to repeat to the entire student body next week when they arrive. However, I want to say a few things before you lose your minds and run out to the celebration."

Some of the kids snickered.

"I tend to pay attention to the small milestones along the way, of which this school has had many," the principal continued. "The one I'd like to pay particular attention to tonight is something I'm not sure will happen again during the history of this school. Unless, of course, they make the same choices for themselves next year during winter break."

"What the hell is she talking about?" Summer grumbled through the corner of her mouth. "Who cares about Glasket getting a little sentimental?"

Amanda shrugged, trying to ignore the growing pit in her stomach.

This announcement is gonna be either really stupid or totally the wrong thing to say right now. I can't even guess.

Glasket clapped her hands together and settled her gaze on the picnic table beneath the pavilion where Amanda sat with her friends. "You, upperclassmen, are the only original Academy students who remain here. As we celebrate the end of this last cycle to beckon in the new year, I'm pleased to say we have every single student from the Academy's first year with us for the celebration."

The outdoor cafeteria fell completely silent. None of the students could figure out what the heck she was talking about. Mr. Petrov snorted loudly and stuffed his mouth with more filet mignon.

Please don't. Please don't. Please don't.

Amanda slumped on the table bench, trying to make herself as small as possible. Summer folded her arms and stared the principal down, her nose and lips wrinkling further by the second into a disgusted snarl.

"Miss Flannerty and Miss Coulier are spending their first winter break here on the Academy grounds with us." Glasket grinned and gestured toward their table. "And maybe the last. So, with only this year's upperclassman on campus, let's give them a New Year's Eve party worth remembering, huh?"

Everything was so quiet, Amanda could clearly hear Petrov's rapid chewing from across the cafeteria. He was the only one who touched his food now. Then Evan leapt up from his seat, threw a fist in the air, and let out a warbling battle cry that made his voice break halfway through.

The cafeteria erupted into laughter, and some of the junior boys threw pieces of their dinner rolls at the kid.

Glasket smirked, then turned to return to the faculty table.

"Jesus Christ," Summer muttered.

"Let it blow over." Amanda stared at her plate. "It's not a big deal—"

"Are you kidding? If I don't do something about this right now, shifter girl, everyone's gonna *know* something's up."

"What kind of something?" Jackson asked, his lips lifted in a half-smile while the rest of his face looked like he'd have to run off to the bathroom at any second.

"Don't worry, guys. I got this."

"Wait. Summer—" Grace tried to grab the other witch's arm to hold her back, but Summer moved too quickly.

Amidst the laughter and excited cheering—plus a few tossed pieces of food scraps that hadn't quite turned into a full-on food fight—Summer stepped up onto the picnic bench and hoisted herself onto the table. Her combat boots knocked over Jackson's plastic cup, which was fortunately empty, and scattered the last of his brownies onto the surface.

"Oh, come on." The wizard reached for his desserts and

scowled when Alex snatched up the last one and popped it into his mouth.

"What is she doing?" Grace whispered. "Make her stop."

"You think *anyone* can make her stop?" Amanda leaned away from Summer's boots clomping past her across the table. "It's Summer."

Someone decided to chuck a piece of a roll at Summer, and she ducked it easily before pointing across the tables with a snicker. "I saw that, Bread Boy. I'll take care of you later. You all heard the witch running this place! Party for me and the shifter girl!"

More laughter and flung food came Summer's way.

"What are you *doing*?" Amanda hissed.

The rainbow-haired witch ignored her and spread her arms. "Don't wanna disappoint the principal so we *all* get detention first thing, right? So let's make this place *lit*!"

The cheer that rose up from the junior and senior classes was so wild and abrupt, Amanda started and almost fell backward off the bench.

Glasket stood immediately and shouted, "Within reason, everybody! This does *not* give you permission to break campus rules, winter break or not."

Summer strutted back and forth across the table, flapping her arms in rhythm to the chant now rising from the upperclassmen.

"Let's get lit! Let's get lit! Let's get lit!"

"Oh my God." Grace buried her face in her hands, then immediately whipped it back up again. "What does that even *mean*?"

Jackson laughed. "It means Glasket and the teachers are gonna be pulling double-duty now trying to make sure nobody sneaks any booze into the school."

Grace groaned. "They all think they're throwing a party for Amanda and Summer. How are we supposed to...you know. *Do the thing*?"

Amanda shook her head and stared at Summer living it up as

she walked across the picnic table, and the faculty didn't instruct her to get down. "Maybe it's time for a Plan B? Just in case."

"We spent all *day* yesterday on Plan A," Grace griped.

Alex slapped the table and stood. "Anyone want more brownies?"

The girls didn't say a word. Jackson nodded. "Yeah, dude. One for me and one for *mine* that you ate."

"Anyone? No? Cool." The Wood Elf took off toward the banquet table.

"Dude! What the—" With a growl, Jackson leapt to his feet and headed after his friend. "Don't even think about taking all of them. Hey!"

Laughing and chanting, the upperclassmen started to filter away from their tables to throw trash away and dump dishes in the bus tubs. With a wild grin, Summer hopped back down onto the bench, then spun and sat. "There. I'd call that one hell of a success."

"Are you kidding?" Grace gaped at her. "It was bad enough Glasket called everyone's attention to both of you. Now you made yourself the center of the party."

"Relax, Blondie. I gave 'em a little…" The rainbow-haired witch barked out a laugh. "A little something extra. Not bad for my first school pep rally, huh?"

"Except everyone's gonna be watching us and wanting to make this *our* party instead of ignoring us like we wanted," Amanda added. "Our whole plan is—"

"Okay, fine. How 'bout this, huh?" Summer flung her arm around Amanda's shoulder and jostled her. "I promise it's better this way. But if I'm wrong about this, I'll let Blondie take a free shot."

"Of what?" Grace asked.

"My face."

"Wait, why does *Grace* get to hit you if you ruin the plan for *my*…" Amanda cleared her throat. "You know."

"Because it's only fair, shifter girl." With a harsh clap on Amanda's back, Summer stood again, this time on the ground. "You've knocked me around plenty of times. It means more to Blondie anyway. See you at the party."

She passed Alex and Jackson on their way back to the table and snatched a brownie from the stack of them piled on the wizard's plate. "Nice."

"What the hell?" Jackson stared at the missing top to his brownie pyramid, his entire body growing rigid. "Does anybody know how to get their own food anymore?"

"That was pretty cool," Alex said through a mouthful of dessert.

"Yeah. Totally cool." Grace rolled her eyes. "We're screwed."

Amanda eyed the other upperclassmen racing out of the outdoor cafeteria toward the central field. No one paid any attention to Summer. The idea of going nuts for New Year's Eve had them too riled up.

"Maybe she's onto something, though."

"She's onto something, all right." Grace folded her arms. "Ruining your internship. And letting a mutated monster run free all over the world because the idiots who want you to grow this plant are gonna sack you *when we fail.*"

"Wow. You really are on board with this, aren't you?"

"Of course I am." Grace stood and snatched up her dishes. "I wouldn't have agreed to do this with you if I wasn't."

"See you at the party," Alex called after her.

The blonde witch shook her head and stormed away.

"I think it could work." Jackson stuck a brownie in his mouth. "Everybody's already freaking out."

"Yeah, it might. As long as nobody tries to make us give a speech or something." Amanda snorted, then turned toward the wizard and eyed his plate of brownies. "You gonna eat *all* of those?"

He froze halfway through chewing, then fixed her with a pleading gaze. "Aw, fine. Go ahead."

"Thanks." Grinning, she snatched up two brownies, then hurried away from the table. "Don't forget the plan, guys. We're still doing this."

"All in!" Alex called after her, then reached for Jackson's desserts.

"Hey, screw you!" The wizard jerked his plate away and slid farther down the bench before shielding his brownies in a circle of both arms. "I'm making a stand right here."

"More like a sit-in, but okay." With a shrug, Alex returned to the rest of his food and watched the beginning of the chaos before the Academy's New Year's Eve party.

CHAPTER SIX

The faculty hadn't quite gone all-out with this much smaller celebration the way they usually did for Halloween or the school dances, but the setup in the central field that night was still pretty impressive. Surprisingly enough, the music didn't suck.

Amanda and her friends had to make an appearance at the party. That way, no matter what happened, at least they'd have almost fifty alibis. The party itself wasn't exactly a bore, so the first hour they'd agreed to stay there and mingle went by much faster than any of them expected.

When it felt like the right time to make a break for it, Amanda found Grace at the refreshments table, staring at the giant punch bowl filled with HardPull. The witch looked like she was at a funeral instead of a party on school grounds.

"You okay?"

"No." Grace sighed heavily. "I haven't been okay since you brought this up yesterday."

"Hey, if you don't wanna do it, I guess we—"

"And let *all* of you get busted and maybe even kicked out? No. I might be uptight, but I'm not an asshole."

Amanda forced back a laugh and nodded. "No, you're not. Thanks."

"No thank you's 'til it's over."

"Okay." The shifter girl gave her friend a gentle nudge. "For that to happen, we have to get started. So..."

"Right now?" Grace stared longingly at the bowl of HardPull. "This better still be here when we finish."

"If it's not, I'll buy you a whole case next time we hit the kemana, okay? Come on." Amanda had to draw the other girl away from the refreshments table so they could head across the field toward the girls' dorm.

They passed Summer, who did some kind of head-banging move to the music with a group of kids.

"Hey, we should get Summer," Grace started.

"She'll be there. Trust me."

"Oh, yeah. I trust *you*. Not her."

"It's fine, Grace. Just act normal, okay?" Amanda regretted saying it the second it left her mouth.

The blonde witch tugged her arm out of the other girl's gentle grasp and scoffed. "I *am* normal. Maybe the only normal magical at this entire school, okay?"

"Sorry."

"It's fine." Grace drew a deep breath as they walked quickly across the grass, trying to steel herself. For a moment, she looked completely composed until she squeaked. "Oh my God, I'm so freaking nervous."

"*You* don't have to do anything, okay? At least until we have everything we need. Just watch the hall."

"Yeah. Yeah, I know."

They rounded the back of the girls' dorm and waited. Less than thirty seconds later, shadows moved across the grass from the far corner of the boys' dorm building. Grace squeaked again and pressed herself flat against the wall behind them. "Shit. Somebody found us."

"Um…yeah." Amanda patted her friend's shoulder and tried so hard not to laugh. "Because they're supposed to, remember?"

Jackson and Alex came into view, partially illuminated by the starlight once they rounded the other side of the boys' dorm. Even from where the girls stood, it wasn't hard at all to see how weirdly the guys were walking toward them—waddling with their arms folded awkwardly across their chests.

"What's wrong with you two?" Amanda asked.

Jackson peered around the corner of the girls' dorm and shook his head. "You have no idea how hard it is to make it look like you're *not* hiding something under your shirt."

Alex lifted his shirt and pulled out one of the huge canvas sacks Nurse Aiken used to store infirmary supplies and chucked it on the ground. "And super itchy."

"Are you serious right now?" Grace gaped at them.

"You said hide the bags…"

"Not under your *shirts*. You guys look like idiots. You were supposed to shrink them."

"We tried." Alex shrugged. "I think there's some kind of enchantment that makes it—"

Grace pointed at the sack on the ground, and a snaking line of lime-green light burst from her finger. The sack flashed once, then slowly shrank until it was the size of a washcloth. "There's no enchantment. Did you guys even *look* at the spell I told you about?"

The boys stare at her with wide eyes.

"Uh…Jackson?" Amanda eyed his bulging stomach, and the wizard jumped before jerking another huge sack out from under his shirt.

"Yep." He tossed it on the ground. Grace shrank that too, then she waited for the guys to pick up the stolen and shrunken sacks.

When they did, she gave them each a disapproving once-over, then stormed off toward the back of the boys' dorm.

"I hope this doesn't, like, affect what's supposed to happen on the inside," Jackson muttered, staring at the tiny cloth in his hand.

"Just the size." Amanda nodded after the witch. "Everything should go back to normal when she blows those up again."

"Oh, so now she's taking *our* job?" Alex asked though he didn't look remotely disappointed.

"Well, when she's the only one who can do the spell, then yeah. Come on." She peered around the corner of the building to check for any straggling students before heading quickly across the grass after Grace.

The guys followed, and Jackson leaned toward Alex to whisper harshly, "Dude, you said you knew the spell."

"I do."

"So why didn't you *do* it? Now they think we've never stolen anything before."

The Wood Elf shot glanced sidelong at his friend. "I thought I could do it. Didn't work. And you *haven't* stolen anything before."

"Whatever, man. That's not the point."

They all stopped again behind the boys' dorm, then crossed the biggest gap in buildings between this one and the main building housing all their classrooms, the storerooms, and Glasket's office on the top floor. If any of the other upperclassmen partying it up on the central field had bothered to look out across the grounds between the buildings, they would have seen little more than four dark, blurry silhouettes creeping across the grass.

Nobody looked. A new song came on, and the other kids exploded into wild cheers.

Amanda and her friends stopped at the back door of the main building's west wing and had nothing left to do but wait.

The quick, nonsensical lyrics of the echoing song reached them, and Jackson snickered. "I can't believe Glasket agreed to play that again."

"Wait, is that…" Grace cocked her head. "Is that Pete rapping?"

"Yep."

"Huh. I thought he would've gotten better by now."

The guys cracked up, snorting and grunting in an attempt to keep quiet.

Grace shoved them both away. "Get it together, already. Weird laughter that sounds like you're choking on something *definitely* counts as a suspicious noise."

"What do *you* know about rap?" Alex asked.

"Oh my God." Grace headed toward Amanda, who stood directly in front of the back door on her tiptoes, trying to see into the dark hallway beyond. "She's coming, right?"

"Probably."

"Yeah, that answer doesn't make me feel any better."

"It's fine, Grace." Amanda thought she saw a flicker of movement at the end of the hall, which would have been seriously bad news for them. Nothing else moved again, and she figured it was a trick of the light or a reflection in the window. "She'll be here."

"She was *head-banging* when we left the field…"

"And we're gonna keep waiting."

Alex and Jackson passed the next five minutes doing some head-banging of their own and whipping out the most ridiculous dance moves in hushed, strained silence, even when they burst out laughing at each other again. Grace kept peering around the corner of the building and growling in impatience. Amanda folded her arms and leaned back against the outer wall beside the door. "She'll be here."

"So what's taking her so long? I wouldn't be surprised if she decided the party was way more fun than this. Nothing at stake for *her*, is there?"

"Nothing really at stake for any of you guys, either." Amanda shrugged. "It was her idea."

"That doesn't mean anything."

"Grace, I know Summer has her own…thing going on. But she's never broken a promise."

"Not yet."

Amanda bit her lip to keep from laughing. "I hope you're able to see her a little differently after this all works out. She's not that bad—"

"I know she's not," the witch hissed. "I actually like her sometimes. I just… I feel like I'm gonna puke."

"Gross." Jackson pointed at the grass behind the building. "Do it over there."

"Shut up. I'm not really—"

A soft *click* came from the back door, and they all froze. The doorknob turned with agonizing slowness. Then the door followed suit. Amanda and her friends stared at the slowly widening door and the darkened hallway inside—and nothing else.

"Creepy," Jackson muttered.

"Summer?" Grace peered into the hall. "That's you, right? Please tell me that's you."

There was no reply whatsoever.

Amanda rolled her eyes. "It's her. Come on."

She stepped into the hall, smirking as the hairs on the back of her neck prickled. Definitely creepy. Especially because she could *feel* Summer watching her, but the witch was obviously taking her role in this seriously.

Jackson and Alex looked at each other, then headed wordlessly through the door.

"Got the baggies," the wizard whispered, dangling the shrunken sack from his fingers and gazing around. "Seriously, where the hell is she? It's creeping me out."

"Guys," Grace whispered harshly outside, still refusing to step through the doorway. "Guys, what if it's not her?"

"It's her," Amanda said. "She's messing with you."

"Why would she do that?" the witch muttered under her breath. "Why? This is already the most nerve-wracking thing I've ever done in my life." She walked through the door anyway with jerky steps. As soon as she cleared the doorway, it slammed shut with a startling *bang*. Grace jumped and squeaked before clapping a hand to her mouth. Then she slowly stepped forward, gazing all around the dark hallway. "Summer? Seriously, where are you—"

"Right here!"

Grace screamed. Amanda and the guys whirled around to see the blonde witch scrambling backward along the wall. Then Summer's wild cackle echoed around them.

"Oh, *man*. You should've seen your face, Blondie! This isn't even a haunted house!"

"Right in my ear? *Right* in my ear? Are you insane?"

"I'm having a little fun." A little thump without a visible body joined Summer's laughter, and one of Grace's shoulders jerked down under the weight. "You're way too uptight."

"And *you* are the definition of the worst magical to teach that illusion to," Grace hissed.

"Probably. But I'm the only one who mastered it. So there's *that…*"

Huffing out startled, angry breaths, Grace forcefully brushed off her shoulder and turned to follow the others down the hall.

"Okay." Amanda stopped in front of the storeroom full of Zimmer's alchemy supplies. "This is it."

"I know where she keeps the good stuff, shifter girl."

Amanda stepped back with absolutely no clue where Summer actually was.

"Wait." Jackson headed toward them. "If the front door was open, why didn't we—" He smacked face-first against an invisible wall, stumbled sideways to try getting away, and whipped a hand up to his nose. "What was—"

"Quit standing on me, man," Summer growled. Then the wizard reeled and staggered backward, hunching over like he'd gotten blasted in the gut by a heavy-duty weapon.

"Come on!" His back thumped against the opposite wall of the hallway, and he immediately realized his loud outburst before lowering his voice again. "I can't even *see* you."

"That's the point." The rustle of fabric filled the hall, followed by the *clink* of thin metal pieces. The door handle to the storeroom jiggled slightly.

Alex stared vacantly at the wizard and snickered.

"Anyway." Jackson jerked his shirt down and pulled himself back together. "If the front door was already unlocked, why didn't we come in that way?"

"It wasn't," Summer muttered.

"Oh, really?" Grace folded her arms and stared at where she guessed the other witch was standing. "Are you trying to tell us you know *another* high-level spell that works against Glasket's security and locks on the door?"

"Nope." A flash of orange light came from the doorknob, followed by a gentle patter of silver liquid spilling out of the keyhole and onto the hallway floor.

Jackson wrinkled his nose. "Ew."

The air in front of the door shimmered as the knob turned and the door opened. Then Summer's illusion broke away, and she stood there with a black case in one hand, a lockpick and an empty potions vial in the other, and a crazed grin. "I have *these*."

Grace's staring mark had been off by three feet, and she immediately turned to face Summer where she stood. "You have lockpicks. Why am I not surprised?"

"What's the goo?" Alex asked, staring at the silver puddle on the floor.

"Pretty cool, huh?" Summer pushed open the storeroom door and walked backward into the room. "Got it off a guy at the kemana. Doesn't do anything for physical locks, but he said it works on alarm wards. You have to use them both at the same time, though."

"Let me guess." Grace folded her arms. "You didn't buy that stuff from an actual store owner selling *legal* magical things."

"Hey, this is great, Blondie. It's like you know me or something."

Amanda bumped her shoulder against Grace's, which was as much of a distraction as she could come up with at the moment. "Nothing we're doing right now is, like... You know, *approved.*"

"I know. But she didn't buy that anti-alarm potion yesterday after we came up with our plan. She already had it."

All Amanda could do was shrug and follow Summer into the storeroom. "Which is why she's good to keep around, right?"

"Oh, jeeze." The blonde witch stepped aside to let Jackson and Alex pass. "Wait, guys. Hold on."

"What?"

She pointed at their tiny cloth bags again and reversed the spell until the heavy and already enchanted items had returned to their normal size.

"Hey, check it out." Jackson lifted his with both hands and shook it. "Me and my giant sack."

Alex snorted and walked into the storeroom. "You wish."

"Yeah, because—hey. Dude, what's *that* supposed to mean?"

"Okay, seriously, be quiet." Grace stepped into the middle of the hall and nervously eyed the opposite end. Everything was still dark and without any sign of someone else in the building. "Otherwise, I won't be able to hear *if someone's coming.*"

"Just keep an eye out, Blondie." Summer gazed around the room. "We got this."

"How about some light in here, huh?"

The witch spun toward Jackson with wide eyes. "Wait, wait. Don't—"

A brilliant burst of light came from overhead, and Summer immediately crouched, staring up at the ceiling. Then the white light flickered and dimmed as the floating orb shrank to half its size and illuminated enough for them to read the labels on Zimmer's pristinely organized and labeled drawers.

Jackson grinned. "What?"

Summer scowled and pointed at him. "Play me like that again, Romeo, and your ass is mine."

"I wouldn't turn on the light. Zimmer probably has another alarm on those or could find my fingerprints or something. I'm not stupid."

"No, you're an idiot."

He laughed at her attitude and kept his finger raised toward the illumination orb overhead.

"Nice work with the lights," Amanda told him.

"Right? Took me forever, but I think I got it."

"Okay, shifter girl. We're in, so pull out the list."

CHAPTER SEVEN

With four of them searching for the needed ingredients and equipment at the same time instead of only Amanda and Summer —or just Amanda as she'd first assumed—the work went a lot faster than anyone expected.

Jackson directed his floating orb of light anywhere someone asked for it and even found some of the more hidden items before anyone else. It didn't come as a surprise to anyone that Summer knew exactly where to find most of the alchemy reagents most commonly used for explosive combinations. To keep any of them from breaking their necks by trying to climb the already precarious shelves built around all four walls, Alex's mastery over his Wood Elf magic came in particularly useful for grabbing what they needed from the highest shelves.

As he finished retrieving one such piece of equipment—a giant cylinder the size of a microscope but definitely not with the same purpose—Jackson held open one of Nurse Aiken's enchanted storage bags and grinned. "Dude. You finally found a use for those things that doesn't include kicking my ass."

The glowing vines Alex had snuck through the one window in the storeroom creaked and groaned as they carried the piece of equipment down from the top shelf. The huge cylinder settled into the bag with a flash of muted silver light and a soft *clink*. "Not nearly as fun, though."

As soon as the vines were free, they snaked out to brush against Jackson's cheek. The wizard leapt away from the bag and spread his arms. "Come on."

"I think that's it." Amanda studied the list from Wallace. "I think we got everything."

"Yeah, better make sure, though." Summer snuck a glance through the open door. "Blondie's gonna have an aneurysm if we have to come back."

Out in the hall, Grace's foot tapped nervously against the tile floors, and she sucked in quick breaths before blowing them slowly out again.

Amanda grimaced. "No, I think we're good."

"Then let's get the hell outta here." Summer pointed at the open storage bags as she passed the guys. "Don't break anything."

"That's why we grabbed these." Jackson tried to pick up his bag by the handles, surprised when it wouldn't budge. So he tugged again. "Throw it over a cliff, and whatever's inside still wouldn't move around or get broken."

Alex squatted beside his bag with the handles hooked over his shoulder and heaved the whole thing up to rest on his back as he hunched forward. Despite the bag being full of glass jars and vials and all kinds of breakable alchemy-ware, it didn't make a sound. "Looks like yours is enchanted not to move, dude."

"What? No. They're the same freaking bag." The wizard pulled on his handles again and still couldn't lift it off the ground. "Okay, come on. This isn't the freaking sword in the stone."

"I got it." Amanda stepped up behind him, pulled out the key to the greenhouse, and handed it over with a nod. "Go open up so we don't take forever hiding this stuff, okay?"

He snorted but took the key. "Listen, Coulier. I know you're strong and everything, but there's something up with that—"

She hauled the bag up over her shoulder like Alex had and rested it against her back. "It's gonna be pretty awkward if I get there before you."

"Damn." Jackson stared at her, then snapped himself out of it and leapt out of the storeroom. As he moved quickly down the hall toward the greenhouse, he turned the key over and over in his hands and muttered, "Okay, I get the shifter thing, but how is the *Wood Elf* stronger than me?"

Amanda stifled a laugh and hauled the second bag into the hall. Grace looked frantically over her shoulder and waved everyone toward the greenhouse. "Go, go, go."

Summer pulled the door shut and messed around with her lockpick again. "Why? Someone coming?"

"Not yet, but I do *not* want to get caught standing here with two stolen bags of stolen things and all of you guys looking incredibly guilty."

Summer snorted. "Well, we are..."

"Go."

Amanda hurried after her friends, and when Summer finished all their work with Zimmer's storeroom, Grace scurried after them, turning around every few steps to check over her shoulder.

By the time they reached the greenhouse, Jackson had already unlocked the door and now held it open for them. "Hey, check it out. Phase One complete, right?"

"Wouldn't have been if we didn't have a shifter to carry that other bag," Alex muttered.

"Without the *shifter*," Amanda said as she swung the heavy bag off her shoulder and dropped it as gently as possible on the floor, "none of us would have to do this in the first place. Which I still really appreciate, by the way."

"What's not to appreciate, shifter girl?" Summer flicked on the lights, making everyone grimace and blink rapidly beneath the sudden glare. "We freaking did it."

"It's not over until Amanda has her magical…whatever." Grace pulled the door shut behind her. "There's still that part."

"Hey, Blondie." Summer stuck her thumb out toward the door. "Want me to take your place now and play super-paranoid lookout who may be the worst spy on the planet?"

"I'm not *trying* to be a spy."

Jackson nudged Alex in the shoulder. "Yeah, or she would've gone to spy school instead."

They both snickered, and Grace fixed them with a warning glare.

"We don't need a lookout." Amanda headed toward the green metal cabinet along the righthand wall. "I'm the only one with a key."

"Probably not," Grace said. "Glasket wouldn't let you have the whole greenhouse without a backup key. Like, what if something awful happened in here and someone had to get inside?"

"You mean like if a bunch of kids broke into Zimmer's supplies and stole at least a thousand dollars worth of ingredients to make a secret potion for the Coalition of Shifters? Like that?" Amanda pushed the seriously heavy cabinet across the floor with a shriek from the rusty wheels and the thunderous rumble of so much weight moving a few feet on the floor. When she finished, she dusted off her hands and frowned. "I don't even think it's a real potion. Just don't have a better word for it."

"Jesus," Jackson whispered. "You on some kinda steroids or something?"

"What?"

Grace socked him in the arm. "What kind of question is that?"

"I don't know." He let out a nervous laugh and spread his arms, smiling sheepishly. "I mean, I get that she's strong, but she picked up that bag like it was nothing, and now she's shoving heavy-ass cabinets all over the place."

"That's all shifter girl, Romeo." Summer winked at him. "What, is it a deal-breaker for you?"

Jackson clapped his mouth shut and looked at Amanda.

She was busy walking back toward the uncovered trapdoor of her cellar. "I guess you haven't seen me actually...you know. Move heavy stuff before. This is nothing. This one time, I ripped a guy's hand completely off his arm with my teeth. Like, one good shake and the whole thing came off. Bone, muscle, tendons. Not as easy as tearing someone's throat out, believe it or not." When she turned to face her friends, she found all four of them staring at her. Only Summer didn't look like she'd just seen Amanda do exactly what the shifter girl had described. "What? Too much?"

Summer grinned. "Not a deal-breaker, huh?" She glanced sidelong at Jackson. "How 'bout now?"

"Uh..." The wizard blinked rapidly and hadn't yet gotten over the shock.

"Amanda," Grace whispered. "Did you... I mean, you really *did* that?"

"Yeah. That was two and a half years ago. I'm probably way stronger now."

A flicker of a smile crossed Alex's lips. "Epic."

"No, it's not epic, Alex." Grace shook her head. "It's...traumatizing."

Summer snorted. "Yeah. For the bastard who got his hand ripped off."

"You know what?" Amanda forced a tight smile onto her face and clapped her hands together. "Let's forget about what I did way back when and focus on what *we're* trying to do right now, okay?"

"Wait a minute, though." Grace slowly walked forward, studying the shifter girl's face with a sympathetic frown. "I think we *should* talk about it. I mean, that's some seriously awful stuff, right? Why haven't you told us any of this before?"

Amanda nibbled on the inside of her lower lip.

Me and my big mouth in the greenhouse. There's a difference between talking to plants and making confessions to your friends, *Amanda. Come on.*

She shrugged. "Just never seemed like the right time, I guess."

"And this *does?*" Jackson's voice broke at the end, and he cleared his throat. "And this does?"

"Not...particularly." Amanda widened her eyes at Summer, hoping for a little backup here because the rainbow-haired witch was the only other kid at this school who knew most of the facts about Amanda's past. But Summer stood there, arms folded, and smirked as she looked back and forth from one of their startled friends to the next.

"Look, maybe I felt like... I don't know. Like I already had to spill the Coalition beans to get your help. Maybe keeping all the other secrets after that doesn't feel so important. Or whatever. So can we get back to—"

"How many other secrets like this have you been keeping over the last two years?" Grace asked.

"Yeah." Jackson cleared his throat again and narrowed his eyes. "And did you *really* rip out someone's throat?"

"Jackson."

"What? Don't tell me you're not curious too."

"Guys, can we please focus on *this* right now?" Amanda pointed at the supply bags behind them. "Kind of on a time crunch here for growing this plant, and I need you guys to help out with making this thing, so—"

"Wait." Jackson tilted his head. "Have you *killed* magicals?"

Grace rolled her eyes. "If she ripped out someone's throat, Jackson, what do you think?"

"I don't know. Maybe it was, like, a little rip."

Alex snorted. "That's the dumbest thing I ever heard. How do you get your throat a little ripped out?"

"Guys, I'm hearing about this now for the first time..."

Amanda drowned out their argument and shot Summer an exasperated glance. This time, the other girl didn't seem nearly as amused by the conversation and instead actually looked a little sorry. She shrugged, and Amanda heaved a sigh before stooping to grab the trapdoor's handle. She threw the door up and let it fall against the wall with a loud *bang*.

It should have been loud enough to get the rest of her friends' attention, but they were still arguing—or trying to wrap their heads around what Amanda was and wasn't capable of and yelling about it. She had no interest in trying to follow that train of thought, so she folded her arms and stared at them, waiting.

This is ridiculous. I'm showing them one of the biggest secrets in this entire school, and nobody notices a thing. I seriously never thought I'd say I made the best choice by telling Summer *about all this crap. She's the only one who can handle it.*

Summer looked severely uncomfortable now as she sidled away from the argument, which was mostly between Grace and Jackson, while Alex threw in the occasional comment that only fueled the fire.

Finally, Amanda had enough. "Guys."

Apparently, they'd completely forgotten she existed.

"Hey! You can fight each other later. Can we just—"

"Alex, tell him how stupid he is right now," Grace shouted.

The Wood Elf shrugged. "Why?"

"Oh my God. Neither of you sees how this is a *serious* issue? We're supposed to be her friends, and we're the worst—"

"Shut *up!*" The snarl in Amanda's voice would have been enough to jerk their attention away from the bickering and back to her. But with her outburst came a surge of shimmering white light, and the larger-than-life head of a ghostly white wolf blasted away from her to barrel across the room toward her friends.

The furious snarl coming from the open mouth of her projected magic made Grace shriek, and she clutched Jackson's arm before skittering behind him. The wizard froze, and Alex ducked.

The snarling ghost-wolf head dissipated right before it would have reached them, and then the greenhouse was perfectly, blissfully silent again.

Summer's grin returned with full force. "*That* was epic."

Amanda ignored her and drew a deep breath. "I get it, guys. I said some weird stuff without thinking. Now that I opened that can of worms, I guess you wanna hear about the rest of it, which is fine. Just not right now. Please. I still need your help, and I'm putting a lot on the line already by getting you involved."

Maybe I shouldn't even have brought them to the greenhouse. There goes having any secrets at all, right?

Grace lifted a finger but couldn't quite manage to point it at the shifter girl. "You weren't trying to, like...hurt us or anything, were you?"

Amanda sighed. "No. Honestly, I didn't even know I could do *that*."

"If she'd wanted to hurt you, Blondie, you'd be on the floor."

"Not helping, Summer." Amanda pointed at the bags on the other side of the greenhouse. "Can someone bring those over here? I'm pretty sure this is all gonna work out the way we want it to, but just in case, I'd rather not make this stuff up here."

"What do you mean?" Jackson asked.

"You know. Like, where anyone could see the evidence. If there is any."

"Yeah, but I mean *up here*. As opposed to..."

Amanda pointed at the gaping hole in the ground beneath the lifted trapdoor. "The opposite of up is down, right?"

Grace finally released her death grip on the wizard's arm and took two steps forward. "Is that..."

"Where you keep the bodies?" Alex finished.

"Okay, I know you're not serious." Amanda pointed at him. "Go get the bag. I have to clear the rest of this stuff out."

"What *is* that?" Jackson muttered as the Wood Elf slinked off to haul a supply bag over his shoulder.

"Secret hidey-hole under the greenhouse." Summer bobbed her head in amusement. "Pretty freaking sweet, right?"

Grace blinked at her. "You knew about this?"

"Duh."

"I don't even know what to say to that."

Amanda hopped down into the cellar and bent to retrieve the first potted plant she'd been secretly growing for the Coalition. Trying not to let any of the leaves brush against her face, she hefted the entire pot up and out of the hole, then slid it across the floor. "Hey. Can one of you shove this thing against the wall or something? I need to make more room in here."

"I don't know, Amanda." Alex dropped off the first bag with a grunt. "Is it gonna kill us or something?"

She glared at him. "I know you're trying to be funny, but you're really failing here."

He shrugged and turned to retrieve the second bag.

"Okay, Jesus." Summer stormed toward the first plant. "I got you, shifter girl. Apparently, the *innocents* need a little more time to scoop their brains up off the floor. Where do you want this thing?"

"Just, like, by the window. I'll figure something out later." Amanda ducked back into the cellar to grab the second plant and paused.

This is a lot harder than I thought. I bet this is how Johnny felt when he brought me home with him and I wouldn't stop going through his stuff. Not like I would've stopped if I'd known...

CHAPTER EIGHT

After clearing out the underground cubby of all the plants Dr. Caniss had finally deemed "useless" on their own—and repeating to her friends at least a dozen times that she'd explain whatever they wanted to know *after* they made the damn accelerant—it was finally time to get to work.

Alex stood at attention behind the open bags, which he'd dragged to the edge of the hole in the greenhouse floor. Amanda dusted off her hands and nodded at Grace. "Your turn."

"To do what?"

"Not get buried alive," Summer muttered. "Probably."

Alex snorted and stuck his fist toward her, which she pounded with hers. Neither of them looked away from Grace.

"You know what? You two deserve each other." The blonde witch spun before either of them could say a thing.

"I need your skills down here, Grace," Amanda added. "The alchemy part. And I, uh…wanna run a few things by you."

"You want me to jump down into the hole under a trapdoor with you."

Amanda grinned. "I mean, the door's propped open."

"Fine."

As Grace scooted toward the edge and hopped down into the shallow cellar, Jackson rifled through the supplies they'd pilfered from down the hall. "Just call out what you need down there, okay? I got everything ready to go."

"Thanks, Jackson. Hold on a sec." Amanda ducked beneath the cellar's ceiling and waved Grace forward with her. "I want you to be perfectly honest with me, okay?"

"Yep." Grace propped her hands on her thighs and leaned toward her friend. "Why are we whispering?"

"Because I want you to take a look at this without anyone else freaking out. There's been enough of that for one night." Amanda pulled out the list she'd copied by hand from Wallace's email and handed it over.

Grace lifted the list toward the UV lighting rigged around the inside of the cellar and squinted. Then her eyes widened. "Are you crazy?"

"Shh." Amanda shuffled toward her and gestured to keep their voices down. Whatever conversation Summer and the guys were getting into now, it had nothing to do with Amanda, and they apparently hadn't heard Grace's outburst. "What do you think?"

"I think you're crazy," the witch hissed. "Which is why I asked. What were you thinking?"

"Oh, I don't know. Maybe that the Coalition wants this plant in two weeks *maximum*, and every plant I've used this stuff on has taken at least a month for full maturity."

"At least *something* in this greenhouse has reached maturity."

"Grace."

The witch blinked furiously and stared at the list. "Sorry. I just...I mean, a month is pretty fast for some of these plants. Maybe this new one they gave you has a shorter germination period or whatever."

"Probably not." Amanda sighed. "I don't care what the regular grow time is. I need to do it in two weeks *now*. Like, without any mistakes. And I want a second opinion."

Grace lowered the paper and raised an eyebrow. "You're gonna do it anyway, aren't you?"

"Well...yeah. But depending on what you tell me, I'll either do it feeling pretty good about my chances or holding my breath in case a little puff of air makes me blow myself up."

"Oh my God." The witch rolled her eyes. "You didn't tell Summer about this, did you?"

"Tell me what, Blondie?"

"She's asking about the Fatethistle down here," Amanda covered without missing a beat.

"Oh, *yeah.*" Summer chuckled. "Hey, you guys ever heard of this plant that's great for shifters but is basically like a narcotic on both planets for anyone else? Super illegal."

"Amanda, is she serious?" Grace whispered.

"It's not a drug. Summer, cut it out! Yeah, I'll tell you guys the rest of it *later.*" Amanda drew a deep breath. "So?"

The blonde witch reluctantly returned her attention to the list. "You can't jack up the amount of an ingredient like Dolorous Agate by three times what you're supposed to use and *not* expect it to backfire. Or at the very least do something completely unexpected."

"Yeah, I know." Amanda rubbed her clammy hands on her jeans now because this was the moment that pretty much defined whether she was thinking outside the box or being so incredibly stupid. "But... Okay, if *you* were trying to make this and wanted to double the timing on the potion's effects, what would you do?"

Grace blinked furiously, scanned the list a few more times, then closed her eyes. "I'd triple the Dolorous Agate. Maybe even quadruple it, but *not* with this amount."

"Thank you." Grinning, Amanda let out a heavy sigh and took back the list. "Don't worry. We can't quadruple it anyway. Didn't steal enough."

"Oh my God. You had us steal more than we needed?"

"I'm pretty sure it's exactly what we need. Hey, Jackson."

"Yeah."

"Start pulling out the equipment first, okay? We're gonna set up down here."

"No problem, Coulier. I'm your guy."

Summer and Alex looked him up and down. "Seriously, Romeo?"

"Dude…"

"What? No, I don't mean *her* guy. I'm just…the guy. With the stuff. To help with the… Shut up." The wizard knelt beside the equipment bag and drew out one fully protected, unmarred, stolen piece of equipment after another before handing them down into the cellar. Fortunately for him, Grace was the one who took everything and passed it to Amanda, so he didn't have to worry about the shifter girl seeing the damning flush rise up his neck and cheeks yet again.

The last item lowered was the huge metal cylinder Alex had taken down from the top shelf. Grace grunted as she brought it to the cellar floor and stopped. "Okay, come on."

"What?" Amanda finished hooking all the various parts together and smiled sweetly. "It's perfect."

"Yeah, and not even a little subtle. You don't think Zimmer's gonna think there's anything weird about a missing *centrifuge*?"

"Oh, *that's* what it is?" Jackson rubbed the back of his neck and tilted his head to peer into the cellar. "I thought it was, like, one of those toaster-oven things."

"What?"

"You know, to keep eggs warm."

Amanda burst out laughing. "You mean an incubator?"

He pointed at her and grinned. "That's it."

"Definitely not an incubator, Jackson. I don't even wanna know what might happen if any of this gets too close to the wrong kinda heat."

"I bet I can guess what'll happen." Summer rocked on her

heels and wiggled her eyebrows. "Come on. Anyone wanna ask me?"

"Even without how excited you sound," Grace grabbed a handful of reagents from Jackson next and arranged them carefully in the cellar, "I already know the answer."

"Hey, don't ruin it for the rest of us, Blondie." Summer waved her off and jerked her chin up at the guys. "Boom."

"Wait, if it gets too hot down there?" Jackson asked.

"Oh, yeah…"

Grace drew a deep breath to compose herself and shot Amanda a dubious glance. "That's the actual reason she wanted to help you with this, isn't it? For the chance to see a few explosions."

Amanda couldn't think of anything to say that didn't make Summer sound like a lunatic, so she shrugged and kept setting up their makeshift alchemy lab in her secret hidey-hole.

"I swear, Summer," Grace called, "if you stole anything that *isn't* on Amanda's list, I'll make you forget all about explosions."

"Nice try, Blondie. I don't think you can hit that hard."

"No, I mean wipe the memory of how much you like them. Got it?"

Summer straightened and stepped away from the hole. Then she looked at Alex with wide eyes. "She can't actually do that, right? No way is there a spell for that."

"There's a spell for everything, Summer." Grace poked her head up again to grab the last jars of reagents from Jackson and widened her eyes at the other witch in warning. "So make good choices."

Ten minutes later, Grace and Amanda had measured all the proportions perfectly and got to work following Wallace's instructions for making the stuff. Summer and the guys waited relatively patiently, though Amanda had to shout from the cellar more than once not to touch the plants in the troughs. Ever.

Fortunately for her little experiment tonight, the cellar's electrical wiring was already perfectly convenient for plugging in the portable centrifuge. The girls filled eight vials with the thick, sludgy yellow liquid they'd concocted, then secured those in the machine's slots and double-checked everything one more time.

"Go ahead." Amanda gestured toward the start button. "I know you want to."

Grace bit her bottom lip and stared at the machine. "I really do."

"Then do it!"

Laughing, the witch knelt and pressed the button. The centrifuge roared to life, picking up speed quickly as the top half rotated and let out a low whine rising steadily in pitch.

"What was that?" Jackson sprinted across the greenhouse and almost slid into the cellar's hole before stopping to investigate. "Shit. Is it supposed to make that sound?"

Grace shot him a playful frown. "Yeah. It's weird that we haven't used this once yet in class. Zimmer has to know how many awesome things we could make if she gave us professional equipment to work with."

"What, you mean like this?" Amanda spread her arms with a goofy grin.

"Okay, fair point."

Summer sat on a worktable at the end of one of the troughs, gripping the wooden edges and kicking her legs back and forth. "This is the last part, right?"

"Why?" Alex looked her up and down. "You have an appointment or something?"

"Yeah, with the New Year. And I would *really* like to not spend it in a stuffy greenhouse with all of *you* losers."

Jackson scoffed. "Come on. Who are you gonna find on campus cooler than us?"

The witch smirked. "Who said I was staying on campus?"

"Wait, kemana party?"

"It's almost finished." Grace stared eagerly at the centrifuge. "There's one more step after this, and it's pretty simple. So if you want to leave now, you totally can. We'll be fine."

"Simple, huh?" Summer kept swinging her legs and stared at the wall in front of her. "Nah. I put in all this work to help you get down there, Blondie. No way am I passing up the chance to see your face when something goes wrong."

Grace clenched her eyes shut and huffed out a laugh of disbelief. "You know if you'd said that a year ago, I'd believe you. Except I know you like me, so I know you're lying." She abandoned her post at the centrifuge to pop her head aboveground again and grinned at the other witch. "Because you want to stick around to share in the celebration when we pull this off. Which we will. Nothing's gonna go wrong."

"Ooh…" Summer wiggled her head. "Look who broke out of her goody-two-shoes shell."

"I'm not…that."

"You were about to puke when we started this thing, Blondie. Now you're super cool, huh? Don't get me wrong, though. I dig it. You're a lot less annoying when you're not worried about getting busted for something awesome."

"You're always annoying."

Amanda grimaced, thinking she'd have to jump out of the cellar any minute to break up whatever weird fight was about to erupt between her friends. Which made the sound of both witches' laughter make her question her sanity for a second.

Okay. Maybe they have *worked out their differences. Hasn't changed the way they talk to each other, but I guess if they're both laughing it off, that's a good thing. Right?*

The centrifuge let out a soft *beep* and wound down with another low whine.

"Hey, this is it." Amanda grabbed the empty beaker for their last step, and Grace dropped back into the cellar.

"I can't believe we're doing this."

"Yeah, that's what you're saying, but your face says, 'I've been waiting my whole life for this.'"

"Shut up." Grace smirked and grabbed all the vials out of the machine to divvy them up. Then the girls uncorked the vials and dumped the concoction—now almost as thin as water and a much paler yellow—into the beaker.

Finally, Amanda grabbed the small jar of Dolorous Agate, pulled out the stopper, and measured out triple the amount Wallace's recipe had called for.

"Are you nerds done already?" Summer groaned. "It's almost midnight."

"So leave, Summer." Amanda slowly tilted the jar and let the shimmering liquid that glowed a bright blue trickle into the beaker. "No one's forcing you."

"Fine." Summer hopped off the worktable and headed for the door. "You guys can geek out over a dumb machine in your little cubby. I can't believe I wasted the whole—"

"Whoa." Amanda stared at the liquid bubbling and fizzing once she finished pouring in the last reagent. "That's...doing a lot right now."

"Yeah, it'll settle down." Grace slowly moved the beaker farther away from her. "Any second now. It'll—"

A few small pops threw sparks from the surface of their concoction, and Grace shrieked. "Nope. It's getting worse. So much worse."

The foam flashed with intermittent yellow and blue light, and the next burst of sparks went up almost to the cellar's ceiling.

"Well, don't keep it down *here*," Amanda shouted. "I still have two plants in here."

"Why didn't you take them all out?"

"Because they're illegal! Take it up there!"

Whining in trepidation now, Grace held the beaker out in front of her as far as her arms would reach and hunched over as she scurried toward the cellar's opening. "Hey! Hey! Take this!"

"I got it." Summer strode jauntily back across the greenhouse with a wide grin.

"No, not *you*."

"Find something to put it in," Amanda shouted, trying to get a good look at what was happening despite Grace now blocking the view through the hole. "Seriously, if it spills down here, no one will see it, but we can't hide that stuff on the floor up there!"

"Yeah, yeah. I got it." Jackson leapt to his feet and darted haphazardly around the room, looking for anything to use as a bigger container.

"Ah! Hurry!" Grace stared at the boiling mixture, which now threatened to spill over the beaker's lip and all over her hands.

"What is it, like, acid or something?" Alex asked.

"Do you seriously think I'd be making magical acid without wearing gloves? Jackson!"

"Got it! I got it!" The wizard raced back with an empty five-gallon bucket in hand. He slammed it onto the floor in front of Grace, then grabbed the beaker from her and practically dropped it into the container. "Whew."

"Okay." Grace swallowed thickly, checked her hands for accelerant spills, then sighed with relief. "That did it."

As the blonde witch climbed out of the cellar, Amanda rolled her eyes with a sigh of her own. "There you go, Summer. Happy now?"

"Not really." Summer tilted her head. "That was super anti-climactic."

"Yeah, well, it's just alchemy."

CHAPTER NINE

Amanda shuffled forward toward the hole above her, then popped up out of the cellar and rolled her shoulders back. "Now we can go back to the…"

"Party. Great idea, shifter girl."

"Guys?" Amanda pointed weakly at the orange five-gallon bucket, which was definitely not where she left it. "Did you put the beaker in there?"

"Yep." Jackson puffed out his chest and grinned. "I can be pretty quick on my feet too, Coulier. I mean, obviously not as quick as *you*, but—"

"Oh, no, no, no." Amanda hoisted herself up over the side of the cellar. "It's plastic!"

"Yeah… You said to make sure it doesn't get on the floor."

"Shit. Get away from the bucket!" She spun away from the cellar and scanned the greenhouse for a better option. Her friends slowly backed away from the orange bucket.

"Something you didn't tell us?" Grace squeaked.

"Yeah, because I didn't write it down on the stupid list."

The potion inside the beaker popped even louder now, bright lights flashing inside the bucket. The subtle splash of liquid boiling over onto the bottom of the bucket made Amanda's gut twist into painful knots.

Not now. We can't screw this up now. This is literally my last option—

A startling loud explosion came not from the bucket but from outside on school grounds. Bright lights flared on the other side of the greenhouse's windows, followed by *bang* after cracking *bang*.

Summer's shoulders slumped, and she gestured toward the wall of windows. "Great. We missed the fireworks and—"

A high-pitched scream rose from the orange bucket before the loudest pop of all sent a column of blue and yellow light shooting up to the ceiling.

Grace and Jackson screamed. Alex tried to scramble backward and jammed his hip painfully into the corner of a workbench. Summer stared with wide eyes, and her grin returned.

"Shit!" Amanda spun in circles as *pop* after deafening *pop* rose from the bucket, and a spray of wet, foamy specks spewed all over the room. The next burst of light was blinding, and the force of the ensuing explosion sent a chunk of the plastic bucket up into the air to *crack* against the curved glass ceiling.

With a snarl, the shifter girl launched herself toward the potted plants for the Coalition and grabbed the closest one. Fortunately, it didn't hold a plant that could have done serious damage to someone dumb enough to handle it without warded gardening gloves. She dumped the plant and all the soil out onto the floor, then darted back to the destructively malfunctioning accelerant.

"What are you doing?" Grace shrieked. "You can't—"

"It's the plastic, not the potion." Amanda reached into the bucket, hissed when another flare of sparks shot up against her hand, then withdrew the beaker and settled it quickly into the ceramic planter pot.

The bucket was smoking now and still sent up sparks but not nearly as many.

"Why are you all just standing there?" she shouted.

No one said a thing, so Amanda grabbed the only other thing she could think of to help. Except her fingers kept slipping on the seal of the giant bag of potting soil. With a furious growl, she slashed her hand down across the bag. A burst of white smoke and a ghostly wolf paw with claws outstretched raked across the bag and ripped it wide open. Amanda spun, hauled the soil with her, and dumped the whole thing onto the smoking, exploding, melting magical mess.

A puff of steam rose with a hiss, followed by a few more stubborn explosions bubbling to the surface of the giant pile of soil. Then it stopped.

Amanda couldn't bring herself to look away in case this epic screwup hadn't finished. Apparently, it had.

She tossed the empty soil bag on the floor and swiped her hair out of her face. "You guys okay?"

Grace's lower lip trembled, her face completely white. Jackson had hunched into himself by the greenhouse door. Alex had opted for the duck-and-cover option and now huddled beneath the closest planting trough.

Summer, though, clapped and let out a wild cackle. "Happy Fucking New Year! Am I right?"

Amanda gave her a warning look. "Maybe hold off on that for a bit."

"Hell no. That was *amazing*! See? I knew there was a reason to stick around 'til the end."

"What..." Grace swallowed, her eyelashes fluttering. "What happened? We did everything perfectly. I mean, theoretically, at least. That wasn't... It shouldn't have..."

"Yeah, that was my bad." Grimacing, Amanda rubbed the back of her neck and shrugged. "Plastic containers are a big no for this stuff."

Jackson groaned. "Man, I would've gotten something else."

"It's not your fault. I forgot to say something about it. And I had no idea the stuff would start boiling before we had to put it in something else."

Grace's eyelids fluttered shut. "The Dolorous Agate. With that much more of it, we should've added it *before* the centrifuge. It was too strong."

"Wait, wait, wait." Summer looked back and forth between the other two girls like she'd walked in on her own surprise party. "You guys screwed with the recipe?"

"Yeah." Grace shook her head. "It wouldn't have been a big deal if we'd known about the plastic."

"I'm sorry." Amanda kicked at the loose soil beneath her feet. "That's my fault. I should've remembered."

"Yeah. That would've helped."

"Wait, and Blondie *approved*?" Summer added.

"Why are you still on that?"

"Because you're breaking so many rules tonight, I'm waiting for your head to explode any second." Summer barked another incredulous laugh. "Or *mine*."

"Oh my God. Explosions." Grace darted forward, stopped, then spun and headed for the door. "We need to get out of here. Like, right now."

"Yeah, the bathroom's down the hall, Blondie!"

"I'm serious. You saw how bright that thing was?" Grace glanced at the ceiling and the walls made entirely of glass. "The fireworks maybe covered up the noise, but there's no way the entire school didn't see the light from those explosions. Someone's probably on their way to check it out right now, and if we're still here—"

Summer scoffed. "The whole school's not even here."

"You know what I mean!"

"Whoa, whoa. Grace. It's fine." Amanda headed toward her,

but instead of listening, the blonde witch had started hyperventilating.

"Oh my God. I'm gonna get kicked out of school. Where am I supposed to *go*? I don't even... My life is over. I can't... I'll never come back from this—"

"Okay, calm down." Amanda slowly approached her friend and wrapped an arm around the girl's shoulders. Grace was trembling.

Man, she's serious about this.

When she met Jackson's gaze, the wizard grimaced so hard it bared all his teeth. Then Grace broke into sobs, and he slowly backed away, shaking his head.

"Oh, come on, Blondie," Summer added. "If they didn't kick *us* out for stealing a soul stone and unleashing a pissed-off spirit, you're not going anywhere. Relax." She stepped away from the worktable and dipped her head to find Alex still huddled under the trough. "Comfy down there?"

"All good." He stared at the heap of spilled soil. "I'm good."

"Okay." She shrugged and headed toward one crying Grace and one seriously uncomfortable Amanda, who had no idea how to handle this.

Exploding potions and flying shards of plastic? No problem. My crying friend? I got nothing.

"Nobody saw the explosion, Blondie." Summer clapped a hand on Grace's shoulder and nodded. "For real. And nobody's coming to snatch us out of here and kick us out of school."

"You don't know that." Grace buried her face in her hands and drew in a shuddering breath.

"No, but Amanda does." Summer met the shifter girl's gaze and raised her eyebrows. "So go ahead. Tell her."

Wait a minute. She's right, but how the hell does she know?

"She's right, Grace."

The blonde witch sniffed multiple times, then slowly looked

up, her eyes blotchy and her lips still trembling. "You're a bad liar."

Summer snorted. "You know, I tell her that all the time."

"Thanks, guys." Amanda rolled her eyes. "I'm not lying, okay? Nobody saw the light. Nobody knows anything is going on in here. The whole greenhouse is enchanted so nobody can see *inside* the windows from the outside."

"Wait…" Grace scrunched up her face and slowly stepped out from beneath Amanda's arm. "Why would the greenhouse be enchanted like that?"

Amanda puffed out her cheeks. "I don't know. I guess Glasket didn't want anyone to see what was going on in here and get a bunch of ideas about stealing my plants and selling them. Or something."

"Oh, nice." Alex finally crawled out from under the trough and stood, dusting off his hands like he hadn't been scared out of his mind two minutes ago. "First logical conclusion. Blame the juvenile delinquents who used to live under LA."

Jackson snickered. "Does kinda sound like that, doesn't it?"

"Glasket, man. So skeptical."

"Amanda." Grace stared at her friend, her cheeks stained with tears. "Please tell me you're not making this up."

"Why would I make this up? I don't wanna get thrown out of here any more than you do. I promise. That's the truth. So, as long as we get out of here in probably the next ten minutes, we'll be fine."

"Okay." The witch drew a deep breath, nodded to steady herself, then shook out her hands. "We'll get out of here. As soon as we help you clean all this up."

"Say what?" Summer wrinkled her nose.

"Wait, five seconds ago, you were trying to disappear," Jackson added.

"I'm not leaving Amanda here by herself to pick up this giant mess we *all* made." Sniffing again, Grace stalked across the greenhouse to grab another plastic bucket and brought it back with her. She paused and cocked her head. "That soil's not gonna blow this up, right?"

Amanda gestured toward the beaker's temporary new home. "Not with the accelerant in that other pot."

"Good."

"You guys don't have to stay around for this. I can take care of it."

"Don't be stupid." Grace grabbed a shovel from against the wall and turned to start scooping up dirt. "We're already this deep into it. Might as well finish it."

"I like this side of you, Blondie." Summer headed toward the overturned plant lying on the floor and grabbed it by the roots before dragging it back to the bucket. "Remind me to talk to you first if I ever need help burying a body."

Grace slammed the shovelhead into the mound of soil and looked at the other witch with a deadpan expression. "You mean like yours?"

The serious faces only lasted a few seconds before both girls burst out laughing again.

Jackson shook his head. "They totally lost it."

"Chicks, man," Alex muttered.

Amanda ignored the commentary as she grabbed the potting planter full of newly alchemized magical accelerant to take back into the cellar. Just in case.

Okay. Maybe letting go of a few secrets isn't all that bad. Not looking forward to all the questions after this, though.

CHAPTER TEN

Amanda spent the first few days of the brand-new year splitting her time between checking the new plant for Dr. Caniss—which hadn't even come with a name on the hastily scribbled note in the package—and trying as best she could to answer all her friends' questions. The plants were easy enough to deal with. They didn't talk back, they didn't get surprised by anything, and they didn't ask questions.

Trying to placate Grace, Alex, and Jackson with satisfying answers was a lot more complicated.

Some of them were about her work with Omega Industries and Dr. Caniss' team. Most of them were about Amanda's past before she'd become a student at the Academy of Necessary Magic. Yes, before she was the shifter girl on campus, she was Johnny Walker's ward for a little over an entire summer. Before she was Johnny Walker's ward, she was the daughter of Bruce and Denise Coulier, twin sister to Claire, and a heck of a lot more clueless.

"I can't believe you went through all that and actually...you know." Grace lifted her plastic cup to her lips at lunch and shrugged. "Turned out pretty normal."

Amanda seriously hoped this was their last group session of Ask the Shifter Girl. She shoveled more food into her mouth and tried to write the whole thing off.

They've done way more than enough to help me. This is the least I can do.

"I'm not *that* normal," she muttered.

"Okay, maybe normal isn't exactly the right word." Grace tapped her fork against her plate. "Well-adjusted, maybe? I mean, all things considered, that's a pretty big accomplishment."

"Not sure any of *us* could have gone through all that and come out on the other side without seriously freaking out," Jackson added.

"Shifter girl's seen some shit." Summer thumped her on the back. "We all have, right? That's why we're here."

Grace stared at the other witch in complete bafflement. "Just when I think you're completely clueless, you come up with something like *that*."

"What?" Summer raised an eyebrow. "You don't think *I'm* well-adjusted?"

Alex snorted and covered his laugh with a large bite of roast beef sandwich. Then everyone around the table burst out laughing.

Summer thumped her forearms down on the table. "Oh, come on. You guys used to live under LA."

"Yeah, and we're still paying for it." Jackson swept both hands out to include the entire campus, and the group shared another good laugh over that.

"I've been meaning to ask," Grace added, chuckling as she wiped a tear from the corner of her eye. "Why are *you* here over break?"

Summer's eyes widened. "Oh, no. This is about the shifter girl, okay? We don't have anywhere near enough time to cover all *my* problems."

"Wait, you mean you have more problems than Coulier?"

MARTHA CARR & MICHAEL ANDERLE

Jackson swallowed his food and washed it down by draining his iced tea. Then he slammed the cup on the table and grinned. "This I gotta hear."

"Well, get used to disappointment, Romeo. I mean, even more than you're already used to."

"I think it's awesome," Alex muttered.

Everyone at the table turned to look at the Wood Elf still munching away on his sandwich.

Grace let out an exasperated sigh. "Please tell me you're not talking about everything Amanda's been telling us over the last few days. Because then there'd be something seriously wrong with you."

"There's something seriously wrong with all of us." He shrugged. "I'm talking about all of it, I guess. We all have our issues, and yeah, that's why *we're* here. Amanda showed up for something else, though."

Jackson scoffed. "Yeah, to not get kidnapped and tossed around by a bunch of crime lords—"

Grace smacked him on the shoulder.

"What?" The wizard shrugged, a small flush creeping up the sides of his neck but not going any farther than that. "She just told us everything."

"That doesn't mean you can bring it up again whenever you want." The blonde witch gave him a warning look. "That stuff's still private, Jackson. Not exactly easy to talk about."

"It's cool, you guys." Amanda wiped her mouth, then chucked her napkin on her empty plate. "I think it's better to talk about it anyway. Kinda feels good, you know?"

When I'm not trying to focus on making it through the next life-or-death thing that pops up way more than I want.

"Yeah, that's a lot to carry around with you for almost three years," Grace muttered.

"I did come here for a specific reason, though," Amanda added. "Johnny didn't try to force me into going to school.

Honestly, I think he kind of wanted me to stay home and…I don't know. Train with him or something."

"Isn't he a bounty hunter with tons of work for the government?" Grace asked.

"Ha. Not anymore."

"So why'd you come to *this* school?" Jackson had forgotten all about his food and now stared intently at the shifter girl. "I mean, no one forced you. You have a place to live and a new family, right? You could've picked any magical school in the country, but you chose bounty hunter school. Why?"

Amanda held his gaze for as long as she dared, then let out a heavy sigh. "To be a bounty hunter. Pretty simple, right?"

"Makes sense." Alex shrugged. "Some people like the idea of going after the bad guys and bashing their faces in. I'm cool with it."

Summer barked a laugh, and Grace tried to send warning glares at them both.

"A few specific bad guys, yeah." Amanda glanced down at her empty plate until she felt all four of her friends' gazes settling on her. "My family's killers still haven't been found. So…I mean, if that's still the truth once I graduate, I guess that'll be my first case."

The picnic table fell completely silent amidst the buzzing drone of all the other junior and senior students having conversations over lunch. When she looked up, she found her friends watching her in various stages of shock.

Great. That's my cue to stop answering all the questions with full transparency.

Summer slapped her hands down on the table and stood. "Looks like this is about to turn into a full-on therapy session. So I'm outta here."

"What are you talking about?" Grace shook her head. "Nobody asked you anything."

"We're keeping it that way. See ya." The rainbow-haired witch grabbed her dishes and hurried away from the table.

"I still think it's awesome," Alex muttered. "Better reason to be here than any of us have."

"Well…thanks." Amanda's gut squirmed now at the thought of the year and a half she had left until she could even consider making that a reality. "I guess I'll have to figure out the rest of it when I get there, right?"

"Hey, if anyone can find them, Amanda, it's you." Grace nodded, her blue eyes wide in an attempt to look reassuring.

Maybe. There's still a long way to go, and I have to keep my head in the game. First the stupid Coalition plants, then that monster the mutated mermaids want me to find. If I can prove myself enough with the Coalition now, maybe I'll have what I need to go after the assholes who killed my family.

The Saturday before the spring semester officially started, Amanda left breakfast early to sneak off to the greenhouse one more time and check on the last emergency-order plant. Once she'd pulled aside the green cabinet, opened the trapdoor, and hopped into the cellar, for a minute, she thought she was seeing things.

The last plant without a name that didn't exist in *Magical's Guide to Magical Greenery* had officially reached maturity.

"Holy crap." Grinning, she squatted beside the potted plant and studied its pulsing orange glow. The thing was covered in dangerous-looking spines two inches long, the budding flowers only the size of a penny but clearly in full bloom now. "It worked. Ha!"

We actually grew a full plant in a week!

Thinking of it as a team effort now surprised her, but it felt right. She couldn't have done this without her friends' help, and they definitely wouldn't have helped her if she hadn't come clean about why she was doing all this in the first place.

Okay. No more secrets, then. Now I have to convince Caniss that her last resort is as useless as all the others. We need to get after that monster.

Amanda pulled out her Coalition phone and sent a text to the number she assumed reached some kind of hotline at the Canissphere.

It's ready.

As soon as she sent it, she wondered if she should have been more specific.

I should tell them one more time it's not gonna work. Not like they'd suddenly listen to me the hundredth time...

Her phone buzzed in her hand, and she immediately answered the call. "Hello?"

"What does that mean, 'It's ready?'" Rick asked gruffly.

"Um...that it's ready?" *Definitely should've been more specific.*

"The most recent seed we sent you last week." The shifter man cleared his throat. "It's at full maturity?"

"Yeah."

"How do you know?"

"I mean, I'm staring at it right now. Hold on." Amanda took a quick picture of the orange-glowing plant and sent it to the same number. "Just sent you a picture. Let me know if you—"

"This is excellent work, kid. Way more impressive than I expected."

"Thanks?"

"We need you to harvest every flower on that thing right now, plus four ounces of the thorns. When you finish with that, get on the next train to Colorado. We have work to do."

"Wait, today?"

"Yes, today. Jenkins needs our help, and you're the one who made it possible."

Amanda stared at the plant and couldn't for the life of her figure out how she was supposed to get there on time. "Can't you send somebody out here to—"

"We'll be expecting you." Rick ended the call, and she glanced down at the home screen of her phone with a snort.

"It's one thing after another with you guys, isn't it?" Rolling her eyes, she shoved the phone back into her pocket and hoisted herself out of the cellar to get her magical plant-harvesting tools.

Once she'd pulled a pair of gardening shears, an extra burlap sack, and the warded gloves from the metal cabinet, Amanda paused and stared at what looked like nothing more than an empty area of greenhouse floor in front of the curving wall of windows. With a glance at the door, she headed toward the windows and slowly swiped her foot along the tiles in front of her.

Her shoe *thumped* against something heavy, and the air shimmered where she'd made contact with one of the other Coalition-commissioned plants potted right there. The three others sat behind the illusion, along with one enchanted bag of alchemy equipment they hadn't had a chance to return to Zimmer's storeroom yet. The other bag, fortunately, had been returned to the infirmary the night after New Year's Eve.

Summer really did master that illusion. I'm gonna have to get her some kind of thank-you present for this.

Smirking in satisfaction, she turned back to the mouth of the cellar and hopped down to start harvesting a plant she had no idea what to call. She had to do it quickly, or she'd miss her chance to get out to the Starbuck's train.

Thirty minutes later, Amanda raced across the central field toward the end of the gravel drive inside the Academy's front gates. Shep's magic school bus was in the lot, the bright Academy school colors standing out amidst the rest of the campus that looked fairly dull in comparison. The wizard driver dusted his hands off and headed for the driver-side door, the keys jingling in his hands.

"Mr. Frederick!" she called, the burlap sack thumping against her back as she raised a hand to catch his attention. "Wait!"

"Miss Coulier." Shep's eyes widened in his wrinkled face, and he gave her a gap-toothed smile. "Why're you runnin' on out here like someone done lit a fire under you, girl?"

Amanda slowed as she reached the van and gave herself a minute to catch her breath. "I didn't want you to leave yet. I have a favor to ask."

"Is that so?" He wheezed out a laugh. "Well, I'm 'bout ready to head out to Everglades City to grab the first load o' kiddies comin' in on the train. Suppose I can help you out after—"

"Actually, that's the favor." She put on her sweetest smile and shrugged. "I hoped I could get a ride from you to...the Starbucks."

Shep snorted. "Jonesin' that much for a latte, huh?"

She playfully rolled her eyes. "No. I have to meet somebody out there. Please? I don't really have any other way to get down there."

The wizard looked her up and down, then nodded toward the van. "All right. Hop on in. Feel free to sit up front with me, girl. I ain't gonna bite."

"Thanks, Shep. Really."

"Mr. Frederick until we're off school grounds, girl." He winked at her. "Let's get a move on."

Amanda hurried around the front of the bus and hopped into the front passenger seat. She stuffed the sack of harvested plant on the floor by her feet and quickly buckled up.

When Shep got in beside her and revved the engine, he paused to look her over, his gazing landing briefly on the sack. "Anythin' in there I oughta know 'bout before we hit the road?"

"Just some plants."

"Uh-huh. This got somethin' to do with your weekend outin's last semester?"

She shot him a coy smile and shrugged. "Maybe. I'm not supposed to talk about it."

"Oh, sure, sure. That's fine. I'm just the driver, after all, ain't I?"

CHAPTER ELEVEN

The drive to the Everglades City Starbucks seemed a lot shorter than when Amanda had made the trip in the back of this same van at the beginning of last semester.

Only then I was in the magically enlarged bottom level.

Shep was his usual chatty self as he drove them away from the campus hidden in the swamp and toward the small Florida city that housed the closest train stop for miles. "You lookin' forward to this next semester?"

"I guess."

"You done made it through two 'n a half years at this place, and you're *still* guessin', girl?" He let out a high-pitched giggle. "Reckon you got plenty of unknowns rollin' 'round the bend for ya, ain't that right?"

"Why? Did you hear something?"

"Aw, hell, Amanda. Don't take a rocket scientist to see you're as busy as all get-out with your extra-c'ricc'lers." Shep glanced at her sidelong and drew a deep breath. "This lil' ride here, now. This changin' things for the semester? Am I gonna be pullin' driver duty out to the Starbucks every weekend now 'stead of shippin' you out on the airboat to that there kemana?"

"Oh." She couldn't help but laugh. "No, I'm pretty sure this is a one-time thing."

"Uh-huh. 'Til you get what you need to start takin' yourself off-campus when the time comes, eh?"

"What?"

The wizard blinked furiously, shook his head, and kept his eyes firmly fixed on the road. "Nothin'. I ain't said nothin'. Too easy to talk to you, girl, and here I go on the edge of spillin' all the beans."

"Shep, if there's something I should know…"

"Naw." He shot her another wink. "Don't let it niggle atcha. Ain't fair to be givin' one of y'all extra information the whole lotta y'all juniors is gonna be hearin' soon enough when it's time anyhow."

"Right." Amanda settled back into the passenger seat and tried to let that go.

Something about getting ourselves off-campus that the rest of us are gonna hear about anyway? Sounds like Shep and Glasket are working on some secret plans of their own. I seriously hope it's nothing like the monster squad.

<hr>

When he finally pulled the van around to the parking lot behind the Starbucks, Amanda was practically already out the door before the wheels had even stopped moving. "Thanks, Shep!"

"You bet, girl. Should I be fixin' to wait here 'til you pop back on out?"

"No, I'll be fine. See you on campus."

"Uh-huh." With another wheezing laugh, the wizard got out of the van and watched the shifter girl sprint around the front of the Starbucks to head for the train station's entrance.

Amanda had been through this particular Starbucks more

times than she could count. Heading down to the actual train station through the supply closet beside the bathrooms was second nature at this point. Only this time, she was doing it all on her own without Fiona's escort.

She cranked the elevator lever, and the supply closet dropped with heart-stopping speed to the train entrance however many miles underground. The doors opened in front of her with a *hiss*. Fortunately, the train cars had all emptied before she stepped into the one in front of her and slumped down on the plush red cushion.

The freshmen and sophomores were probably now rising out of the stairwell leading to that weird garage door in the Starbuck's back parking lot. Here she was, on the train all by herself, making her way to Colorado so she could deliver a sack of useless plants to the Coalition's smartest and still blindest head scientist.

Not a useless plant for everyone else, probably. Only for Jenkins. If they don't believe me after this doesn't work, I'm in the wrong internship.

The trip felt like it took forever, even with the train's obnoxious speed as it barreled away from Everglades City and made two more stops between there and what Fiona had called "the stop in downtown Denver. Probably." Amanda hefted the sack of plant matter over her shoulder when the car doors *hissed* open again and led her into the long, dark hallway stretching out beneath the city she could only assume was Denver.

Now all she had to do was get to the valley in the Rockies and—

"Crap." She spun in the dark hall, her eyes wide as a group of gnomes hurried down the hall toward the train, fully immersed in their hushed, hurried conversation.

How could I be so stupid? I can't teleport myself to the lab!

She walked down the hallway a little longer, trying to figure out how the heck she was supposed to make the last leg of the trip on her own when she'd always had Fiona Damascus to get her from this stop to the giant dome of the Canissphere shielded from view in the middle of nowhere.

She's gonna kill me when I tell her I still need her help. Caniss is gonna kill me if I'm late.

Stopping in the hall to lean against the dark, smooth wall, Amanda pulled out her thin Coalition phone. For the first time, she didn't know exactly who to call.

They can't be pissed at me if I'm doing my job, right?

Fiona wasn't involved in all this extra plant-growing stuff for the Coalition. It might get them both in trouble if she called her mentor for a last-minute teleport. Beyond that, Fiona was always busy and hardly ever answered her phone.

Screw it. If they can't send somebody to pick me up, they're missing out on their magical plant delivery.

So she pulled up the Canissphere hotline number instead. A split second before she sent the call, a burst of blue light filled the hallway three feet in front of her. When it faded, a scowling shifter man in a white lab coat stood there instead and snarled.

"Let's go. I'm busy, and you're wasting my time."

"Oh." Amanda frowned and walked toward the scientist. He didn't move toward her, didn't reach out to grab her hand or anything. The guy stared at the opposite wall of the dark hallway.

Great. They sent the scientist who hates me for cleaning up his mess with the rampaging rhino-squirrel in the exam room.

"Hurry up, kid. There are a million other places I'd rather be right now."

"Then why'd they send *you*?"

He shot her a sidelong glance. "Supply and demand."

Without warning, he clapped a hand roughly on her shoulder, and the whole world lit up in a bright-blue glare.

The world spun around Amanda, her breath caught in her throat, then she stumbled forward across the dead, brown grasses

JINX IN THE HINTERLANDS

of the valley in the Rocky Mountains. The chill in the air would have made her breath catch in her throat if she hadn't already been unable to breathe through the teleport.

She managed not to fall face-first on the frost-covered ground, then pulled herself quickly together. "What does that even mean?"

The scientist grunted and trudged across the ground toward the edge of the lab's outer cloaking illusion. He disappeared a second later within a shimmering ripple of light, and Amanda forced herself to hurry after him. By the time she stepped through the illusion and into one of the branching hallways that connected every dome in this Coalition facility, the shifter man was nowhere in sight.

Supply and demand, huh? He couldn't come out and say, 'Not every shifter can teleport other magicals, so I was next on the list?'

As she hurried down the long tube of a tunnel toward the central dome she knew waited for her on the other end, she couldn't help but wonder what exactly that implied.

Not every shifter has the same kind of magic. That's what that means. I happen to have a mentor who can teleport. Jeeze, if the guy didn't hate me enough already, he definitely does now.

She finally reached the end of the hall and the central dome beyond. The place bustled with activity as the shifters employed by Omega Industries raced back and forth to tend to their various duties. Despite her frustration with being summoned the second this last-resort plant was ready, being back at the Canis-sphere made Amanda smile.

Okay, fine. I kinda missed this place after two months.

"Amanda." Dr. Caniss' assistant Lucy stepped forward with her tablet in hand. The shifter woman's expression was as blank as ever, but when she saw the sack of plant matter hanging over Amanda's shoulder, her eyes widened. "Dr. Caniss is waiting for you. Follow me."

Lucy spun smartly on her heels and marched across the giant

central dome, not bothering to check that the fifteen-year-old intern was following.

Amanda puffed out a sigh and hurried after her. "Yeah, good to see you too."

The farther they went down the series of winding corridors, the busier the commotion around them became. Shifters shouted directions to each other, moving back and forth from one laboratory room to the other. The second that they emerged into another huge central dome that looked like the first—only filled with twice as many staff—Dr. Caniss looked up from the table over which she practically loomed and nodded. "Oh, good. The Godvein's here. Corey, take those to the med bay so they can get started. Amanda, come with me."

"Whoa, what?" Amanda stepped away from the middle-aged shifter with a giant handlebar mustache and wearing a baseball cap as he reached toward her.

"Just need the package," he grumbled, then snatched the burlap sack out of her hand and hurried away down another branching hallway.

"I did mean now, Amanda," Caniss called over her shoulder. The doctor was already walking across this dome, and the shifter girl jumped before weaving her way through the chaotically milling scientists to follow her boss.

"Where are we going?"

Dr. Caniss didn't say a word.

"Hey, I brought the Godvein. That's what it's called, right? There wasn't even a name on that little note, by the way. It would've been nice to know what I was growing for you—"

"Did not having the name of the plant deter you from growing it to maturity in record time?" Caniss asked without turning around to look at her intern.

"Um…no. But—"

"Then I suggest you direct your energy elsewhere. You

performed what we required of you with precision. I expect the same of you in every endeavor from here on out. Including this one."

"This one?" Amanda caught up to the doctor as Caniss stopped at a large steel door without a handle. Instead, it had a large control panel mounted on the wall beside it.

Caniss swiped a keycard across the panel's face, then lowered her head for a retinal scan. As soon as the red light finished flashing across her eyes, she nodded, and the door slid open with a hydraulic hiss.

"Dr. Caniss, I just came to drop off the plants. That's it. I mean, not like they're gonna work anyway, but I can't—"

"I highly recommend wiping everything else from your mind, Amanda. Instead, pay attention." Caniss gestured toward the room, but when Amanda stepped forward to enter, the doctor brushed past her to get inside first.

Sure. No one will let me finish a sentence, but I'm the one who has to pay attention.

Shaking her head, Amanda stepped inside and spun when the heavy steel door *hissed* again and slid shut. A series of loud *clicks* resounded from the mechanism in the walls, and she gritted her teeth.

Pretty sure they forgot to give me a keycard for getting back out again.

She was about to ask the doctor what exactly she was here to do, but the scene in front of her made her stop.

This was a room she hadn't seen before.

Rows of touch-screen panels with flashing lights lined every single wall of the darkened room. Four other Canissphere employees in white lab coats moved from hub to hub, typing in commands, checking readouts, and confirming data. None of them looked at her, but that wasn't anything new in this place.

What *was* new was the large circular table in the center of the room. It wasn't so much a table as a giant central computer bolted into the floor. Its surface was individual access stations in front of the ten chairs also fastened to the floor. A group of shifters who looked as out of place in the Canissphere as Amanda felt occupied five of those chairs.

There were four men and one woman, all of them in dark clothing. Some of it was leather, all of it was dirty-looking and bulky, and Amanda noted three giant trekking backpacks on the floor beside the shifters. One of them had an automatic rifle resting against it.

What the heck did I just step into?

A Canissphere employee stood in front of the gathered shifters, scrolling through a tablet on her arm and pulling up image after image on the holographic display rising from the center of the table. Dr. Caniss stood a few feet away from the other shifter woman, scanning the faces of the five rough-looking shifters who'd come in for a meeting Amanda couldn't begin to understand.

"As you can see," the woman with the tablet concluded, "the necessity for tact and discretion is as high as the threat. Even higher, honestly. We'll leave it up to you to devise the tactical strategy in the field, but know that we'll have eyes and ears out there with you the entire time."

The rough shifters sitting around the computer table had turned to watch Caniss' entrance when the door had *hissed* open, and now two of them faced Amanda head-on in their chairs.

"Any questions?"

"Yeah." One of the men staring at Amanda—his thickly muscled forearms completely covered in tattoos beneath the rolled-up sleeves of his shirt—nodded at the shifter girl and smirked. "Is this her?"

"I find it slightly insulting that you would even consider the possibility of me having brought the wrong shifter," Caniss interjected. "Yes. This is her."

"She's a kid."

"That has no bearing on her skills." Caniss frowned. "Nor should it pose a detriment to your team's operation. Unless I misjudged your abilities."

"We got nothing to hide." The bearded shifter man sitting at the table with a set of dark-lensed goggles pulled up onto his head looked Amanda up and down, then turned to address the doctor. "But nobody said anything about adding babysitting to the job description."

"If you doubt my ability to vet my operatives in this, MacMillan, feel free to show yourselves out." Caniss gestured toward the door. "Otherwise, I suggest we return to the matter at hand without any further disruptions."

The shifters at the table exchanged slightly amused glances. The woman sitting among the men, who looked equally as rough and unapproachable, snickered as she leaned over the computer touch-screen in front of her. "What is she? Ten?"

Amanda clenched her fists at her sides and couldn't help but stare at the five shifters she knew now definitely didn't belong here.

What are they doing? Why am I a part of this at all?

"You may continue, Carol," Caniss said, and the woman with the tablet nodded.

She swiped across her tablet's screen again, and another image appeared on the central holographic display. "This is the area where our satellite sweeps last spotted TS-0513. It was difficult to trace with what we had, but the last *ping* on our system showed high spikes of magical activity. Fortunately, we're looking at the middle of Elk State Forest, so civilian involvement isn't our top concern."

"It *will* be if TS-0513 is not apprehended and returned here to Omega Industries for further study," Caniss added. "Is that clear?"

"Sure." MacMillan snorted. "Simple bag and tag. We got it."

"Nothing about this operation is simple." Caniss fixed him

with her sharp, gray-eyed gaze. "Our intel on TS-0513 leads us to believe this particular specimen is aggressive and dangerous, not to mention highly capable of stealth maneuvers beyond the realm of what we've previously seen. If you narrow in on the target—"

"*When* we narrow in," the shifter woman at the table interrupted with a low chuckle. "We will."

Caniss stared at her, her nostrils flaring slightly, then continued. "You will proceed only to apprehend. Incapacitate if you must, but only temporarily. That's your top priority for this operation. If I hear TS-0513 is mortally injured, or you bring back a corpse instead of a breathing specimen, I'll make sure none of you find work in this industry again. Understood?"

"Absolutely, doctor." MacMillan spread his arms and grinned. "When do we start?"

"First thing in the morning. I'll ensure whatever resources of ours you need are at your disposal. I expect a prompt return when it's finished. I want a debriefing the second you step foot back in my facility."

"No problem." The tattooed shifter stood from the table and grabbed the automatic rifle and the backpack serving as its prop. "I'm guessing you don't want us to sleep in your war room, right?"

"Don't call it that." Caniss gestured toward the door again. "My assistant will show you to your lodgings for the night."

With a round of sniggers and grunts, the five shifters grabbed their things and headed toward the door. The shifter man wearing a stained brown leather jacket with a snarling wolf's-head patch on the back looked Amanda up and down and sneered. "You gotta be kidding me."

The door opened with a *hiss*, and Lucy's voice greeted the stomping shifters on the other side. "Right this way, please. I'll have to ask you not to touch anything until we've reached your rooms for the night."

The shifters erupted into raucous laughter that echoed behind them down the hall.

Amanda stared after them until they were gone, then turned to confront Caniss. "What's going on?"

"Exactly what you've been waiting for." The doctor nodded at the woman with the tablet. "Shut it down, Carol. I don't want them thinking they can come back to interfere with our system."

"Dr. Caniss." Amanda tried to approach the doctor, but Caniss brushed past her again to leave the room and move swiftly down the hall. With an aggravated growl, the shifter girl followed her. "I have no idea what's going on. What do you mean 'exactly what I've been waiting for?'"

Caniss spun sharply, and Amanda reeled backward to avoid running face-first into the head scientist. "We've pinned the location of TS-0513, Amanda. As such, you—"

"I don't know what that is, either."

The doctor rolled her eyes. "The specimen you were made aware of after your communion with the Subject UM-43562 representative."

"Wait, the monster with their power source?"

"If you must refer to it as such, then yes. So gather your things. You'll be assisting the acquisition team tomorrow in Philadelphia."

As the woman walked briskly away again, Amanda found herself standing stock-still in the middle of the hallway, her mind spinning. "My things? Hold on. I didn't *bring* any things. I came here to drop off plants!"

"Oh?" Caniss looked over her shoulder, then clasped her hands behind her. "Yes. Well, I suppose that was an inconvenient oversight on our part. But you're here now, and that's what matters."

Amanda darted after Caniss, her stomach churning and rolling over on itself. "Wait, let me get this straight. You want me to head out *tomorrow* with those…with that team to go hunt the monster."

"Yes."

"Okay, but I didn't even know this was happening. I don't have time to—"

"It won't take much time at all, Amanda. You'll be tracking TS-0513 from its last known sighting. I don't see this taking more than three days, four at most, excluding your return to Omega Industries and the necessary debriefing."

"Four days. Four *days*? I have school."

"As much as I don't agree with abandoning one's schooling, I'd say this is much more important, wouldn't you?"

Amanda huffed out a sigh and gestured aimlessly down the hall in her frustration. "Yeah, but the agreement when we started this was that I wouldn't *miss* any school. And *you* said we'd be going after this monster over Christmas. Now you want me to tag along with a bunch of mercenaries?"

"The terms of our agreement have changed." Dr. Caniss raised her eyebrows, her lips pursing as she fixed the shifter girl with the same disapproving look Amanda had grown more than used to over the last semester. "If it interferes with your school schedule, it interferes. I recommend you make your peace with that insignificant detail because you'll be leaving before dawn with that team either way. And they're not mercenaries." The woman cocked her head. "At least not that I am aware."

"Are you serious?"

"Perfectly. Enjoy your afternoon, Amanda. Get some rest. I'll imagine you'll need it."

With that, Caniss stormed away again and turned swiftly down a branching hallway on the right.

"Wait. Dr. Caniss!" Amanda hurried after her, but by the time she reached the hall, the doctor had disappeared again. "Oh, come on!"

She stood there in the hall, completely alone with only the

echo of urgent footsteps and muttered conversations from any number of other hallways to break the silence.

How the heck am I supposed to explain this *one to Glasket? If I don't clear this up, I'll be kicked out of this semester before I can even start it.*

CHAPTER TWELVE

Amanda didn't bother trying to find Bill the resident zookeeper, Dr. Blane, or any of the other shifter scientists she thought of as pseudo-friends during her brief and unexpected stay at the Canissphere. She couldn't justify spending time with any of them to get her mind off this impending *operation* tomorrow. The only people she wanted to talk to right now, she realized, were her friends.

No way that was happening because campus rules forbade student cell phones. Not like that stopped her anyway, but she was pretty sure she was the only one who'd bothered to break that rule in the first place.

When she realized she hadn't brought her room key with her —as she hadn't brought a change of clothes or any of her things, expecting nothing more than a simple drop-off of the plants before heading back to the Academy—Amanda exhausted all her options. So she wouldn't have to embarrass herself any further, she refused to ask any of the staff about additional ways to open their cramped rooms. However, she did find an app on her Coalition-issued phone that held all the information the Canissphere's system needed.

It was a long shot but still worth a try. When the green light flashed on the door panel, and the door slid open to reveal her tiny temporary room at the lab, Amanda uttered a short laugh.

A QR code. Seriously? What else can this phone do? Make me dinner?

Unfortunately, there wasn't an app for that. So Amanda had to leave her cramped quarters that evening to get dinner from the mess hall, which she wolfed down without looking at any of the staff. Nobody approached her, either, and the team of weird mercenary shifters she'd be working with tomorrow was nowhere in sight.

That night, she lay wide awake on the small mattress inside the recessed dome of her room and tried not to think about how crazy this whole thing had become.

If they wanted me to go out with a team of hired bounty hunters, they should've had me training with those guys over the last six months. Not here mucking out creature cages and practicing my magic in the biodome.

The dim lights coming from the ceiling of her bed nook didn't do anything to help her get to sleep, so she contented herself with scrolling through the shifter app on her phone again. They'd be going to Pennsylvania tomorrow, and that was all she knew.

Lots of shifters in Pennsylvania, apparently. I wonder how many of them know about the Canissphere or whoever those weirdos are I'm supposed to team up with.

The app's home screen disappeared under a notification for an incoming call as the phone vibrated in her hand. When Amanda saw Fiona's name pop up as the caller, she almost bolted upright in the bed before remembering how badly she didn't need a good bump and a headache. So she slowly crouched her way into sitting and swung her legs over the edge of the bed before answering the call.

"Fiona, *what* is going on?"

"Hey, kid." The shifter woman chuckled. "Nice to talk to you too."

"Yeah, I think we're past that at this point. You won't believe what Caniss has me doing tomorrow. She *tricked* me into showing up at the lab today because she has to know I wouldn't have come here to do this on my own. She wants me to—"

"Okay, calm down for a second." Fiona's amusement only made Amanda grit her teeth even harder. "First of all, it wasn't a trick. Just one of the brightest minds in shifter history leaving out a few tiny details."

Amanda snorted. "Yeah, that's what she called it too."

"Don't blame her too much for it. The doc has a lot on her plate, and this thing with your monster is one of them."

"It's not my monster."

"It kind of is, though, kid. Without you, Caniss never would have figured out what the thing looks like or where it is. I'm guessing that without you, she wouldn't have a chance in hell of bringing it back."

"She said four days, though." Amanda heaved a sigh and leaned forward over her lap to rub her forehead. Apparently, *not* hitting her head on the ceiling of her sleepy cubby wasn't the only thing that could give her a headache. "Classes start the day after tomorrow. What am I supposed to do? Show up mid-week and say, 'Sorry, I was doing this thing I can't talk about. Guess you'll have to trust me?'"

Fiona chuckled. "Don't worry about school, kid. I've already taken care of it with Glasket."

"Wait, what?"

"Yeah. She knows you'll be a little late, and no, I didn't spill the beans on why."

"She was okay with it?"

"Eh...not really. But it's not like she has a choice. Listen, the first week of a new semester isn't that important anyway. You won't miss much. So go on the hunt tomorrow. Bag that mutated monster. Make Caniss happy. Then you can come right on back and jump into classes like it ain't no thang."

Amanda wrinkled her nose. "Don't say stuff like that. It sounds weird."

"I'm trying to lighten the mood here, kid. Come on. You're covered. It's all good."

"Well, thanks, I guess. You know, I could've used you showing up at the last second like, twelve hours ago too."

"How's that?"

"It's not like I can take the train all the way out to Colorado and teleport *myself* out of the station."

Fiona cleared her throat. "Huh. Yeah, we're gonna have to come up with a better way to handle that. Looks like you figured it out, though."

"More like Caniss sent my biggest enemy in this place to come get me instead."

"Ha. Enemies. Why would you have any enemies in a shifter lab?"

"Oh, I don't know. Maybe because I saved the day and rained all over his parade when he couldn't figure out that rhino-squirrels grow into giant rampaging beasts when they lose their eggs."

Fiona cackled into the phone. "Anyone who can't see the value of what you bring deserves everything coming to 'em, kid. Focus on tomorrow, okay? I look forward to hearing all about it."

"Yeah, don't get your hopes up. Thanks, Fiona."

"Anytime. I mean, you know, when I can."

They ended the call, and Amanda swung her legs back up onto the bed before lying back on the pillow.

So Glasket and all my teachers know I'm pretty much not showing up for the first week of class. Convenient, I guess. Except for I doubt Fiona made a visit to tell my friends what's going on. Oh, man, they're gonna freak out...

She didn't remember setting any kind of alarm on her phone before passing out, but it went off anyway at exactly 4:00 a.m. With a groan, Amanda slapped around on the floor beside her bed to find the offending alarm and bash it into oblivion. The second she managed to turn it off, a brisk knock came at her door.

"Amanda? It's Lucy."

"I'm up," she grumbled.

"You're to report to the main dome in twenty minutes. If you aren't out of your room in the next ten, I have access and permission to drag you out. Understand?"

"I said I'm up!"

There was no reply from the other side of the door. Now that she'd yelled at her wake-up call, Amanda was completely awake.

She slid carefully out of the sleeping nook, glaring at the obnoxiously low ceiling, then hurried around the small room to get ready for the day.

Four days.

Four days of running around Pennsylvania with a gang of shifter mercenaries she didn't know who laughed at her because of her age.

This is gonna suck.

Without any of her usual belongings—or any belongings besides the Coalition phone—she did the best she could with combing her fingers through her hair, splashing water on her face, and jamming her feet back into her sneakers.

Haven't had to wear the same clothes multiple days in a row since the Boneblade kidnaped me. Honestly, this doesn't feel much different right now.

Scowling, she opened the door to her room and found Lucy standing right there in the hall, looking wide-awake and all put-together, even this early. "Oh, good. Do you have your belongings ready to go?"

Amanda blinked once and gave the shifter woman a deadpan stare. "Just the clothes on my back."

Lucy looked her up and down, then cleared her throat. "Well, I suppose that's a lesson in preparedness for you. This way, please."

Everyone in this place is insane. And I'm the one who gets crap for not playing along.

What Amanda wanted to do was shout in the woman's face that nobody had given her any warning about this whatsoever, so why was *she* the one who had to learn a lesson in preparedness? But that would have only made her anger flare more, not to mention probably wake up every other shifter sleeping snugly in their cramped quarters lining the residential hall. So instead, she bit her tongue and stomped after Caniss' assistant, glaring at the back of the woman's perfectly straightened and tied-back hair.

"You'll find whatever information you need on your cell phone," Lucy muttered, her voice hushed as they hurried toward the center dome beyond the residential quarter. "Of course, the operatives accompanying you have already been sufficiently briefed as much as our system security allows. You'll maintain constant contact with us through your phone, so don't lose it while you're running around out there after TS-0513."

Amanda shook her head. "What's the T for?"

Lucy shot her a confused look. "Target. We only apply that naming system to specimens with the highest threat levels. Obviously, there have been far fewer of those than the more common UM classification."

"Target." Amanda swiped the loose hair away from her face,

still trying to blink out the last remnants of fatigue. "Do the shifters with guns know it's not a shoot-to-kill kinda thing?"

"They've been made aware."

"I don't think that means much to—wait." She reached toward her back pocket with the slim Coalition phone resting almost invisibly inside it. "All the information already on my phone?"

"Yes."

"I thought this was straight from the Coalition. Like, the board or whatever."

Lucy scowled and lowered her voice. "I know you've been told not to mention them here, so you're lucky Dr. Caniss isn't around to hear you."

"Okay, but—"

"Yes, we received the directive from...*them* to supply you with a phone, Amanda. Including permission to link your device to our system here at Omega Industries. You didn't think it was a piece of highly advanced technology with no strings attached, did you?"

"I mean, I didn't actually think about it." A disturbing thought entered Amanda's mind, and she grimaced at Caniss' assistant. "You guys aren't, like...you know. Listening to my phone calls and stuff, right?"

"We have access to all activity on that device. How else do you think you would have woken up at four o'clock in the morning?"

"What? You went into my phone and..." Amanda shook her head. "Okay, fine. I guess that part was probably helpful."

"To answer your question, no. Dr. Caniss has more important items on her agenda than spying on your private conversations. Though be aware that once you and the operations team land in Pennsylvania, your phone will be activated to continuously ping your location back to the lab until you return. We'll monitor audio and visual as well."

"Great. What else can you control from my phone?" Amanda rubbed the back of her neck. "Wow. You know, if you guys don't trust me this much, maybe you shouldn't send me on this *mission.*"

They reached the end of the hall opening into the mess hall dome, and Lucy paused to stare at the five hired shifters gathered by one of the tables. "Don't flatter yourself, Amanda. You've done more than enough to earn Dr. Caniss' trust over the last six months."

"You know, that'd be nice to hear from *her* every once in a while. Which probably won't ever happen. So why do you need..." Amanda's gaze settled on the mercenary monster hunters, and she narrowed her eyes. "Oh. Wait a minute. You guys are sending me out with a bunch of hired guns you don't even—"

"That's enough for now, thank you." Lucy lifted her chin and strode purposefully across the dome toward the five shifters donning their gear and getting ready to head out for a monster hunt.

Amanda stood back at the mouth of the hallway a moment longer.

Caniss isn't sending me out with this team because she thinks I can do this. She's sending me out as a spy. I mean, I guess I'm a better choice than Lucy, *but seriously?*

"I assume you have everything ready for your departure," Lucy called as she approached the shifters.

The woman mercenary with half her head shaved—who honestly could have passed for Summer fifteen years in the future if she were a witch instead of a shifter—snorted and fixed Caniss' assistant with a sneer. "We have a handle on our stuff, lady. Just waiting for you to pull your weight."

Lucy cleared her throat. "We have a transport waiting for you outside the facility. It will get you as far as the Denver train station. I imagine you can take it from there."

"Yeah." The bearded shifter with the goggles—MacMillan—

hauled his tactical pack over one shoulder and snickered. "Bet that's a helluva stretch for your *imagination*, huh?"

The other shifters snickered with him, strapping on their gear. The tattooed shifter brandished his automatic rifle as if they were heading into a battle right then and there, though the way the other packs bulged, Amanda had a feeling they were packing a lot more heat than the one firearm.

Lucy maintained her poise as she ignored the comment and gestured toward another branching hallway. "This way, please."

Then she led the team forward with the crisp *click* of her short-heeled pumps across the tile floor.

Amanda glanced at the basket of protein bars laid out on the table beside the cafeteria window, which was closed this early in the morning.

Caniss can't get pissed at me for taking some of those now. Call it my rations for the next four days.

She snatched up as many wrapped bars as she could, stuffing them into the pockets of her jeans and her zip-up sweatshirt before racing after the mercenaries she was supposed to spy on for the foreseeable future.

Lucy took them only as far as the end of the hall, which looked like a dead-end but was only enchanted that way. Probably to make guests that much more confused. "This is where I leave you. Good luck."

"We don't need luck, lady." The woman on the team scoffed and walked right through the wall.

"Don't wait up for us, huh?" The mercenary with dreadlocks boldly winked and sneered at Lucy. A flash of silver came from one metal tooth, and Amanda wrinkled her nose.

This is nuts.

The team disappeared one by one through the illusion of the hallway's end. Then only Amanda stood there with Caniss' assistant.

"I'd hurry if I were you," Lucy muttered. "They don't strike me as the particularly patient type."

"Yeah. Okay. Hey, did Caniss tell them—"

"Right now." Lucy surprised them both when she shoved the shifter girl in the back and sent Amanda stumbling through the illusion.

The icy chill of January air in the Rocky Mountains made Amanda gasp, and she spun to glare at what looked like nothing but an empty valley surrounded by craggy, snow-covered peaks. *I'll remember that.*

A gust of cold air buffeted her from behind, and she turned to stare with wide eyes at the private jet resting there in the valley. At least, a private jet was the closest thing she could think of to call it.

It looked more like a military jet, though obviously, the Coalition of Shifters wasn't exactly working with the US military or government. The thing's outer hull was a sleek matte black, the wings close enough to the ground for her to touch if she stood on her tiptoes. She wouldn't have even known the engines were on if it weren't for the constant gust of air pummeling her from the rear of the craft. The thing was that quiet.

"Look at this." The shifter with dreadlocks gestured toward her and shook his head. "Like she's never seen a private jet before."

The others chuckled and stepped up onto the rear cargo ramp into the aircraft.

Gritting her teeth, Amanda booked it across the frost-covered grass and barely managed to make it up the cargo ramp before the door's system engaged and drew it up to seal them in with a *bang.*

The team tossed their gear into lockers along the walls, laughing and shoving each other around. Since Amanda had nothing whatsoever to lock up during their flight, she headed for the rows of flight seats lining the cargo bay walls closest to the cockpit. Figuring out the harness was easy enough, and she had herself strapped in before the other five shifters joined her to take their seats.

The rumble of the engines didn't rise in volume, but the steady vibration kicked up a notch as more harnesses clicked into place and the shifter team sneered at her. The craft jolted, shuddered, then took off right there without having to taxi or build up speed.

Amanda studied the cargo bay and the supplies secured tightly to the walls and ceiling.

This is why the Coalition doesn't work with the military. They don't need to. How come nobody else in the magical world knows about this stuff?

As the team of five shifter mercenaries and one teenage shifter girl bounced up and down in their fight seats, Amanda didn't bother trying to hide her stares. She'd be getting to know them a lot better than she wanted over the next four days anyway.

It's not like they're trying to be subtle about anything.

The bearded shifter with the goggles—MacMillan—sat directly across from her. On his right was the woman, and the guy with dreadlocks sat on her other side. On MacMillan's left was the tattooed guy, and the last shifter of the bunch was completely bald and wore nothing over his tight black t-shirt despite this being the middle of winter.

That's real mature. Nobody wants to sit next to the intern.

"So…" Amanda cocked her head and eyed each of them in turn. "I guess you guys don't exactly work for Omega Industries."

The bald guy snickered. "Do *you?*"

Whatever answer she might have had for that, she knew they'd laugh at her either way. So she didn't answer.

Dreadlocks snorted. "For real, though. What are you doing here, kid?"

"Caniss sent me to come with you."

"Uh-huh. You know this isn't a field trip, right?"

The team broke into snorting, grunting laughter.

"Yeah, I know." Amanda tried to steel herself against their judgment. *I bet she didn't tell them a thing about who I am or what I can do. Or how they even know where to find this monster in the first place.*

"So you're the one who found this thing, huh?" the woman asked.

"What?" Amanda stared at her, now filled with the eerie sensation that the shifter woman had read her mind.

That's not a thing, though. It can't be.

MacMillan fixed her with wide eyes and a not-very-friendly grin. "Hanging out at a petting zoo in that lab and going after monsters in the field ain't the same thing. This shit gets crazy. I'm not so sure you can handle it."

Amanda narrowed her eyes. "I guess you're about to find out."

The other shifters burst out laughing again. "No shit, Mac. Listen to this. Kid's got a mouth on her."

"Sounds like it. Bet it won't be so easy to put that attitude in action once we're on the ground."

The tattooed shifter leaned as far forward as he could in his flight seat, laughing silently and shaking his head. "Man, Caniss has *got* to be kidding us with this one. Sending along a ten-year-old because she can talk to animals?"

"I'm fifteen!" Amanda shouted.

The cargo area fell silent for two seconds before the shifter team burst out laughing again.

"Yeah, much better," Dreadlocks said through his grunting, snorting chuckles. "Green *and* hormonal."

The woman stared at Amanda with a grin of her own. "I bet she's tagging along to keep us in line."

Another uproar of laughter ricocheted around the hull, and Amanda angrily whipped a protein bar out of her sweatshirt pocket. She ripped off the cellophane wrapper, tossed it on the floor, and glared at the team she was supposed to be working *with* as she chewed on the rectangle of processed animal meat.

This is the only thing that's gonna taste even remotely good on this trip, isn't it? Fine. They can forget me sharing food with them anyway. They'll see what I can do. This is my chance, and I'm not screwing it up.

CHAPTER THIRTEEN

As weird as it was to be in a private Coalition jet that made the trip from the middle of the Rockies to downtown Denver in eleven minutes, it was even weirder to be dropped off on an empty construction site three blocks down from a Starbucks. The pilot didn't say a word to the team clomping from the back of his aircraft before lifting silently back up into the night sky again.

Amanda forced herself not to shiver in the frigid air as she followed the team into the Starbucks, which shouldn't have even been open this early anyway.

It wasn't. MacMillan pulled a device from his pocket—definitely not a Coalition phone like hers—and punched in some kind of code that unlocked the side door to the building before they all piled in.

As they all crammed together into the supply closet of this particular Starbucks, Amanda pressed herself against the wall and waited for the looming drop into the train station.

This makes riding the train with Fiona look like the best thing in the world. I gotta tell her that at some point.

The actual trip on the train couldn't have gone by any faster for Amanda's liking, even if the Starbucks train had someone kick up its unbearable speed to brain-splattering velocity. Every time the car jerked to a halt at the next stop on the route, the shifter team fell into another round of uproarious laughter, this time most of it aimed at the guy with dreadlocks. He didn't find it so amusing.

"I swear, the next asshole to look at me like that is gonna get my fist in their face."

"If you saw *your* face right now, Hob, you'd be laughing too," the woman jeered.

"I mean it."

"Want us to find you one of those paper barf bags?" Tattoo asked. "I mean, I'd ask the baby shifter over here, but she's not looking half as green anymore compared to you."

They all laughed again, and Amanda pressed her back against the cushion behind her.

I better not spend the next four days as the butt of all their jokes.

Even after that thought, she couldn't help but say the next part out loud. "It helps if you hold your breath."

"Ha! You hear that?" MacMillan thumped Hob on the back. "Just stop breathing, and all your problems disappear!"

"Shut up."

"This train is now departing for the next destination," the robotic female voice warned through the ceiling speakers. *"Please remain seated. Thank you."*

"Aw, shit…" Hob drew a deep breath and held it. The rest of the team's laughter cut off abruptly as the train zipped away toward the next stop.

Amanda clenched her eyes shut and hoped the guy found her suggestion helpful. If he didn't, she'd probably made it a lot easier for all of them to write her off as dead weight on their team without anything useful to add.

When they finally reached the last stop on their route that morning, the Starbucks train had filled with a lot more magicals heading across states and countries for their morning commute. MacMillan stood, tugged his pack onto his shoulder again, and nodded at the doors *hissing* as they opened to the station. "This is us."

The whole team was on their feet and following him closely down the long dark hallway, ignoring the wary glances cast their way by every other magical making their way to the train.

Amanda hurried to keep up, slipping past the milling magicals who didn't pay any attention to a seemingly lone teenage shifter girl trying to get through on a Sunday morning. No one on the mercenary squad checked to make sure she was following, which was probably for the best.

When they emerged from the hallway, she stopped briefly to take in the sight she almost couldn't believe was real.

They now stood on a platform overlooking the Philly kemana. Magicals swarmed across the main avenue far below them, shouting to each other, grabbing to-go meals from the food trucks, and opening up their shops.

On their left was an elevator made entirely of glass, and a painted sign beside it had a green arrow pointing straight up and the word, "Coffee." A narrow staircase descended into the kemana proper in front of them, but MacMillan hadn't yet given the command to take either one.

"What's the matter, kid?" the shifter woman asked with a snort. "Never seen a kemana before, either?"

"I've seen kemanas before." *Got myself in trouble with a crime boss Saithe too, but they don't need to know that.*

"No time to stop in this one," MacMillan grumbled before heading down the stairs.

"Wait, don't we need to go up?" Amanda pointed at the elevator sign.

Tattoo clicked his tongue and shook his head. "Bunch of shifters looking like us coming up through a coffee shop? Don't think anyone's gonna buy it."

"I mean, you guys could pass for hipsters. Maybe."

He stared at her, and Hob burst out laughing. "Hipsters with automatic weapons. Just what Philly needs more of. Shit…"

Amanda couldn't help but smirk at the tattooed shifter's scowl before she followed Mac and the others down the stairs.

Not my fault if they can't take a little of what they've been dishing out to me the whole time.

For the first time since she'd been a shifter walking through a kemana for everyone to see, Amanda was scrutinized by every single magical they passed as Mac led them to…wherever they were going. To be more specific, the mercenaries were the ones getting most of the odd looks. Amanda was only the kid tagging along behind them, and that might have worked to her advantage.

Yeah, they don't exactly look like your friendly neighborhood shifters, huh?

The other magicals down here made it a point to give the team a wide berth as they stared, but nobody tried to greet them. Even the street vendors stopped shouting when the mercenary team stomped past, and Amanda hoped Mac had a plan for getting out of the kemana that didn't include making a giant scene.

When he finally stopped at the far wall of the kemana, there was no visible route for them to take.

Mac stepped aside and nodded at the bald shifter. "Wally. Do your thing."

Wally grunted and stepped around his team members to approach the wall. Only then did Amanda glimpse the utility cover settled vertically into the wall. "Wait, we're going up through the sewers?"

The shifters snickered and shot her weird looks. "That a problem, kid?"

"Well, I mean, I don't have anything else to wear, so yeah."

The device in Wally's hand sparked around the outside of the cover, which finally fell with a *clang* and repeatedly wobbled before settling.

"Not the sewer," he grumbled before climbing into the hole in the wall.

"Best way to skip over Reading Market entirely without being seen," Mac added, glancing behind Amanda at the magicals watching the team of rough-looking shifters breaking out of the kemana like they owned the place. He pointed at the ceiling. "Not a place magicals like us wanna be seen."

Hob, the tattooed shifter, and the woman all disappeared through the hole.

"You guys do this a lot?" Amanda asked.

"We've done it enough. If you can't handle that—"

"I didn't say I can't handle it." With a scowl, she brushed past him and hoisted herself up into the hole. Mac's deep chuckle followed her as he brought up the rear and the entire team crawled on their hands and knees through the tunnels under Philly.

It took them another half hour of crawling before Wally finally stopped in a wide, empty chamber and stood. He grabbed the first rebar rung of a ladder bolted into the concrete wall, and craned his neck to look up at the top of the shaft above them. "Yep."

That was all he said before he started to climb, and the others followed suit.

"Almost there," Mac muttered.

Amanda frowned at him as she waited for her turn to climb the dumb ladder. "The monster's out in Elk State Forest."

"We need a few extra things from a friend. You don't think we carry everything we need to tag a bounty like that with us all the time, do you?" He looked her up and down. "Even if we're way more prepared than you are."

"Whatever. I have everything I need."

"Then climb away, kid. You'll get your monster fix soon enough."

Gritting her teeth, she grabbed the rebar rungs and hauled herself steadily up. A sliver of pale predawn glow spilled through the maintenance hole cover Wally had slid aside at the top of the shaft, and the rush of distant traffic and car horns and pedestrian morning life echoed down toward them.

Everyone needs to stop talking about me *not being prepared. I'm doing pretty damn well for a kid who got a last-minute mission shoved on her without warning.*

After they'd all climbed out of the opening, Mac shoved the cover back into place, and the team looked around to orient themselves in the narrow alley. "Tyler. Where we headed?"

The shifter woman nodded, turned in a slow circle, then pointed down the alley. "That way. Should only be about four blocks down."

"Okay, so get moving."

Tyler led the group down the side streets of Philly, moving confidently as she scanned the surrounding buildings and the signs on street corners. Ten minutes later, her confidence faltered. Then Hob finally called her on it.

"You said four blocks, man. We've gone at least six by now."

"Yeah, well, it's not two blocks back that way." Tyler gestured in frustration the way they'd come. "This place looks way different when the sun's up. And I haven't been here in like... three years."

"Your one job," Tattoo snarled and shook his head. "Get us to the safehouse. That's all you had to do on this one."

"I'll get us there!" she snapped and shoved him out of the way. "Give me a minute."

"We already gave you fifteen," Mac said as the team fell into line again. "I'm not letting this op fall apart because you couldn't remember the place you said you could find in the dark."

"Yeah, it's *not* dark! Shut up." Tyler stormed off down the side street, muttering under her breath.

"Man, we should've had someone check in sooner," Tattoo muttered, leaning toward Mac.

"Let her get her bearings again, huh? She's our nav. Leave it at that."

"Might as well be *walking* to the damn woods. It'll take us that long anyway."

Amanda brought up the rear, knowing now was not the right time to get involved in the discussion.

Looks like they don't have everything as perfectly planned out as they thought. Who's unprepared now, huh?

As she followed these strangers through the even stranger streets of Philly, she pulled the Coalition phone from her back pocket and frowned.

Worth a shot. Especially if it helps us get there faster than she does.

Amanda opened the Global Shift app—available for networking with shifters worldwide—and pinned their location on a map of Philly. The red dots of networked shifters in the city were randomly scattered throughout, but there was a higher concentration two blocks down in the direction they were already heading.

Safehouse. I bet it's a shifter safehouse specifically. If Tyler can't find it on her own, I'll say something.

They reached the right street, but then the shifter woman spun to face her team and spread her arms. "I don't know. It all looks the damn same in the day."

"How does that even make sense?" Wally asked. "We can see everything."

"Yeah, well, I don't know where it is, okay?"

Mac grunted. "You got a number, then?"

Tyler glared at him and barely shook her head as if he'd insulted her with the question. "Why the hell would I have a number? The guy's expecting us."

"Damnit, Tyler." Their leader tugged on his thick beard and

growled. "Now we gotta get Jimmy involved."

"Aw, come on. You don't have to do that. I'll find it."

"Well, we don't have all day. If we're not standing in that safe-house in ten minutes, I'm making the call—"

"It's right there," Amanda interrupted.

The shifter team all turned to stare at her, and she pointed at the long line of row houses across the street.

Mac snorted. "How the hell d'you know that?"

"Look." She offered him her phone, and he looked back and forth between the large concentration of red dots on the map and the houses across the street. "Well shit. Looks like we got a new nav, Tyler."

"Bullshit." The shifter woman stormed toward them and ripped the phone from Amanda's grasp.

"Hey—"

"What're you doing with this shit, huh? You trying to break into our—"

"It's an *app*." Amanda snatched the phone back and returned Tyler's snarl. "Maybe you should check it out. You know, if you have a phone."

"Ha!" Tattoo burst out laughing. "This little pup saved your ass big-time, Ty."

"We don't know she's right."

"It's a better shot than anything you've given us so far." Mac crossed the street and waved them forward. "Let's go."

"Shown up by the baby with a cell phone." Wally nudged Tyler in the ribs and chuckled. "Maybe she'd be willing to give you a few pointers on *apps*, huh?"

"Piss off, man. You're in my bubble." The shifter woman shoved him angrily aside, and he stumbled across the street, laughing.

"We'll be telling this story for *years*," Hob added, gliding his hand across the air in front of him as he read the imagined head-line. "Tyler Gets Her Ass Handed to Her."

"Ha." Tattoo jogged to catch up with them. "Best Nav in the Biz Can't See in the Light. Ten-Year-Old Kid Saves the Day."

Amanda brushed past them all as they reached the stairs up to the front stoop of the rowhouse she'd indicated. "I'm not ten."

Everyone but Tyler laughed. "You gonna do something about it, kid?"

As Tyler headed past them to join Mac at the front door, Amanda spun to glare at Tattoo. "If you get my age wrong again, I might have to, yeah."

"Oh, shit!" Hob pressed a fist to his mouth—hiding the glint of his silver tooth in the process—and guffawed. "Bro, this kid's got balls."

"Yeah, I bet she's nothing but talk."

"That right, kid? Or do you got a little bite to back up that bark?"

"Shut the hell up and save the crap for happy hour," Mac growled. "Is this it or what?"

Tyler tried to inconspicuously run her hand along the top of the doorway, scowling the whole time. When she removed her hand and held a small brass key in it, she hissed and glared at Amanda. "Yeah. This is it."

"We're running the story as soon as we finish this job." Tattoo snickered.

"Bite me." Tyler unlocked the front door, and the team stepped into the dark, empty entryway of the rowhouse. Wally pulled the door shut behind him, and Tyler trudged toward the back of the home without another word.

"All right." Mac looked Amanda up and down and smirked. "Not bad, kid."

"I didn't do anything." She shoved the phone back in her pocket and shrugged. "You guys don't have the shifter app?"

He sniffed and cocked his head. "Never heard of it 'til now. Can't keep up with all the tech crap you kids are into these days." Then he clomped down the hall after the rest of the team.

"It's not just a kid… Whatever." Amanda rolled her eyes and hurried after them, waiting for whoever owned this house to either welcome them into an actual safehouse or freak out and threaten to call the police because they'd picked the wrong one.

Anyone could leave their key above the door, right?

Tyler opened a door at the end of the hallway. Instead of a closet, it held a staircase leading down into the basement.

"You sure David knows we're coming?" Mac asked.

"I know what I'm doing," Tyler spat and headed down the stairs.

The other shifters chuckled and shook their heads but followed her just the same.

Amanda walked down last, wondering what they were supposed to find in a safehouse for shifters. Then the shouting started.

"No, no, no! Put it down, Paul! Jesus, are you trying to blow my face off or what?"

A high-pitched whine rose from the basement, followed by a loud *zap* and a brilliant blue light. There was a small explosion, followed by the sound of multiple heavy metal objects crashing to the floor and a low groan.

"Give me that. You're the biggest moron on two planets, man. You know that? I can't even—hey! Ty!"

The shifter woman spread her arms, grinning as the rest of the team fanned out around her at the bottom of the stairs, and Amanda snuck out to join them. "Been a while, David. Glad to hear you still recognize me."

"How could I forget you?" The shifter who'd been screaming at Paul—apparently the other shifter now pressing himself against the wall of the basement and staring at the newcomers with wide eyes—looked the team over and chuckled. "Don't think I've met your friends, though."

"Don't worry." Mac folded his arms and jerked his chin up at David. "We won't be staying long."

CHAPTER FOURTEEN

The way he said it made Amanda's gut tighten.

That doesn't sound like a couple of friends having a chat in a safe-house. That sounds like he's about to tie this guy up and hold him hostage. Or steal all his stuff.

David waved off the comment with a chuckle and turned to gesture toward the incredibly eclectic stash of weaponry and gadgets stored in his basement. "Stay as long as you want, guys. Doesn't make a difference to me. I've got whatever you need, and if I don't, I have friends who do. Promise."

"Then we'll have a look around, huh?" Tattoo stomped across the basement and snickered at the terrified Paul pressing himself against the wall like he wanted to phase right through it.

"Don't be rude, Wes," Mac called. "This guy's one of the best."

"Hey, thanks." David grinned even wider and tousled his hair. "Nice to get a compliment where credit's due. Whatcha got goin' on this—" He stopped instantly when his gaze fell on Amanda, and the smile disappeared. The shifter man's shoulders sagged, and he shook his head. "No. Oh, no. I don't do kids."

"She's with us," Mac muttered as he lifted the lid of a silver case set it on one of the shelves lining the basement.

"She's with—Are you crazy? How old is she, twelve?"

"Careful, bro." Wally snickered. "She'll kick your ass if you get her age wrong."

"What are you, the age police? I don't care how old she is. I have a basement full of unapproved weapons, and kids are out of the question!" David stalked toward Amanda, brandishing a thick black device in his hand that looked like a commercial-grade flashlight. He swung it toward her, completely oblivious of aiming the barrel of what could have been another weapon at a kid. "What are you doing here?"

"I'm with them. Like he said." She couldn't stop staring at the weapon in his hand because now she knew that was exactly what it was.

"Yeah, I'm not buying it. These guys are professionals. For the most part."

"Hey." Hob turned with a firearm in hand that boasted a massive, wickedly barbed harpoon at the tip. "We're as pro as it gets, man."

"Yeah, yeah, whatever. Pointy end down, genius." David turned back to Amanda and looked her over. "You're not even close to pro. So why—"

"Where did you get that?" She pointed at the heavy, bulky weapon in his hand.

The shifter man's smile flickered back into existence. "Not that these things are exactly a secret, but I doubt you've seen anything like this before. And no, I'm not selling it to a kid, no matter who you're running around with."

"It shoots laser bombs."

"You can't even *imagine* the kind of damage this thing—what?" He looked down at the weapon, then back up at her and blinked. "How do you know that?"

"Did she say laser bombs?" Tyler spun from the shelf she'd been perusing and grinned. "Tell me she said laser bombs."

"Yeah, that's what she said. And lemme tell you right now,

these things are off-limits in the basement, understand? Paul couldn't get that through his thick head, and look what he did to the merchandise. By the way, Paul, you break it, you buy it." David pointed at the terrified shifter man, who lifted both hands in surrender when the barrel of the laser cannon swung his way.

"I said I was sorry."

"Well, say it with your money." David went back to staring at Amanda, this time with renewed curiosity. "The only thing I wanna hear is how you know what this is."

"I know somebody who has one." That was all she could think to say with five mercenaries and a terrified customer within hearing range. "I recognized it, that's all. Where did *you* get it?"

"Where did I—ha!" David waved the laser cannon around again as if it was a perfectly harmless piece of machinery. "Kid, I *made* it."

"You made it." Amanda broke into a wide grin. "I know the guy who bought two of those from you and wishes he made it instead."

"Nah. No way. I don't sell these publicly. Not as anything other than a prototype, anyway."

"Yeah, I know." She looked the guy up and down. "I'm talking about Johnny Walker. You've met him, right? I mean, if you're part of the group that built these things, you have to have met him."

"Johnny..." David's eyes widened. "You gotta be kidding me. How the hell do you know the bounty hunter?"

"The who?" Tyler called as she rifled through a case of weapons.

"Johnny Walker."

Wally shrugged. "Never heard of him."

"These guys..." David stuck a thumb over his shoulder at the shifter gang perusing his wares and shook his head. "Can you believe it? I sure as hell don't. Is that crazy-ass dwarf hiring juveniles as his newest assistants or what?"

"No." Amanda folded her arms, eyeing the laser-bomb gun with interest now. "I'm his kid."

"You're his *kid*? Ha! Didn't think he had it in him to keep a kid around."

"Yeah, well, I didn't exactly give him much choice."

David burst out laughing. "Small world. Man. Not that I'm a huge fan of the guy. He's not easy to work with, that's for sure. Or to talk to. But he saved my ass from one nasty Azrakan about two years ago, and now he has a *kid*!"

"Super touching story," Mac muttered. "Whoever you're talking about. But we got a job to do, so let's get moving, huh?"

"Right. Right. Yeah." David looked Amanda up and down again, then thrust the laser cannon toward her. "You want it? I got plenty more where it came from. Seriously. Have at it—"

"Nope." Hob sidled toward them and snatched the weapon from their host's hand. "I'll take that."

"What?" Amanda scowled at the dreadlocked shifter. "He's giving it to *me*."

"Can you pay for something like this?" Hob jiggled the cannon around. "Didn't think so."

"Well, then give me *something*."

"Sorry, kid." Mac turned with some high-tech gadget in hand and smirked. "No weapons for the kid."

"But I—"

"We'll take all this, David. Put it on our tab."

"Your tab." David raised his eyebrows.

"*My* tab, then," Tyler added. "You know I'm good for it."

With a sigh, David ran a hand through his hair and shrugged. "Yeah... Yeah, fine. But I'm not chasing you all over the country to collect, Ty. Got it? Last time, you left me hanging for six months."

"Last time, we didn't have this client." The shifter woman grinned, looking fully insane, and that seemed to settle it.

The team stocked up on supplies—mainly food from David's kitchen—then Wally reached out to another contact and got them an SUV to drive out to northern Pennsylvania.

Amanda couldn't help but feel like this was a poor attempt to copy a Johnny Walker job.

And none of them know who he is.

By early afternoon, they'd reached the visitor center for Elk State Forest, parked the SUV haphazardly in the empty parking lot, and hopped over the gate that declared the park closed for the off-season. The signs and closed gates and locked-up visitor center didn't matter to the mercenary monster-hunter team heading out after their bounty.

Why would it? These guys don't care about anything but getting the job done. And they still don't take me seriously.

Fortunately for Amanda, David had also kept a cache of random clothing at his safehouse, and they'd managed to outfit her with a much heavier winter jacket and boots. The boots were a little on the big side, but after stuffing them with three pairs of socks, they worked well enough.

Mac led their party through the crust of fresh snow coating the entire park as far as they could see. The fancy tracker in his hand had to have come from the Canissphere. Amanda hadn't seen anything nearly as sophisticated or slim at David's safehouse, and the intel for this monster was coming from Dr. Caniss' team anyway.

The thin, bright, nearly translucent device looked seriously out of place in the lead mercenary's hand.

"Okay, so how about now?" Amanda asked as she scrambled over a fallen log that the other shifters merely had to hop over to keep going.

"Did you guys hear something?" Tattoo cocked his head.

"Didn't think there'd be flies buzzing around my ears in the middle of winter."

"I'm serious," Amanda added. "Dr. Caniss ordered me to come out here like the rest of you. The least you can do is hand over a weapon. You have like...thirty."

"Not happening, kid," Tyler muttered as she ducked beneath overhanging pine branches laden with what looked like pounds of snow. "You wanted a weapon; you should've brought one with you."

"I didn't bring anything in the first—forget it. Mac." The shifter girl jogged to catch up with the hulking, bearded mercenary, her boots crunching as heavily in the snow as his. "Just give me *something*. I'm on the team. Don't you think I should be armed, at least?"

"No, I think you should be quiet." He gave her a warning glance from the corner of his eye. "It's so quiet in this place that the damn monster'll hear you from miles away."

"Come on. I've spent the last two years hunting in the Everglades, okay? With rifles and harpoon guns. I know what I'm doing."

"Sure, but you're still a kid. That was the deal. No weapons to the kid. We're following orders."

"That came right from Dr. Caniss?"

Mac turned his head to scan the surrounding forest and grumbled, "What do you think?"

I think these are the complete wrong monster-hunters for the job, is what I think. Caniss wouldn't even consider *guns like she didn't consider giving me a heads-up that I'd be crossing the country twice in a weekend to do any of this in the first place.*

"Was that seriously the deal?" she asked Wally as the bald shifter stomped through the snow past her.

All he gave her in reply was a grunt as he lifted the heavily modified rifle in his hands and swept it back and forth across the line of trees in front of them.

"Fine." Rolling her eyes, Amanda fanned out with the rest of the team, scanning the forest for any sign of the creature they were here to *apprehend*.

Not like I need weapons anyway. Just wait.

After another hour of trudging through the snow without stopping or slowing, Mac grunted at the tracking device and raised a fist for the team to stop. "This is it. Looks like a quarter of a mile out. You guys know what to look for."

Tyler snorted. "Yeah. Crazy-high magical spikes. Flashing lights. And a power core that either looks like a giant egg or a big-ass pile of seaweed. Honestly, if the fee wasn't what it is, I'd say the doc's completely lost it."

"The briefing was a load of shit," Wally muttered. "Couldn't even show us what the thing looked like."

"That's because it could look like anything." Mac scanned the thickening trees ahead of them. "Shapeshifter mutant. The snow'll make it easy enough to pin down."

"Probably not," Amanda piped up. All the shifters turned to look at her, and she shrugged. "The thing we're looking for can change its shape *and* its density. It's not some brainless beast, okay? It's smart, which is why it took the power core in the first place. If it's that smart, it'll know we're hunting it. It won't leave any tracks—"

Tattoo snorted. "Who asked the brainiac?"

Amanda glared at him. "I'm saying we have to be—"

"*We* don't have to be anything, kid." Mac nodded at his team. "Hob, you're with me. Tyler and Wally, you guys circle northeast." He glanced at Amanda, then jerked his chin up at Tattoo. "Wes, you're staying with the kid."

"No way in hell—"

"That's an order. The two of you stay back. I don't want an eager kid getting in the way, and if things get dicey, you'll be first back out to the car."

"You gotta be kidding me." Tattoo—Wes, apparently—snarled

at his leader. "I'm all geared up, Mac. You think we can spare an extra shifter to babysit the pup who shouldn't have even been on this op in the first place?"

"The doc's paying us what she is *because* we agreed to take the kid." Mac glanced at Amanda, looking as disgusted as Wes. "Didn't say a thing about letting her in on the action. But if anything happens to her, we don't get paid." He waggled the tracking device at Wes in warning. "I can see you the whole time with this thing, so don't do anything stupid. Let's move out."

Mac and Hob broke away to the left, Tyler and Wally to the right. When their swift, relatively silent forms disappeared into the forest, Wes hissed and unstrapped his pack before chucking it into the snow. "Damnit."

Amanda sidled closer to him and eyed the pack. "He doesn't have a tracker on your weapons, right?"

"I'm not giving you a damn thing, kid." He whirled around and shoved a finger in her face. "Shut up and don't ask again. Keep your eyes open and let me know if you hear or see anything that doesn't sit right."

"Okay…" She watched the tattooed shifter lower himself onto his pack in the snow before he unzipped a side pocket and pulled out a small water bottle. "What are *you* gonna do?"

"Apparently, I'm sitting here to babysit your ass." Wes grudgingly handed her his water bottle, and she squeezed a little into her mouth before handing it back. "No talking."

No wonder the Coalition wanted better monster-hunters on their team. These guys don't take anything seriously.

CHAPTER FIFTEEN

It only took another half-hour of waiting in the silent, snow-covered forest before Amanda's senses picked up on something seriously wrong. An icy tingle raced up her spine despite the already frigid air in early January, but she knew it had nothing to do with the cold.

That's the monster. I know it.

Wes had sat quietly on his pack the whole time, his weapon resting on his lap as he diligently scanned the trees. The second she tried sneaking off to investigate, her footsteps as quiet as they could be in the snow, his head whipped toward her and he snapped his fingers. "Where do you think you're going?"

Amanda looked at him over her shoulder. "A little privacy. Unless you wanna *babysit* me while I answer the call of nature too."

Hearing the words from her lips almost made her laugh, but she forced it back down and tried to look at serious as possible.

I sound like Johnny now too.

Wes grimaced and waved her off. "Make it quick."

As she headed across the snow toward a thicker stand of pine trees, she heard him mutter under his breath, "Goddamn teenagers."

You have no idea, Wes.

Once she'd made it far enough away from the shifter that she could no longer see even the dark outline of his figure sitting in the snow, Amanda followed the cold itch of her magic's knowing and headed north. Whatever tracker Caniss had given the monster-hunters, Amanda's magic was stronger. And a lot more accurate.

The farther she crunched through the thick layer of snow, the stronger the wrongness flooding over her became.

I can't keep going like this. If I walk right into that thing's den...

She stopped and spent another two minutes looking for the perfect hiding spot—a mostly snow-less bed of soggy pine needles beneath a massive tree that had shielded its trunk beneath a canopy of thick boughs and more snow. Glancing once more over her shoulder to be sure Wes hadn't followed, Amanda headed toward the tree, hunkered down to crawl beneath the branches, and sat with her back against the rough bark of the trunk.

This is perfect. I can do this.

Inhaling a deep breath, she closed her eyes and called on her magic right there in the woods.

The change from seeing nothing but darkness behind her closed eyelids to viewing the white-crusted world through the eyes of her ghost-wolf was instantaneous. Reveling in the freedom of being able to move this way—without making a sound and without any of the stuck-up mercenaries telling her what she could and couldn't do—Amanda and her ghost-wolf bounded across the silent landscape.

Everything looked so much brighter, the sounds sharper and with so much more clarity. Sunlight dazzled off every speck of snow packed onto the ground and resting on tree branches. Two Northern Cardinals swooped down from the highest branches of a tree in front of her as she moved, disturbing the snow with their wings and sending a flurry of it cascading down toward the ghost-wolf padding silently forward.

Of course, Amanda didn't leave a single footprint this way.

Just like the monster. Caniss should've given me more control on this one. I'm the only magical besides the not-mermaids who even know what this thing kind of *looks like.*

Despite how incredible it was to be back in actual snow again —the crisp air, the cold silence—she couldn't ignore the growing weight of the strange magic in these woods telling her to turn back. Whatever this monster was, it was either seriously deadly or in a lot of danger itself, and she couldn't figure out which option felt more like the truth. So she kept going.

Her ghost-wolf quickly picked up the sour, iron tang of blood, and she pushed herself to move even faster—a white, misty blur across a white landscape.

Before she realized how close she was, Amanda stumbled upon the monster's den without warning. Fortunately, she and her ghost-wolf could stop short on a dime without making a sound or disturbing a single bit of the forest around them. She couldn't move anyway as she stared at the unbelievable sight before her.

The snow had cleared away in a large ring between tall trees —not from a shovel or claw marks or even the monster physically moving the frozen layers but simply melted. As if a giant heatwave had burst away from the center and brought a swift and unnatural thaw.

In the center of the cleared ring of damp earth hunched a creature that only slightly resembled the image Amanda had received in her mind from the mutated mermaid's thoughts. It was a hulking beast the size of an elephant, covered in patches of green and purple fur, bright-orange scales, and blood-red feathers tipped with black. She couldn't make out any specific body parts—no wings, legs, arm, tail, or anything else. Only a heaping mound of flesh and scales, fur and feathers, and so much blood.

That should have been the first thing she saw, but it wasn't. Only when she realized the splotches of dark crimson splattered across the monster's form weren't part of its coloring did she notice the carnage strewn around the creature's heaving body.

Her ghost-wolf took two more quick sniffs of the air to confirm—this was all blood.

From where she stood, she couldn't tell if the blood splattered across the ground and covering the churned-up dirt around the monster belonged to unfortunate forest animals who'd gotten in its path or to the monster itself. It was one giant, tangled mess of blood and guts and what looked like animal parts, almost as if the beast had made itself a nest of entrails.

Then a low, rumbling growl rose from the mountainous thing. Wet crunches and slurping sounds followed, and the beast's sides heaved mightily.

What is it doing? Feeding?

The answer was even harder to discern when a limb shot up from a patch of orange scales on the creature's hide. It could have been a wing or maybe a foreleg, but it stretched straight up toward the sky with another sickening squelch. A thin, opalescent membrane that kept it from stretching to its full span covered it.

No. It has to be shifting.

Amanda and her ghost-wolf padded forward two steps, trying to get a better view of what was happening.

Or it's hurt. What even is *this thing?*

Without thinking about the consequences—and there weren't that many when her body lay safely curled up against the tree miles back—Amanda snuck forward on silent, ghostly paws to investigate further. She felt the abrupt change in temperature beneath those paws when she stepped off the cold snow and into the ring of warm dirt and mud surrounding the monster.

The wet sucking sounds rose again. The monster heaved another massive sigh that could also have been a groan, then she and her ghost-wolf were halfway across the ring.

The monster grunted, froze, and moved faster than she'd expected. The giant, amorphous mass of flesh and scales and fur all cobbled together whirled to face Amanda.

Yes, it had a face—something like a bear's snout with terrifyingly long upper fangs protruding from blood-covered lips. Orange scales and purple fur covered the face in haphazard patches, and at least one foreleg ended in a cross between a paw and a set of talons. The beast raised this single limb and brought it crashing down into the thick, warm mud, sending a tremor through the ground. With a disgusting *rip*, the limb held back by the thick membrane on the monster's back burst free, and out came a single crooked, bent wing lined in more black-tipped crimson feathers.

But the thing's eyes...

It's hurt.

Amanda knew it the second she met the monster's gaze—two giant orbs of silver and gold, swirling like mist in a soft breeze. The pupils flickered into existence behind the constantly changing colors, settling intently on the white ghost-wolf halfway across the ring of cleared mud.

Even if she hadn't intuitively known it, the smell of the beast's fear and pain was strong enough to get across the same message. The thing stank horribly, but its eyes pleaded with Amanda and her ghost-wolf for something she couldn't quite figure out.

Then she saw the bright turquoise orb nestled snugly against the monster's chest. It pulsed with an internal light, sometimes purple, sometimes an eerie green, and sent rippling shudders up the flesh of the monster's underbelly and chest.

That's it. That's the power core. The creature either took it to help itself, or that egg's been destroying it the whole time.

Wanting to help, Amanda lowered her ghost-wolf's head

toward the ground and inched closer. The monster snorted and eyed her warily but didn't move.

We have to get this thing back to Dr. Caniss. They can help it. They can—

A shout pierced the silent forest, followed by the sharp staccato *crack* and brilliant flash of gunfire report coming through the trees.

The monster bellowed and thrashed against the ground, sending up a spray of blood-soaked mud and pieces of flesh Amanda realized were most parts of the thing's shifting body and not the leftovers of animal victims. A high-pitched wail from the thing's gaping mouth made the trees around the clearing shudder and sent down waves of heavy snow to crash to the ground.

"Take it down!" Mac snarled, setting the sight of his rifle on the creature's head.

A volley of yellow and blue lights burst from gun barrels from seemingly every direction, though it was only the four mercenaries firing indiscriminately at the wounded, mutated monster. The creature roared again and spun, flinging what looked like a scale-covered beaver tail the size of a door down against the mud. The ensuing bloody spray blew the mercenaries back, but it only bought the beast a few seconds at most.

What are they doing?

With a snarl, Amanda leapt across the clearing toward Mac. She didn't think before leaping up to grab the barrel of his magitech rifle between her ghost-wolf's jaws. Mac shouted in surprise as she jerked his weapon forcefully down, and his furious growl startled Amanda so much that her ability to touch anything physical with her magic shattered. The rest of her ghost-wolf sailed *through* Mac and his weapon, then he lifted the barrel again and kept firing.

You have to stop! This isn't right. You're not supposed to kill it!

She raced around the clearing, snapping and snarling at Hob

and Wally and Tyler too, but none of them paid her any attention.

The monster bellowed again, and another wet crunch came from its sickeningly mashed-together form. A massive spear that looked like a bone shot from the monster's side and barreled into Tyler's chest, sending the shifter woman flying backward through the trees. Then, ignoring the rapid weapons fire from the other three mercenaries, the bear-faced monster coiled itself around the glowing turquoise egg of the mutated mermaid's power core, and it was gone.

Disappeared, just like that, leaving behind only a circle of upturned mud and the bloody remnants of whatever it had done to itself before being disturbed.

"Damnit!" Mac shouted, spinning around in the mud and scanning the trees. "It couldn't have gotten that far. Spread out and—"

"Mac!" Wally shouted, kneeling beside Tyler's still form half-buried in the snow on the forest floor. "She's hit."

"Well, get her up. We need to—"

Amanda fully intended to run after the shimmering trail of magic she could see through her ghost-wolf's eyes as it zig-zagged across the clearing and into the forest. She could still follow the creature and find out where it had gone. She could still help it.

Then the rough hands clamping down around her physical shoulders resting against the tree sucked her ghost-wolf right out of existence, and she hurtled back to her body without any choice in the matter.

CHAPTER SIXTEEN

With a violent gasp, Amanda returned to her body and reacted instantly. Snarling, she braced herself against the tree and lifted both legs to kick squarely at the chest of the magical looming over her. Her assailant grunted and flew backward out of her hiding spot beneath the boughs. A thick collection of snow slopped down on top of him, and even when she realized it was Wes as he leapt to his feet and shook the snow out of his eyes, her fury wouldn't let her stop.

"What the—" The tattooed shifter had only enough time to see a snarling, furious teenage girl barreling toward him before Amanda's fist came up to deliver a cracking right hook to his jaw. He staggered backward and shook his head. "Are you insane?"

"You ruined it!"

"Stop hitting me, you—Hey!" He fumbled to catch her fists flying toward him, then finally grabbed her by the wrist and jerked her toward him. "I had to track you down, you little brat." He spun her around and wrapped a forearm around her neck. "What the hell are you trying to pull with this—"

Amanda hooked her foot around his ankle, grabbed his forearm as she leaned backward, then ducked and tossed the shifter almost three times her weight over her shoulders and onto his back. Snow crunched with a hollow *thump*, sending thick flurries spraying up in all directions.

Wes coughed and blinked up at her, grunting again when she stuck a boot on his chest and leaned over him with a snarl. "Don't touch me."

"Okay, okay, Jesus." He slowly lifted both hands and stared at her with wide eyes. "You're insane."

"You ruined this whole thing!" she spat. "I could've found that creature again, and you just—"

"Whoa, shit!" Wally's sharp bark of a laugh cracked through the trees, followed by the loud crunch of his hurried footsteps in the snow. "What the hell happened over here?"

Amanda jerked her foot off Wes' chest and whirled to face the rest of the monster-hunter team racing toward them. Mac jogged after Wally. Hob and Tyler took up the rear with her arm slung over his shoulders so he could help her shuffle through the woods. "What was that back there, huh?"

"I could ask you the same thing, kid." Mac scratched his chin beneath his beard and eyed Wes now pushing himself up out of the snow. "You get your ass beat by a twelve-year-old, man?"

"Shut up," Wes snarled.

Amanda didn't even bother to correct the incorrect statement of her age. She stormed toward Mac and thrust a finger in his face. "You were only supposed to *catch* that thing! Not blast it out of existence."

"Relax, kid. It's not dead." Mac slapped her hand out of his face. "What are you, the monster-whisperer?"

"We were supposed to bring it in for observation *only if* we got the power core first. You could have destroyed *that* by firing your guns all over the place. Did you even *think* about it?"

"Wally, get this thing away from me—"

Snarling, Amanda shoved Mac in the chest with both hands

and sent him stumbling backward. "If that power core gets destroyed, Jenkins dies. That's on *your* hands."

"Who the fuck cares about a scientist in a coma, kid?" Mac spat back. "Or the damn power core? That thing was out there lounging around in a pile of shredded bodies! It damn near speared Tyler through the chest and probably would've roasted her over a spit that way!"

Tyler groaned. "Don't be dramatic."

"And don't tell me you didn't see all that out there." Mac stomped toward Amanda again, ignoring his team member's comments. "Whatever the hell that was with your fancy little wolf trick, you could've gotten the rest of us killed if you weren't trying so damn hard to get in the way."

"Could've gotten *you* killed? That creature is hurt. It wasn't trying to kill anyone until you barged in with all your weapons. Now we have nothing."

"Not my fault, kid—"

"No, it's *his*!" Amanda whirled and pointed at Wes, who was on his feet again and dusting snow off his clothes. "If he hadn't pulled me back, I could've followed the creature and found where it went. Now the trail's gone, and I'm stuck here with a bunch of morons who can't think before they shoot!"

When her tirade ended, Amanda stood there in the perfectly silent forest, her breath huffing out of her in thick bursts of hot mist while the mercenary team eyed each other in confusion.

Tyler snickered. "That why you let her kick your ass, Wes?"

"I didn't let her do shit." The tattooed shifter slung his pack over his shoulder and grabbed his weapon. "She was sleeping against the tree."

"I wasn't sleeping. I was tracking the monster and trying to figure out what was going on. Before you all destroyed any chances we have."

The shifters ignored Amanda's protests. Wally turned to search in the direction they'd left Wes and Amanda and snorted.

"Looks like she got away from you first. How the hell'd you let that happen?"

"She said she had to go, man, okay? I'm not watching a kid do her business in the woods."

"You said she was sleeping."

"She gave me the slip, all right? It's not like you have anything to show for all the shots you wasted on that—"

"Shut up!" Mac roared. The forest fell silent again, and he turned in a slow circle with the tracking device in hand once more. His eyebrows drew together, and he scowled. "We lost it."

"Seriously?" Wally asked. "How do we lose the signal?"

"Well, we *are* out in the middle of nowhere," Tyler muttered, grunting as she tried to straighten but couldn't quite manage it.

"Has nothing to do with a satellite signal," Mac growled. "That thing lost us completely. No trail."

"It had a trail," Amanda snarled. "I could've followed it if you hadn't—"

"That's enough out of you." Mac stared her down, then finally turned back toward his team. "You get the scans?"

"Just a few prelims, Mac." Hob shrugged. "Didn't have time to go past Level 2."

"Fine. It's something. If we stay out here any longer, that thing'll come down on us to finish the job. Let's go."

No one argued. Amanda was too furious to bother repeating herself yet again to these single-minded mercenaries. She stood where she was as the team fell in line behind Mac, rooted to the spot. Her entire body quivered, but it wasn't from the cold she hardly felt at all now.

These shifters shouldn't be out here doing this kind of work. We have to study that creature, not mindlessly go open-season on it.

Wes crunched through the snow past her, turning his head to glare at her as he shucked another clump of snow off his jacket.

"Careful, man," Tyler teased. "I'd leave her alone if I were you.

Unless of course, you *like* lying on your back with a fifteen-year-old girl's boot on your chest."

The team chuckled and moved on. Wes snarled at them, and Amanda let the group get a good ten yards in front of her before she could move again.

My first time monster-hunting, and I can't do it right because these idiots think they know everything.

Seething, she tromped off through the snow after them.

She thought they'd return to the lab that night to tell Dr. Caniss of their miserable failure, but she was wrong. For the next three days, Mac and his team dragged themselves back to Elk State Forest and returned to the muddy clearing where they'd found the monster, hoping to track it down again that way.

Amanda could have told them it was useless, but they wouldn't have listened anyway. The creature was gone. Its trail had completely disappeared the first time they returned, and there was nothing the mercenaries' tracking devices—both from Dr. Caniss and from their sources—could do to find it again.

On the third day, she'd finally had enough of watching them make the same idiotic choices over and over. "It isn't even *here* anymore."

Hob snorted. "Says the kid."

"It knew what you guys were trying to do, and it ran away to save itself. I told you it was smart, didn't I? That creature would know you'd come back to try again. It's not ever returning to this spot."

"How do *you* know?" Mac grumbled.

Amanda rolled her eyes. "Because I took the time to *watch* the thing instead of blindly rushing in and trying to kill it first!"

No one had a reply for that, but once they'd canvassed at least five square miles around the ring of dirt—which had started to frost over and now had a thin layer of snow from the flurries coming down—Mac made the call.

"We're done. Looks like the doc'll have to be happy with the scans we got."

"She better pay us," Tyler muttered.

"She will."

When they got back to the Canissphere that night, Dr. Caniss insisted on having them all back in the strategy room for a debriefing the second they stepped into the main dome. That meeting was even worse than the first one when Amanda had no idea what these shifters were plotting or that she would inherently be a part of it.

Nobody wanted to listen to the teenage shifter girl trying to explain what *really* happened. Every time she opened her mouth, one of the mercenaries would talk right over her to answer Caniss' questions. No one let her get more than two words in, so it was impossible to get across any other version of the operation than what Mac and his team wanted to present—the monster was deadly, tried to attack them, they fought back. Then it disappeared and left no trace on any of their tracking devices.

Then the debriefing was over, and the team stood to shuffle out of the strategy room.

"Okay, *now* can I say something?"

The entire group turned to look at her, and Dr. Caniss shook her head. "We're finished here, Amanda. I have all the information I need."

"So I can't have a weapon, I have no say in how to do this, and you won't even let me talk about what I found in that forest. Why the hell did you even bring me into this whole thing in the first place—"

"That's quite enough." Caniss fixed her with one of those

sharp looks that teetered on the edge of a mental breakdown, then nodded at the mercenaries. "Lucy will help you settle the remaining details, MacMillan. Thank you for your time."

Without a single snicker or leer in anyone's direction, the monster-hunter team left the strategy room and disappeared down the hall.

"Dr. Caniss—"

"You've been away from your school long enough, I think. Out to the central dome, Amanda. A colleague of mine is waiting for you there to take you back to the train station. We'll be in touch if we need anything else from you."

Then the doctor left Amanda standing there with literally nothing to show for the last five days spent working for the Coalition but a boiling rage. Still, what other choice did she have?

CHAPTER SEVENTEEN

She made it back to campus before the kitchen pixies had set dinner out on the banquet table. Slouching at her regular picnic table, Amanda stared at the outer wall of the kitchens and waited for them to serve the food. For some reason, the pixies were more punctual than usual today and had the entire dinner spread laid out ten minutes early. She didn't waste any time piling herself a heaping plate of fried chicken, pickle chips, bacon-baked beans, and two dinner rolls before taking it back to the table to get started all on her own.

Being back on school grounds—in the Florida warmth that felt downright sweltering compared to the Pennsylvania winter—hadn't improved her mood at all. In fact, she was sure that being back here with nothing but boring classes to continue, surrounded by a bunch of other teenaged magicals who had no idea what she'd done over the last five days, made everything worse.

By the time her friends made it to the cafeteria with the first wave of chatty, hungry students from their last classes of the day, Amanda was already halfway through her dinner.

"Whoa, hey! Coulier!" Jackson waved at her from his place in line. When the rest of her friends saw her sitting alone at the table, they abandoned their spots and raced toward her instead.

"You're back! When did you get back?"

"You look like crap."

"Where the hell were you, shifter girl?"

"Hey, guys. Chill out a second." Grace slid onto the bench beside Amanda and studied her friend's face. "Are you okay?"

"Not really." Amanda jammed a dripping forkful of beans and large chunks of bacon into her mouth.

"We had no idea where you were, Coulier." Jackson dropped onto the opposite bench and leaned forward. "We thought maybe you'd been, like, kidnapped or something—"

"Speak for yourself, Romeo." Summer punched him in the shoulder, and he winced. "But for real. Glasket wouldn't tell us *anything* about where you were."

"She didn't even seem to care that you missed the first three days of classes," Grace added. "Which means there's either something seriously wrong with Glasket. Again…"

"Or you got Principal High and Mighty to sign off on the shifter girl playing hooky," Summer added with a growing grin. "In which case, I'll go ahead and be the first one to say *what gives*, huh? You got yourself out of the most boring first week of school ever and didn't think it would've been pretty freaking awesome to share that kinda free pass with the rest of us?"

Everyone stared at Summer, who grinned like a lunatic now, her arms spread out to her sides where she'd spread them in her passionate outburst.

She's pissed. Okay, point taken.

Amanda set down her fork, washed down her mouthful with iced tea, then had to clear her throat before she could begin to think about how to tackle this. "Okay, I know I just…disappeared on Sunday—"

"Without telling anyone," Jackson cut in. "I mean, Blake said she saw you get into the van with Mr. Frederick, which would've been seriously creepy if it had been anyone else but him."

"What? No, Sh—Mr. Frederick wouldn't do anything to me. He's harmless."

Summer snorted. "Says the girl who hopped in his Florida Gators van and didn't come back for five days."

"What else were we supposed to think?" Jackson added.

"Don't stick me in that weird paranoia basket with you," Alex muttered. "I knew she was fine."

"Not worrying about her didn't tell us where she went and what she was doing, though, did it." Grace scowled at the Wood Elf. "You don't worry about anything."

"I worry about plenty of stuff." He shrugged. "I don't go running around the school screaming bloody murder about it."

"Oh, come on…"

"Wait." Amanda glanced around the quickly filling cafeteria. "The whole school knows I was gone?"

Jackson scratched the back of his head. "I mean, it's not like you haven't already made an impression here over the last two and a half years. Petrov almost snapped Jasmine's neck when she wouldn't stop hounding him about how the Academy could *lose* a student."

"I wasn't lost."

"Yeah, we know that *now*." He gave her a sympathetic smile, then widened his eyes. "Oh, hey. We didn't run around screaming bloody murder about you either, Coulier. Just to be clear."

"Nobody knows anything," Grace added. "But there are a lot of rumors going around already."

Amanda stared at her. "Great. Like what?"

"Like…the angry spirit you pissed off freshman year came back to get its revenge," Jackson muttered.

"What?"

"And that all your secret trips off campus last year got you caught up in some kind of underground magical crime war," Alex added with a growing smirk.

"That's…" She cleared her throat. "I mean, that's pretty accurate as far as rumors go."

"Candace Jones has been running around telling people she heard you bragging about killing someone over winter break, then *bam!*" Summer smashed a fist into her other palm. "You vanished."

"Oh, come on." Amanda rolled her eyes. "What does Candace know anyway? She has one semester left. Then she's gone."

"I think she's jealous of you." Grace shrugged.

"Seriously? Of me?"

"Yeah. I mean, you saved Rob's life after he broke up with her—"

"Because he was attacked and mind-controlled by the *mutant mermaids*."

"Then you took his place on the Louper team last year and pretty much ran circles around anything he could ever do on the field," Jackson added. "Which was awesome. You sure you still don't wanna be on the team, Coulier? 'Cause you kick serious—"

"No, I don't wanna be on the Louper team." Amanda said it a little more forcefully than necessary, though it wasn't exactly a shout. She ran a hand through her dark hair and puffed out a sigh. "I can't even *think* about Louper right now. I don't even know if I can think about classes. I'm just… I don't even know what to think."

Grace leaned closer and bumped her shoulder against Amanda's. "You can always tell us. I mean, it wasn't so bad the first time, right?"

"Yeah…" Stabbing at her now-cold dinner, the shifter girl realized all her friends had abandoned the meal line to talk to her. "You guys go get some food. Then I'll tell what happened over the last few days."

Alex squinted at her. "You won't pick up and disappear again?"

She wanted to reach for the Coalition phone in her back pocket to reassure herself it was still there.

Would I even answer it if someone else calls to make a bunch of demands without any explanation?

"No, Alex." She shot him a playful scowl. "I'm not disappearing again. Not today."

"How about not ever," Grace said as she stood from the bench. "Because if you miss too many days of school, you're gonna have a hard time graduating with all the credits you need."

"Yeah, maybe." Amanda nodded toward the breakfast line. "We can talk about all that when you guys get back. Better hurry up before it's all gone."

"Oh, hell no." Jackson leapt from the bench and spun to take off toward the line. He skidded to a stop at the end before a group of freshmen boys could add six more plates to the wait before his.

Alex and Summer headed off without a word, but Grace hung around a little longer, drumming her fingers on the tabletop as if she was considering sitting back down again.

"Grace." Amanda looked up at her. "Seriously. I'm not going anywhere."

"No, I know. I'm not worried about that."

"Then say whatever it is you're trying so hard not to say right now."

"Okay. Fine." The blonde witch hunkered toward the table and lowered her voice, shooting one more glance toward the line of students waiting to plate their dinners. "I know it's not any of my business, but I can't exactly say it in front of everyone else."

"Well, they're all gone, so..."

"Yeah. We were *all* worried about you, Amanda. Even Alex and his 'nothing bothers me' attitude. I mean, we knew the accelerant worked, which is honestly the most amazing thing consid-

MARTHA CARR & MICHAEL ANDERLE

ering what we had to do to help you make it. So we kinda figured it had something to do with that, but…" Grace swallowed and grimaced. "She won't say it. Obviously. She'll never actually come out and say it, but Summer was freaking out the worst. Like really, really bad. I thought maybe Glasket would finally cave and tell her where you went so Summer wouldn't do anything stupid, but she didn't. I mean, I've never seen that witch look like she was about to crawl out of her skin the way I thought she would since Saturday."

"You're talking about Summer, right? Not Glasket?"

"What?" Realizing the wan joke, Grace let out a wry chuckle. "Yeah, I mean Summer. Like I said, it's not any of my business, but you might wanna talk to her later. Alone. Just…make sure she doesn't go off the deep end and completely lose it, you know? 'Cause I really thought she would."

"Yeah, I'll talk to her. Thanks, Grace."

The blonde witch shrugged and looked incredibly self-conscious now that she'd let it all out. "We're all friends, right? I mean, yeah, your problems are, like, a million times worse than anything *we* have to deal with—"

"Oh, thanks a lot."

"You know what I mean." Grace nudged Amanda's shoulder and smirked. "But I can help more than one friend at a time. Yeah, if you asked, I guess I'd say I consider Summer a friend. Probably."

"I didn't ask."

"I know. Shut up." Playfully rolling her eyes, Grace headed around the table to join the last of the students getting in line for dinner.

Fortunately, Amanda had eaten most of her meal already, because now she'd completely lost her appetite.

I had no way to let them know where I was or what was happening. If Grace had to say something, Summer must've really been freaking out. That won't happen again. I'll make sure of it.

Her friends' easygoing attitudes had returned for the most part when they rejoined her at the table with their plates of food. Still, it didn't take long at all before the topic of where the heck Amanda had been for five days came up again with full force.

So she told them.

It wasn't a vague glossing-over of what she'd been through, leaving out important details because Dr. Caniss, the Coalition board, Fiona, or anyone else had ordered her to keep everything to herself no matter what. For the first time, Amanda told the story from beginning to end without leaving anything out because she knew her friends deserved to hear the truth.

And she deserved not to feel like a ticking shifter-girl time-bomb as she moved through the motions of her junior year without a single person to talk to.

If I get in trouble for telling them, I don't care. They won't say anything anyway, and I'm tired of keeping secrets.

When she'd finished the story that felt as if it had all gushed out of her, Amanda's friends shared surprised looks across the table. Evidently, she'd answered all their questions before they'd had a chance to ask them.

"If Dr. Caniss doesn't listen to you after this," Grace muttered, "*you* should be running that lab. She's an idiot."

"You said it, Blondie." Summer stabbed her sliced strawberries with startling aggression and waved them on the tip of her fork at Amanda. "It's not like you're some clueless baby walking in there and needing someone to wipe your ass all the time."

"Ew. Do you mind?" Grace gestured toward her food. "I'm eating."

"Yeah. So am I."

"What do you think that monster thing is?" Jackson asked. "'Cause it sounds like... I mean, that thing could probably rip you apart if you find it again."

"I have no idea what it is." Amanda shook her head. "But it won't rip me apart."

Summer snorted. "And you're so sure of that because you had a private chat with it through your wolf magic?"

"Uh…yeah." The table fell silent until Alex snorted a laugh. Then they all cracked up, howling with laughter, and Amanda couldn't have even said exactly why she found it so funny. "So, what did I miss in the first three days?"

"Absolutely nothing, Coulier." Jackson crammed the rest of his fried chicken into his mouth and wiped off his greasy hands. "Same old, same old. I think even the teachers are bored at this point."

"Petrov's game's still going on," Alex said. "Bag the Bounty."

"That's right." Amanda grimaced. "I don't wanna go after fake bad guys to get a stupid artifact. That's, like, the cherry on the Coalition's failure sundae."

"I bet your team can handle it on their own," Grace added as they all stood to clear their plates.

"Yeah." Summer grabbed Amanda's shoulder and shook her. "Or *maybe* they won't even want you in on it because you got eaten by an angry spirit, caught up in a magical gang, *and* murdered someone all since Saturday. No wonder you look like crap, shifter girl."

"Hey, thanks a lot."

CHAPTER EIGHTEEN

That night, still feeling aggravated and wired, she decided to go for a run on the grounds to clear her head and get rid of all the extra energy. First, though, she grabbed her first illegal cell phone and the service box from the bottom drawer of her dresser and slipped it into her pocket before heading into the hall.

Two light knocks on the door brought Summer racing across her dorm room to open it. The witch looked surprised to see Amanda standing there after 11:00 p.m., but she didn't exactly look happy, either.

At least she doesn't look completely pissed.

"What do you want, shifter girl?"

"Can I come in?"

"Why? I don't have any magic potions or secret plants in here, in case you'd forgotten."

Amanda turned to look up and down the hall, but as far as she could tell, they were entirely alone in their conversation. "Well, I have something for you, and it's the kinda thing you don't wanna get in the middle of the hall for everyone to see."

Summer scoffed. "You're not the first idiot who's tried to fix things with a useless present instead of an *actual apology*—"

"Summer, I'm sorry. Really. You know I didn't have any way to get hold of you, and I had no idea I was gonna be gone that long. I thought I was—"

"Dropping off a bunch of glowing leaves to your puppet master. Yeah, I heard the story."

With a sigh, Amanda met her friend's gaze and only had one option left—being honest. "Please? You won't think it's a present. I promise."

The witch rolled her eyes and stepped aside. The second Amanda entered her friend's room, the door shut with a *bang*.

"So, what is it?"

Amanda pulled out the phone and Johnny's black service box and held them out to her friend. "These."

"Ha." Summer folded her arms. "A shitty cell phone people stopped buying, like, twenty years ago and a hunk of plastic. It's like you didn't even try."

"Bear with me, okay? Look." She set the phone and box on Summer's desk, then pulled out her Coalition phone too. "You get to keep the other phone. For now. The next time I have to go babysit a bunch of full-grown idiots trying to be monster-hunters, I'll be able to call you and let you know."

Squinting at the slim, nearly translucent touch phone in Amanda's hand, Summer cocked her head. "Why can't you give me *that* one?"

"Oh, yeah? You want a bunch of shifters teleporting into your private spaces whenever they want because you wouldn't answer the phone I'm supposed to keep on me at all times?"

"Fair point." Summer crossed the room to examine her regifted new phone. "So what can this thing do? I mean, besides call and text."

"That's pretty much it. I mean, it has a camera, but it sucks."

"Jesus, shifter girl. How am I supposed to enjoy this thing?"

Amanda barked a laugh. "That's not why I gave it to you."

"Yeah, yeah. Whatever." The witch smirked. "I guess it's cool. For being so lame."

"And a few rules—"

"Oh, come on..." Summer groaned and rolled her eyes. "You're killing me here."

"You don't get to call or text unless you hear from me first. The last thing I need is Caniss breathing down my neck because my phone goes off in the middle of some meeting when it's not supposed to."

"Is there like a time limit on that, or—"

"Ever. You can call or text me back when I say, 'Call or text me back.' I swear, Summer, if you use that thing for anything else besides talking to me when I'm gone, I'll kick your ass."

"Oh, yeah?"

"You know I can."

"How are you gonna figure out if I used this thing, huh? You'll be off hunting monsters."

Amanda folded her arms and perfectly copied her friend's stance. "It might be an old phone, but it still comes with call records. Which Johnny checks every month, by the way."

Total lie, but there's no way she'll call the bluff.

The girls stared at each other, then Summer snorted. "Guess you got me, shifter girl. Fine. I'll be your freaking lifeline at this boring place while you go running around after shifting monsters that don't actually wanna kill anyone." She tossed the phone onto her bed and stepped closer, lowering her voice. "Did that thing actually just, like...shed parts of its body all over the ground?"

Wrinkling her nose, Amanda shrugged. "That's what it looked like. I have no idea what it does, but if I ever get sent out there again to find it, I'll be answering a lot of questions."

"You mean if that scientist lady ever pulls her head out of her ass."

"Ha. Yeah. But now you don't have to wait five days to hear all about it." Amanda turned to head for the door.

"Where are you going?"

"For a run. Didn't exactly have the time and space to do that at the Canissphere. Or in the middle of the woods in Pennsylvania."

"Hey, Amanda."

She paused with the door halfway open.

It's only Amanda when she drops a giant bomb on me.

The shifter girl slowly turned and found a surprisingly embarrassed-looking Summer standing there with her arms folded and tears shimmering in her eyes. Actual tears.

"I guess... I guess I'm glad nothing happened to you."

"Me too."

"Thanks for this."

"Sure, Summer." Amanda pointed at her friend and grinned. "This means now you have zero excuses to sneak around with that illusion and crash more private Coalition meetings. Got it?"

"Whatever." Summer approached the door to shoo Amanda into the hallway, then closed it quickly again and locked it. At least she was smiling while she did so.

With that out of the way, Amanda could hardly wait to get downstairs, out of the dorms, and out into the cool night air. There weren't many students milling around on the grounds. Either they were all content to be snuggled up warmly in bed, or they were too exhausted during the first week of waking up at 5:00 a.m. every day to bother staying up late.

That means I don't have to tiptoe around every kid sneaking off in the dark so they don't start screaming bloody murder too.

The thought made her laugh as she trudged across the grounds, glad to be back to at least this part of her routine. She found her favorite spot to shift and hide her clothes among the tall wall of cattails at the swamp's edge. Then she was off, racing across the grass and splashing silently through the water and soggy reeds. The nocturnal wildlife was a lot more silent in the middle of winter, but it didn't matter to the gray wolf.

Amanda welcomed all of it—the occasional splash of a frog or fish, the hoot of an owl, the scent of natural decay mixed with the salty brine in the air.

Who knew being in Pennsylvania for four days would make me miss the Everglades so much?

She hadn't run off anywhere close to half her bubbling energy when the next scent she caught on the wind hit her like a thorny bush to the muzzle.

The gray wolf skidded to a halt, halfway on land with her rear paws submerged in the shallow waters of the swamp. It was a musty scent, vibrant and foreign and still so very familiar at the same time.

What the hell? How did another shifter get on school grounds? Glasket's been doubling up on the security wards since freshman year.

Curious and cautious, Amanda slinked fully out of the swamp. She made her way silently through the cattails, sniffing at the breeze blowing down toward her from the north. If she hadn't been downwind, she might never have caught the scent. Then again, it had grown so strong in her senses that she probably would have discovered it on her own eventually.

Whoever it is, needs to get out. If it's one of the local shifters, they're not gonna like smelling me here again. This is a school! Why would they even risk showing up here?

She followed the scent almost desperately now, her hackles raised and her gray tail pointing straight up toward the night sky. Then she saw him.

The red-brown wolf nosed around in the reeds at the water's edge, stepping delicately across the soggy vegetation not nearly as green in January but with plenty of life year-round. He was larger than Amanda, which wasn't saying much anyway, but he wasn't fully grown.

This was another young wolf, prowling the grounds of *her*

school with obviously no regard for the security wards or the fact that he didn't belong here at all.

Amanda crouched, lowering her head to the ground as she watched the red-brown wolf innocently sniffing at the grass and the water and whatever small critter had plopped across the surface. Then the wind changed, dying down enough to stop blowing her scent farther downwind. The young male wolf smelled her now too.

He lifted his head from the surface of the swamp, then slowly turned to fix Amanda with two glowing silver eyes.

That's right. I caught you, asshole.

She let out a low warning growl, but instead of darting away as she'd expected, the other wolf turned and headed toward her. He sniffed the air with playful curiosity, moving slowly toward her but without stopping to gauge the cues coming from the young gray wolf crouching in the starlight.

When he'd gotten within six feet, Amanda growled again, and this time, bared her teeth.

Whatever he thinks he's doing, it's not gonna work.

The red-brown wolf held her gaze and stepped closer, his ears fully erect and swiveled toward her while he dipped his head. The tip of his pink tongue poked out from his muzzle as he panted.

Don't even think about it.

The other wolf kept coming, testing her, wanting to say hi without giving Amanda any reason whatsoever to play nice. Then he crouched, his hindquarters weaving like he meant to pounce, and that was what ripped her out of her indecision.

With a ferocious snarl, Amanda leapt toward the other wolf and snapped at his face. She wouldn't attack him unless he tried it first, but this was *her* school, *her* swamp, *her* nightly run. The other shifter seemed to know that even though he didn't flinch away or cower. He didn't show any sign at all of being scared off, and when Amanda growled again to warn him away, his only response was to sit right there on his haunches and stare at her, still panting.

Hushed voices came from the back of the boys' dorm, and Amanda's ears twitched at the sound.

Screw this.

With a final snarl, she turned and booked it through the closest stand of reeds before splashing into the water.

Let him try to follow me through here. That asshole has no idea who he's messing with. What is he even doing *here?*

She found her pile of clothes and shifted back before tugging them on quickly and silently. Then, she remained crouched in her favorite hiding spot for another twenty minutes at least, scanning the school grounds and sniffing the air for the trespassing shifter's scent. She didn't find it again, and there was no sign of another shifter moving around under the starlight on four legs or two.

I have to tell Glasket about this. Shifters running around on campus like they own the place? I don't think so.

Unfortunately, when she slipped into her bed in her dorm room, sleep was even harder to come by than it would have been if she'd tried to force herself into it an hour ago.

CHAPTER NINETEEN

The next morning at breakfast, Amanda tried to weigh the pros and cons of telling her friends about the strange shifter trespassing on Academy property. She tried to convince herself she might have overreacted, but by the time her friends joined her at the picnic table with their breakfasts, they'd already noticed something was wrong.

"Whoa, shifter girl." Summer rounded the table and sat across from Amanda. "You look even worse than yesterday. What happened? You do something last night you seriously regret?"

The witch winked at her, but Amanda wasn't in the mood for inside jokes.

No, I didn't lose any sleep over giving you my old phone, Summer.

"Yeah, for real." Jackson took a seat beside Summer, and Alex sat on her other side. The boys were already cramming food into their mouths before their plates hit the table. "You look like you saw…I don't know. Maybe that monster again or something."

"Bad dreams?" Grace asked as she stepped over the bench beside Amanda.

"Jeeze, it's that obvious?" The shifter girl tried to laugh it off, but none of her friends were buying it.

"Hey, if you feel sick, go talk to the nurse," Summer suggested. "None of the teachers seem to think it's a big deal if you skip out on classes."

"I'm not in the mood today, okay?"

"Damn." Alex stared at her with wide eyes as he chewed. "Something *did* happen."

"Okay, now you have to tell us." Grace leaned toward her. "You haven't even been back twenty-four hours. Did Dr. Caniss call you again? She has to realize she can't pull you out of school whenever she needs—"

"No, Grace. I didn't get another call."

"So..." Alex waved a fluffy biscuit at her and shrugged. "Spill it."

Great. Now I have no choice, and they're all gonna think I'm some territorial shifter girl trying to start trouble. Grace'll probably have a heart attack knowing someone broke into the school.

After taking a deep breath, Amanda leaned forward over the table and lowered her voice. No one would have been able to hear her over the chattering drone of the entire student body starting their day with a hot meal, but saying any of this at full volume would have made her feel insane. "Okay. So I went out for a run last night. Normal thing."

"I'm guessing it didn't turn out so normal," Jackson muttered through his eggs.

"No, not really. I wasn't even *looking* for anything, you know? I mean, I'm always alone out here at night anyway. Then I caught this scent. You guys, there was another *shifter* out on the grounds last night. Like full-on wolf out on the grounds."

Grace stiffened beside her, and Summer glanced up at something behind Amanda, smirking while she chewed.

"Oh, come on. Nobody thinks that's a little weird? No one else should be able to get onto the grounds, and I'm telling you I found—" Amanda frowned at Summer and spread her arms. "What's so funny?"

The rainbow-haired witch didn't say a thing, but she didn't have to.

Because the scent of the red-brown wolf from last night filled Amanda's senses a split second before the boy's voice rose behind her. "Hey."

She spun on the bench and had no choice but to ignore Summer's snickering. "What?"

The boy with close-cropped auburn hair and strikingly gray eyes looked down at her with a crooked, easygoing smile. "You're Amanda, right?"

"What?" She cursed herself for saying something so stupid a second time, but Amanda literally couldn't breathe. Her heart fluttered in her chest, heat flaring up the sides of her neck and into her cheeks despite the cold knot settling in her gut, and her hands grew instantly clammy.

What is wrong *with me right now?*

The boy laughed. "I said you're Amanda, ri—"

"Yeah, I heard what you said," she snapped. "Who are *you*?"

His crooked smile widened into a flashing grin, and the dimples forming in his cheeks made her mouth run dry.

Why am I staring at dimples? Who gives a crap about dimples?

"Matt." He extended his hand toward her, but she couldn't bring herself to take it now that her palms were practically drenched.

She wouldn't have shaken his hand anyway. This was the shifter who'd been running around on *her* grounds last night. "What are you doing here?"

Alex snorted, but she ignored him. She couldn't stop staring at Matt's shimmering gray eyes.

"Yeah, I know, right?" The boy dropped his hand back down at his side and shrugged. "Always sucks starting a different school halfway through, but I'm used to it by now. This place is way cooler than the others, so I'm okay with it. See you around." He briefly raised his eyebrows at her, not bothering to even look at the rest of her friends sitting around the table, then turned and headed toward another table of junior boys calling his name and thumping the benches for him to sit.

Amanda stared after him, her face contorted in a scowl of suspicion and complete confusion.

Summer laughed. "You should see your face right now, shifter girl. Priceless."

She finally pulled her gaze away from Matt and the other junior boys, then spun on the bench again and whispered, "Who's that?"

"Matt." Alex smirked. "You guys already covered that part."

"He's new." Grace's voice fluttered out of her with a weird, dreamy breathlessness. "And he knew your name."

"You guys swamp buddies or something?" Summer asked as she crunched down on a piece of bacon.

"What? No. We're not friends." Amanda shook her head. "Wait, you mean he's *new*-new? Like, an actual student here?"

Jackson looked her up and down and raised an eyebrow. "We're in serious trouble if Glasket's hiring kids our age to teach our classes."

Oh my God. No. The semester just started, and it couldn't get any worse.

Amanda gritted her teeth and forced herself not to look at Matt's table again. "Were you guys gonna tell me he's a shifter too or did you leave that part out for fun?"

Grace sucked in a sharp breath and blinked furiously. "What? He's a *shifter*?"

"Whoa…" Alex chuckled softly. "That's new."

"Oh, *shit*." Summer stabbed a finger at Amanda across the table. "That's why you're so pissed. Shifter girl's not the only shifter at the good ol' Academy anymore. You're getting *territorial*."

"No, I'm not, Summer. Shut up."

Jackson ruffled his floppy dirty-blond hair and wrinkled his nose. "Another shifter. You think Glasket knows?"

"She has to, doesn't she?" Grace leaned forward to look past Amanda and sneak another peek at Matt's table. "I mean, that *is* part of her job."

Alex shrugged. "Wonder when he was gonna tell us."

"Probably never."

Amanda wiped her clammy palms on her jeans. "Okay, well, don't say anything about it to anyone, okay? That's not... It's none of our business."

"Uh-oh." Summer wiggled her eyebrows. "Sounds like somebody's feeling guilty."

"Wait, how'd *you* know?" Jackson asked.

"Really?" Amanda pointed at her nose. "I could smell him before he started talking."

"Wait, wait, wait." Grace grabbed the shifter girl's arm with a desperate grip, her eyes wide. "*Matt's* the shifter you saw on the grounds last night."

"Obviously."

"You mean you were out there, at night, with him, both of you as *wolves*, and you didn't get his name?"

"Wolves don't talk, Grace."

"Yeah, they do a whole bunch of other wild and crazy stuff," Summer said, then she and Alex burst out laughing.

"Whatever." Amanda shoveled the rest of her food into her mouth, then stood to clear her plate. "Forget it. Nothing's changed, right? I'm back. The semester already started. Doesn't matter if there's another shifter kid here or not."

"I think your face says otherwise," Summer called after her.

Grace chucked her wadded-up napkin at the other witch's face. "Stop. She thought he was someone breaking into the school."

Trying to shut out the rest of her friends' conversation behind her, Amanda tossed her trash, almost hit a freshman in the head when she chucked her plastic cup at the bus bin, and growled as she stomped across the central field toward the main building for their first class of the day with Mr. LeFor.

It's fine. No big deal. There's a new kid here who happens to be another shifter and goes for runs at night at the same time I do. I'll just...lay down some ground rules first. We'll flip a coin or something for who gets to go out which nights—

A group of sophomore girls burst into high-pitched giggles, and Amanda stopped at the main building's front doors to see what the heck all that was about. They clung to each other's arms, grinning and batting their eyelashes and waving weakly at a group of boys passing them toward the main building—Matt among them.

Amanda scowled at the whole display before Matt turned and locked his gray-eyed gaze with hers. Swallowing, she jerked open the door and stormed down the hall toward Mr. LeFor's workshop for Augmented Tech.

Forget splitting up the days. I'll have to make sure he knows he can't run around here whenever he wants. This is a one-shifter school.

She hadn't stopped to consider which class Matt was in. That question answered itself when the new kid walked into LeFor's workshop with Tommy Brunsen, Evan Hutchinson, and Mark DeVolos, all four of them laughing it up and jostling each other before they took their seats at the tall bistro tables.

No. No, no, no.

Amanda didn't realize she was staring at the new kid until he looked up at her and shot her another crooked smile. Then she spun in her chair and stared at the assignment LeFor had laid out in front of every seat.

"Distracting, right?" Jasmine muttered as she stared at Matt's table and chewed obnoxiously on a mouthful of gum.

"What?" Amanda could only quickly look up at the other girl before pretending that she was listening intently to whatever LeFor was saying as he started their lesson.

"The new kid. Matt." Jasmine twirled her pencil in her fingers and didn't seem to care that she wasn't paying attention to their teacher at all. "I mean, wherever you've been the last few days doesn't matter. You can't miss a guy like that even if you tried."

Amanda scoffed and blinked furiously at the worksheet in front of her.

Oh yes, I can.

That was easier said than done.

Amanda was seriously surprised that her teachers didn't pull her aside after class to talk to her the rest of that day or the next. They also gave no indication of being aware of her absence over the last three days.

It was a small relief on top of everything else going on, but Amanda didn't question it. Her only goal now was to keep her head down, move through the rest of her junior year, and do whatever Dr. Caniss and the Coalition wanted when they wanted it. Hopefully, that wouldn't be for a long time.

If Caniss insisted on ignoring everything Amanda had to say, the doctor might as well wait until the end of the semester. That would make Amanda as useful as she was now. Never mind that the shifter girl knew about the mutated mermaids, how to wake Jenkins from his magically induced coma, and what they needed to do to find the grotesquely injured monster and retrieve the mermaids' power source.

She wasn't that useful in or out of her classes right now because the new kid Matt Hardy wouldn't quit *looking* at her.

Everywhere she went, he was there too. Of course, they had all their classes together. Still, the Academy's new shifter appeared in the cafeteria during meals or in the spaces between classes when Amanda was trying to either focus on her homework or spend time with her friends.

To make matters worse, it seemed as though every single girl at the Academy of Necessary Magic was now falling over herself whenever the new junior boy walked past. It didn't matter what grade they were in or which boy they'd been interested in before Matt showed up. Clusters of girls followed him around like he was a rock star, which didn't make sense after the school had *literal* rock stars playing for them on stage last year.

Summer might have been the only one who was immune to the mere sight of the shifter boy, and that somehow made it that much more agonizing. Besides Summer, though, Amanda was the only girl who didn't start drooling or giggling or sighing dreamily over him whenever he made an appearance like all the other regular boys everyone seemed to ignore now. Her pulse quickened, sure. Her hands kept getting stupidly clammy, and she blinked furiously beneath the hot flushes lighting up her cheeks. Yeah, maybe he was one of the better-looking guys at their school, but she couldn't stand the sight of him.

Mostly, it was because he wouldn't stop *looking* at her. No matter where she went or what she was doing, it was impossible to ignore the flurry of giggling, goo-goo-eyed girls who followed Matt everywhere. It didn't matter how many girls tried to get his attention and made complete idiots of themselves in the process. Every time Amanda glanced up to gauge where he was—and to plan a last-minute escape route if he ever tried to talk to her again—she found those startling gray eyes already settled on her face and that crooked smile aimed right at her.

It made the weekend unbearable when the blaring school bell or the teachers telling the entire class to settle down and focus on lessons couldn't save her. She almost considered begging her friends to move to a different table in the outdoor cafeteria, one farther down beneath the pavilion and farther from the table where Matt now sat for every meal with the most obnoxious boys in the junior class.

That would have given her away completely. Not like her friends hadn't already picked up on how much the new shifter kid affected Amanda too. They just thought it was in a completely different way.

"I don't get it," Grace said during dinner in the middle of the semester's third week. "Why do you hate the guy so much?"

"I have no idea who you're talking about." Amanda shoveled more spaghetti into her mouth, her hand clamped tightly around the napkin beside her plate.

"Really? You have no idea, huh?"

Summer snorted. "You know, it *is* super easy to miss all the drooling yahoos following him around everywhere he goes. Sometimes, I forget they're even there."

"I thought it'd blow over," Jackson muttered as he cast Matt's table a dubious glance. "You know, new-kid-itis or whatever."

Alex smirked around his mouthful. "That's not a thing."

"Yeah, apparently not. Almost three weeks in, and the whole school's still going nuts over this Matt guy." The wizard shrugged. "I mean, yeah, he's cool, I guess. He has more self-control than I do, I'll tell you that much. Man, if I had girls clawing at each other to talk to me, I'd completely lose it."

"And run away screaming, Romeo. We get it."

He glared at Summer and shook his head.

"Okay, I get why *you guys* wouldn't like him." Grace wagged the tines of her fork back and forth between Jackson and Alex. "He's basically in the spotlight twenty-four-seven."

"And?" Alex raised an eyebrow. "Doesn't make a difference to me."

"Yeah, I'm not trying to be the center of attention, either," Jackson added.

"Oh, wait." Grace's fork swung toward Amanda. "Is that it?"

"Probably not."

"No, seriously. Because Matt's the center of attention here?"

Summer laughed. "Yeah, right. Because the shifter girl can't stand it when everyone's not looking at her."

"That's not what I mean, Summer. Cut it out." The blonde witch slowly scooted toward Amanda and studied her friend's profile. "I'm talking about Matt being everyone's favorite new junior boy and *Amanda* being the only girl he ever looks at."

Jackson choked on his water and pounded a fist against his chest. "What? That's the dumbest thing I've ever heard."

"Well, maybe you should pay more attention." She raised her eyebrows at him, and the wizard instantly downed more water. "That's it, though. Isn't it? Matt *likes* you, and that's why you can't stand him."

"This is a stupid conversation," Amanda muttered. "Stop talking about Matt liking me or not liking me. If anyone else hears you saying crap like that, I'm gonna have girls lining up to fight me for him, and that's the last thing I need."

"Why?" Summer bit down loudly into a round, crisp, bright red apple. "You could probably kick all their asses at the same time."

"Yeah, but I don't want to. That's the point."

"Because you could take them in under ten seconds, or..."

"Because I'd feel bad, Summer. Okay? I didn't come here to fight other kids. I came here to learn and to be a bounty hunter and—"

An ear-splitting screech from half a dozen voices blasted across the outdoor cafeteria, following by bursts of giggling and exaggerated coos of, "Hi, Matt..."

Amanda grimaced and clenched her eyes shut.

I don't need to turn around to know where he is at this point.

"I have way more important things to worry about than some dumb shifter kid who shows up in the middle of the year and thinks he can get my attention with all that...smiling." When she noticed her friends' dubious expressions, she cleared her throat and stood from the table. "If you guys need me for anything, I'll be in the greenhouse."

"Wait, alone, right?" Jackson called after her.

Summer burst out laughing.

"Just like always," Amanda called over her shoulder, but she couldn't stand to turn around and look at her friends before throwing her trash away. She couldn't stand to look up in front of her either, because she knew she'd find Matt Hardy standing there somewhere in a flood of fawning girls, not even bothering to fend them off because he was too busy staring at—

"Hey, Amanda."

She saw his black sneakers on the grass in front of her a second after she heard his voice and reeled away so quickly, she almost fell over backward right there. The first thing that sprang to mind was to tell him to leave her alone. Whatever he wanted from her, she wasn't interested. More than anything, she wanted to tell him to quit going for wolf-out runs every night because the scent of him on the salty swamp breeze had kept her cooped up in the girls' dorm for almost two weeks.

She didn't. Instead, when she looked up like a startled animal into his wide gray eyes above that crooked smile and the stupid dimples, the only thing that seeped out of her was, "Uh...hey?"

They stared at each other, and she felt like her head was going to explode.

What are you thinking, Amanda? Run. Punch him. Do something!

Matt chuckled and glanced briefly up at the scattered groups of Academy girls clinging to each other and watching him talk to Amanda Coulier instead of them. "Listen, we haven't exactly gotten a chance to talk since the night you found me..." He scratched his head and shrugged. "You know. I'm not a fan of being watched all the time, either. So maybe we could—"

"Miss Coulier." Glasket walked briskly across the central field toward the outdoor cafeteria, frowning and doing double-takes at the fawning lowerclassmen and upperclassmen girls going weak in the knees the closer they crept toward Matthew Hardy. Shaking her head, she stepped in a wide circle around the closest group, caught Amanda's gaze, and cleared her throat. "Sorry to interrupt, but I need to see you in my office, Miss Coulier. Right now, please."

"Yeah, okay." Amanda brushed past Matt, moving quickly after the principal who seemed completely baffled by the other girls' reactions around them.

Matt spun. "Hey, wait. Can't we just—"

The girls closest to him swarmed in like vultures, talking and giggling and babbling all at once, and whatever he'd tried to say to Amanda was lost under the noise.

She swallowed and didn't turn to look as she followed the principal across the field toward the main building.

Serious points for Glasket right now. She just saved me from having to deal with the worst conversation I can possibly imagine.

As the relief of being whisked away from Matt's gray eyes with perfect timing faded, though, a new wave of guilt bubbled up beneath the butterflies in her stomach.

He was only trying to be nice, right? We're the only two shifters in the whole school. Maybe he doesn't wanna be alone. I've been avoiding him...

Glasket pulled open the glass door of the building, and when Amanda caught it, she finally turned to look over her shoulder at the crowded grass between the outdoor cafeteria and the central field. From here, it was impossible to see Matt in the sea of other students.

It'll be impossible to talk to him too without every girl in the school trying to strangle me with a stare. Forget it.

CHAPTER TWENTY

Amanda assumed Glasket wanted to talk to her about something related to the Coalition, her internship at Omega Industries, or her recent mission as a monster-hunter that made her miss the first three days of the spring semester. When she stepped through the door of the principal's office and found Mrs. Zimmer sitting in an extra chair beside Glasket's desk, she knew she'd been wrong.

Crap. I'm so busted now. Play it cool. Don't say anything. If they had proof, they would've kicked me out instead of bringing me up here.

"Have a seat, Miss Coulier." Glasket gestured toward one of the empty chairs in front of the desk, and Amanda sat stiffly without a word. "We thought we'd give you some time to process everything you've been through over the last few months before we brought this to your attention. I had hoped you would have come forward willingly about this, but now we don't have much choice."

Both women stared at her, and Amanda's skin tingled with apprehension. "Okay…"

"Miss Coulier, a significant number of items have recently gone missing from Mrs. Zimmer's storeroom in the west wing,"

Glasket continued. "Taken sometime between the end of last semester and the first few days of this semester."

Amanda glanced back and forth between them, nibbling on the inside of her cheek. "Bummer."

"That's one way to put it, yes." Zimmer eyed the list on the principal's desk and shook her head.

Glasket sat back in her office chair and folded her hands on top of the desk. "Miss Coulier, if I were to take a wild guess—and it honestly wouldn't be that wild, in my opinion—I'd say you know something about when and how these items belonging to the *school* went missing. And most importantly, *why* they went missing."

"Oh. Well, I can't tell you anything about that, Dean Glasket." Despite knowing she was between a rock and a hard place here, she couldn't help but pile on the sweet attitude and call the principal by the title the woman preferred. "I mean, I wasn't even here the first few days of the semester, so if you think it's me, there's kind of a big hole in your timeline, right?"

The second she said it, she wanted to take it back.

I'm gonna try to argue *this? They know. They have to know.*

Glasket dipped her head in agreement. "You have a point."

Amanda blinked and couldn't believe what she was hearing.

"No, we don't have any hard evidence that you were involved in this," the principal continued, "but I'm hoping Mrs. Zimmer and I aren't too far off the mark. Because if it *wasn't* you, that means it was someone else. Most likely someone with far less access to these supplies and, I can only assume, a far less developed conscience."

"Well, yeah." A nervous laugh escaped the shifter girl. "I mean, if someone's stealing all that stuff, their conscience probably didn't have anything to do with it."

Shut up, shut up. What are you doing?

"Possibly." Glasket and Zimmer shared another look, and the Alchemy teacher lifted one shoulder in a "do what you have to do" shrug. "That would leave us with only two other options, Miss Coulier. The first is that someone breached the security wards around this school, and we're dealing with a magical thief running at large around the Everglades. The second, however unfortunate, would be that we have something of a repeat crisis like last year on our hands. Another mutated magical species has managed to affect one of our students or faculty members, much like Mr. Mackey last year, and these creatures are now using whoever it may be as a way to pilfer the Academy's potent supplies."

"Not to mention highly volatile," Zimmer added.

"Exactly." Glasket nodded curtly. "In which case, I'm sorry to say that it would force the Academy of Necessary Magic into another lockdown scenario, this time much more strictly enforced now that we know the possible dangers of this sort of situation. The safety of our students here is and always has been the top priority. Still, I hate to think of the disruption severely heightened security would cause to everyone's experience this semester."

"Hmm." Zimmer leaned back in her chair and crossed one leg over the other. "No trips to the kemana."

"A reinforcement of Lights Out and the enchantments around both the girls' and boys' dormitories."

"Probably have to cancel the Spring Fling dance. Oh, right. And pull the Gators out of the Louper season. Just when things were starting to get good, too."

"They really are getting better, Mrs. Zimmer. You're right."

Amanda wanted to sink through the floor of Glasket's office to get away from this torture. Instead, she swallowed thickly and kept her mouth shut.

Glasket shrugged. "That's only one option, of course. The other is that you've done some work on improving your poker face, Miss Coulier. Either way, I can promise you right now that we will not punish *you* if you tell us exactly what happened. As you understand the series of events, of course."

"Any little thing you might have seen," Zimmer added. "No detail's too small to help us put these pieces together."

The office fell incredibly, painfully silent. Amanda looked back and forth between her teachers and held her breath.

Worst deal ever. But the rest of this semester's gonna be a whole lot worse for everyone if Glasket shuts down the school to look for a criminal on the loose or another mutated creature specializing in mind control. Because they don't exist.

"Okay, fine." She puffed out a huge sigh and lowered her gaze to the edge of Glasket's desk. "Yeah, it was me. I took the stuff from the storeroom."

A small smile flickered across the principal's lips. "Thank you for your honesty."

"I mean, you didn't really give me a choice."

"Oh, there's always a choice, Miss Coulier. If anyone knows that, I'm sure it's you."

Zimmer uncrossed her legs and leaned forward over her lap to scrutinize Amanda with her steely, unflinching gaze. "Anyone else involved in this?"

"Nope. Just me."

"So you disarmed a highly sophisticated security ward around the doorknob without leaving a trace of evidence behind, picked the lock, gathered thousands of dollars worth of alchemical reagents and laboratory equipment—including from the highest shelves in that storeroom—and snuck away with every single item all on your own?" The Light Elf teacher sat back in her chair again and puffed out her cheeks, her eyes wide. "Wow. That has to be close to eight hundred *pounds* of inventory. All by yourself."

"Yep." Amanda tried to smile, but it felt way too tight, and she abandoned the attempt immediately.

I guess they're not buying the whole shifter-strength thing. But they don't have proof.

"I still find that pretty hard to believe," Zimmer added. "That you didn't have help from *anyone* else."

"Well, what can I say? I've learned some pretty awesome stuff at this school so far."

Glasket surprised everyone when she snorted a laugh and immediately clamped her hand over her mouth. Zimmer shot her a disapproving glare, then shook her head. "I'd love to believe you, Miss Coulier. But your story isn't exactly—"

"Yeah, okay. Here." Amanda rattled off from memory all the ingredients and equipment from Wallace's list she'd copied by hand and read over countless times, as well as what she remembered of where each item had been among Zimmer's stored supplies. "I stuck it all in Nurse Aiken's medicine-cabinet bags and carried it all away myself. Yeah, it was heavy. Not *that* heavy."

"All without turning on the lights to see what you were doing," Zimmer muttered.

"Yeah, I know there's magic and everything, but flashlights still exist." Amanda shrugged. "That's what happened."

"Where's the rest of it?" Glasket asked, looking like she was on the verge of either busting out laughing or leaping over her desk to strangle her student. "The leftover equipment, I mean."

"You don't need any more proof than what I gave you." Amanda looked back and forth between them. "I'll return the equipment. I was always going to. But I'm not gonna show you where it is. That's... I mean, I can't really—"

"That's fine, Miss Coulier." Glasket whisked a paper off the surface of her desk and handed it to the Alchemy teacher. "How does it compare?"

Zimmer scanned the list, and her eyes widened until she finished and handed it back. "Apparently, we can add a photographic memory to the long list of Miss Coulier's other unique skills."

"Well, then. I suppose that settles it." The principal slipped the sheet of paper into the top drawer of her desk and leaned forward again, raising her eyebrows. "I have one more question."

"Okay…" Amanda grimaced and waited for the final bomb to drop.

There's no way they won't give me detention or tell me I can't work with the Coalition or something. I should've paid more attention to getting all that stuff back into the storeroom.

The firm line of Glasket's tightly pressed lips softened, and she fixed her student with a sympathetic frown. "If you needed these supplies badly enough to steal them, Miss Coulier, why didn't you ask for permission to use them first?"

"I… What?" That was the last thing Amanda expected to hear, and she still couldn't wrap her brain around this *not* being the setup for a punishment.

"Asking permission. I know you're familiar with the term, however rarely you might put it to practical use."

"Um…" The shifter girl glanced at Zimmer, and Glasket seemed to read the full sentiment behind the brief look.

"It's all right. Mrs. Zimmer knows enough about your internship not to be too terribly shocked by whatever you might say."

I seriously doubt that.

"Well, I mean, I didn't ask because they told me not to."

Zimmer scoffed. "So your…acquaintances asked you to steal from the school, is that it?"

"Not…exactly." Amanda shrugged. "But it's pretty much implied when somebody tells you, 'Do whatever it takes and get it done *now.*'"

The Alchemy teacher bit down on her bottom lip and shook her head. "Tell me it was at least successful."

"Excuse me?" Glasket turned an incredulous look onto her employee.

"If she went through all that, it had to be incredibly important. Those are incredibly dangerous and volatile alchemical reagents. I'm trying to find a silver lining in all this."

"Yeah." Amanda cleared her throat. "Yeah, it was successful. Didn't have any problems at all."

They don't need to know about the exploding bucket because I forgot to tell my friends no plastic.

Zimmer folded her arms and sighed. "Well, at least we know you're paying attention in Alchemy."

"One of my favorite classes."

Both teachers frowned at her, and she immediately folded her arms too just to keep from squirming around.

Okay. Taking it too far with the brown-nosing. Noted.

"Well, I suppose that lifts a little weight from my conscience," Glasket said. "Mrs. Zimmer and I expect the missing equipment and useable materials to be returned to her Advanced Alchemy classroom in the east wing by Sunday night. No, this isn't a ploy to catch you in the act to which you've already confessed."

"Got it. Sunday night. No problem."

"Good. And next time you need something for your... extracurricular endeavors, Miss Coulier, come to me first. We'll figure something out together *without* the need to sneak around the school to pilfer the storerooms. No questions asked."

For a moment, Amanda thought she'd misheard the principal and could only blink in surprise. "You mean you won't ask me what it's for or why I need it?"

"Correct."

"Wow, that's... Okay. Thanks."

Glasket lowered her chin and fixed her student with a stern gaze. "Can I trust you not to abuse this arrangement?"

"Trust me. It's not like I *like* stealing a bunch of supplies for last-minute potions that could probably blow up the whole..." Realizing she'd gone too far, Amanda plastered a thin smile onto her lips and nodded. "Yep. Totally. I won't abuse it."

"Excellent."

"No more stealing," Zimmer added. "I want to see you apply yourself. In the right way."

"Got it."

The Alchemy teacher pushed herself out of her chair and headed for the door. "I'm looking forward to finding that equipment in my office Monday morning."

Then she slipped into the hallway on the top floor and closed the door again behind her.

Amanda practically leapt to her feet and couldn't get out of there fast enough. "Good talk, Dean Glasket. I won't let you down. I mean, not again—"

"Amanda."

She stopped at the sound of her first name on the principal's lips and turned slowly with a grimace. "Yeah?"

"I imagine the work you're doing with the Coalition on the weekends—and the occasional few weekdays, when necessary—takes its toll. If you'd like to talk about it, I'm here. Not as your principal meting out discipline. Just as an open door and someone willing to lend an ear. Whenever you need it."

"Um...thanks. I think I'm good for now."

"All right. Just know my door's always open. How are things going with the internship, anyway? There must be some exciting new improvements if they asked you to brew the kind of potion requiring everything you...found in the storeroom."

"Not that exciting."

More like infuriating when I went through all that thievery for a big fat whopping load of nothing.

"Oh, I'm sure that's not true. It doesn't have anything to do with a new evolved species, does it? Ms. Damascus informed me you had a few new assigned tasks at the—"

"Sorry, Dean Glasket." Amanda shrugged and inched her way backward across the office. "I *really* can't talk about it. Not even with you."

The principal's eyelids fluttered as she tried to mask her disappointment. "Understood."

"But I promise I'm not trying to make explosives at school for fun, okay?"

"Funny. Hearing you say that doesn't exactly put my mind at ease." Glasket huffed out a wry chuckle and waved toward the door. "Enjoy your weekend, Miss Coulier. Don't forget Mrs. Zimmer's equipment by—"

"Sunday night. Yeah, I got it. Thanks." Amanda practically leapt through the office door and made it a point to close it quietly and softly again behind her. Then she raced down the stairs to the ground floor, her hands shoved deep into the pockets of her light zip-up sweater.

I can't believe I got a free pass on that one. No detention. No shakedowns to search everybody's rooms. They didn't even try to find out where I'm keeping the rest of those supplies.

The corner of her mouth twitched, then she snorted a laugh and broke into a wide grin.

Okay. I guess there's at least one advantage to working with the Coalition.

CHAPTER TWENTY-ONE

The weeks after that flew by in a blur of classes, extra time spent in the greenhouse, and Amanda going out of her way to avoid Matt Hardy completely. She even made excuses for why she couldn't join her friends on the central field to watch the Louper matches because of course, the other shifter kid would be there. On nights when she had to go for a run, she chose the complete opposite direction of where she'd run across the Academy grounds as a wolf for years, so she wouldn't run into the young red-brown wolf again.

Despite all the extra care taken *not* to be the center of attention for the junior boy who was still the center of attention, she surprised herself by acing her assignments in Advanced Alchemy and Augmented Tech specifically.

Zimmer didn't seem like she was making an effort to give Amanda good grades—which might or might not have resulted from Amanda returning all the stolen equipment—but the shifter girl wasn't about to complain. And she didn't feel the need to tell her friends about how close she'd come to almost ruining the rest of the year for everyone with her denial of the storeroom supplies theft. That would have only worried them even more.

She had no clue who her team was trying to go after for the current round of Petrov's Bag the Bounty game, and no new grow orders came into the greenhouse. Ms. Ralthorn's History of Oriceran classes seemed to have skipped over considerable gaps in the last century. That was probably to avoid any mention of monsters, mutated species, or groups of shifters networking one giant society dedicated to helping other shifters rise in the world. Possibly because she now had *two* shifter students in the same class.

Most importantly, Amanda received zero calls on her Coalition phone. Nothing from the hotline number, nothing from Dr. Caniss, and nothing from Fiona. Half of her was relieved to have that extra headache off her hands so she could focus on being a junior at the Academy of Necessary Magic.

The other half of her couldn't help but constantly wonder if something had gone seriously wrong at the Canissphere or if the teenage shifter intern had been kicked off the roster altogether and would never be a part of the lab's operations again.

When March arrived, the Everglades warmed right up, true to form. The campus buzzed with excitement over the upcoming Spring Fling dance and their opportunity to let loose a little on school grounds in the middle of the semester.

The weekend before the dance, Glasket made a special point to call an assembly for a short announcement about the upcoming months. For the first time since the school had opened, Shep stood on the stage with the principal, and no one could figure out why.

"Now, as most of you are aware, the Academy's Spring Fling dance is next weekend. Attendance isn't mandatory by any means, but it's highly encouraged. I think you'll all be extremely pleased with what's in store for you this year.

"We also have a new addition to the extracurricular activities offered to students this year." Glasket cleared her throat and gestured at Shep, who stood slightly hunched over on the stage with a crooked, toothy smile, wringing his wide-brimmed hat nervously in both hands. "Mr. Frederick, our resident driver, chauffeur, airboat captain, and groundskeeper, has agreed to help us with this for as long as the program is viable. Or until he's tired of pulling his hair out from the effort and the lot of you drive him away from it."

The principal snickered into the floating microphone at her head, but the central field remained completely silent.

"Did Glasket just try to tell a joke?" Grace asked as she leaned toward Amanda and stared at the stage.

"I can't tell."

"Anyway, starting this year, from here on out, the junior class at the Academy of Necessary Magic will enjoy the luxury of receiving driving lessons from Mr. Frederick. Yes, before you start gloating, the seniors have already received their lessons. So thank you, seniors, for being our willing guinea pigs!"

Again, none of the students responded to what might have been another attempt at a joke.

"Man." Summer snickered and leaned forward, her grin widening. "She's really bombing this."

Alex shook his head. "So this is what happens to standup comedians who don't make it."

Both of them screwed up their faces and failed miserably to hold back their laughter.

"Right." Glasket cleared her throat again. "Driving lessons for juniors start next week after the Spring Fling dance and will be at the end of the day after your last class. Don't be late. There's no makeup work on this and no extra credit. So let's give Mr. Frederick a round of applause and our gratitude."

The student body clapped politely, and Shep whipped his hat out in front of him before bending over it in a graceful bow.

"*That's* why she's trying to make jokes," Amanda muttered. "She's terrified of having a bunch of juniors behind the wheel of a car."

"You think he's gonna let us practice in the Gatormobile?" Jackson asked.

"I mean, unless he's hiding a sportscar somewhere in one of his sheds."

Amanda had no desire to go to the Spring Fling dance at all that year, and she couldn't pretend to convince herself that it had nothing to do with Matt Hardy.

It had everything to do with Matt Hardy.

So when the dance arrived and the girls' dorm fluttered with excitement—girls squealing over each other's hair and dresses, swapping makeup tips, and yes, gossiping about Matt—Amanda couldn't have been in a worse mood.

She let Grace and Annabelle pull her along down the stairs to the common room in the swarm of girls heading out to the central field. Once they hurried through the dorm's front doors and into the cool night air, she completely lost her nerve. "Hey, guys?"

"Come *on*, Amanda." Grace tugged on her arm. "Glasket said she *thinks we'll be pleased*. That means this has gotta be better than all the other dances put together."

"I'm not sure that's what it means, but okay." Amanda pulled her wrist out of the witch's grip and plastered on a tight smile. "I left something up in my room."

Annabelle looked her up and down with a pitying frown. "You mean your entire outfit?"

"Stop," Grace chided, then fixed Amanda with wide eyes. "You sure you're okay?"

"Totally fine. I'm fine. Go and wait for the veil to open. I'll find you later."

"Okay…"

"Come on." The dwarf girl grabbed Grace's hand and tugged her across the grass. "They have to have HardPull again, Grace."

"Then we should *definitely* get to that table first."

Amanda heaved a sigh and stepped away from the dorm's entrance, which kept spitting out more and more girls in their formal wear, who giggled obnoxiously and squealed and fawned over each other's hair. To be sure none of them saw her—and decided to either drag her along or try to fight her so she wouldn't make it to the dance to distract *Matt*—she snuck around the outer wall of the dorm building, pressing her back to the smooth concrete and sticking to the shadows.

Why do we even need dances in the first place? This is ridiculous.

She watched the swarms of students gathering in front of the arch that blocked them off from the central field until it was time to reveal the dancefloor and felt a small pang of longing. No, she hadn't been as excited about school dances as the other girls, but at least she'd enjoyed them. Most of them, anyway, when they weren't interrupted by magical-plant fiascos or wild boar storming the campus. Now that she'd decided to sit this one out, she wondered if she'd end up regretting the decision.

Heavy panting echoing along the sidewall of the girl's dorm caught her attention, as if someone had been running and now stopped to catch her breath. Curious, Amanda moved slowly down the outside of the dorm toward the back, trying to separate the sound of a frightened animal in pursuit from the chaotic excitement filling the air over the central field.

When she reached the end of the wall, she stopped at the corner and muttered, "Hello?"

Matt's face poked out from behind the back corner, his eyes wide as he scanned the empty grass around them in the darkness. At the sight of Amanda's surprised expression, he disappeared around the corner again and plastered his back against the wall beside the rear door. A heavy sigh of relief escaped him.

Jeeze. Doesn't look like this guy's enjoying Spring Fling any more than I am.

As she was about to sneak away again to find a *different* hiding spot—one that didn't include the shifter boy she was trying to hide from in the first place—Matt whispered, "Are they gone?"

Amanda froze. "What?"

"They're not coming over here, right?"

She scanned the darkness with a frown, instantly on the alert. "Who?"

"Anyone. Everyone." He swallowed thickly and let out another sigh. "Just tell me if anyone is heading this way, okay?"

"Um… Nope. I'm pretty sure everyone's going in the opposite direction."

"Okay. Good."

He didn't say anything else, and Amanda's curiosity got the better of her. She stepped slowly around the corner of the building and found Matt standing there with his back still pressed against the wall, his eyes closed and his face tilted slightly toward the night sky. "You okay?"

He jumped at the sound of her voice, then chuckled and ran a hand over his close-cropped hair. "Ha. Yeah. Now I am."

When he looked at her, his gray eyes glinted in the moonlight, and it almost looked like the same silver glow flaring behind any other shifter's eyes before they brought out their wolf. But Matt Hardy didn't shift. He held Amanda's gaze and fixed her with that crooked smile again. "Thanks."

"I mean, I didn't do anything." She turned to peer around the corner of the dorm building again, but the coast was still clear. "Who exactly are you hiding from?"

Matt snorted. "Anyone. Everyone. It's impossible to get any peace around here, you know?"

Frowning, Amanda eyed him up and down. "Like, from every girl in the school?"

"Yeah…" A self-conscious laugh escaped him. "I didn't do

anything either. They won't leave me alone, and it's kinda starting to get to me."

"Right." Wiping her clammy hands on her cut-off shorts, Amanda swallowed when she found herself staring way too intently at his face. "Sorry to barge in on your hiding spot. So... I'll just—"

"Wait." Matt pushed himself away from the wall and stepped toward her. His gaze still flicked around this part of the campus behind the dorms, though no one had bothered to look for him behind the *girls'* dorm. "You didn't barge in. I mean, yeah, it's a little embarrassing for you to find me out here *hiding* behind a building, but I'm glad it's you."

Amanda's heart fluttered in her chest. "You...you are?"

What am I doing? I should've run away the second I saw him. Get out of here, Amanda.

"Yeah. Listen, are you..." He shrugged and stuck his hands in his pockets. "Are you still going to the dance?"

No, no, no. He can't ask me to the dance right now after he's been hiding from Matt-crazy girls.

"Not really." She started to walk away, her legs wobbling like Jell-O. At least, it felt that way. "You should go if you want, though. They can be fun sometimes."

"Not fun enough for you to be out there with everyone else, though, huh?"

"I guess."

"Amanda, hold on." Matt caught up to her again in one long stride and took her completely off-guard when he set a hand on her shoulder. That shoulder seemed to flare with instant heat, even after he removed it. "If *you're* ditching the dance and *I'm* ditching the dance, maybe we should ditch it together. You know, two pairs of eyes are a better lookout than one, right?"

That made her frown. "I'm not trying to be anybody's body-guard right now, so—"

"What? No. That was supposed to be a joke. Obviously not a

very good one." He fixed her with that crooked smile again and nodded toward the northeast edge of the swamp. "I meant it'd be cool to hang out with you. You know, without all the screaming and giggling…" Matt grimaced, then shook it off instantly with another unsure laugh and stuck his thumb out toward the open ground behind them. "You could show me the swamp?"

He wants me to show him the swamp. For Spring Fling. Alone.

For a moment, Amanda couldn't get her mouth and her brain to line up and work together like they were supposed to. When she finally managed to find her voice again, the first thing she blurted out was the exact opposite of what she wanted. "Yeah, okay."

Wait, what?

Matt's face instantly lit up, and he nodded. "Awesome. Come on. Let's get outta here before somebody figures out I'm not heading to the dancefloor."

He turned quickly to head for the water's edge, and Amanda was sure that if he glanced back to look at her, he'd see her trembling.

What am I doing? This is so stupid. I can't walk around campus with another shifter. It's too…

She couldn't finish that thought. She couldn't even think straight. Matt had caught her completely off-guard, and after almost three months of avoiding him completely, she didn't exactly have a choice now. Somehow, Amanda's feet moved all on their own until she caught up to him. They made their way toward the open ground on the north end of campus, away from the buildings, the dance, and every other student at the Academy.

This is the worst idea ever. The last thing I need is to be alone *with him right now. Or ever.*

CHAPTER TWENTY-TWO

"I did mean what I said, by the way."

"Huh?" Amanda blinked furiously and looked up at the shifter boy walking so close beside her.

"That I'm glad *you're* the one who found me. You don't freak out like all the other girls here."

"Yeah, I don't do magic like all the other girls here, either."

She hadn't meant it as a joke, and Matt's low laughter made her stomach curl up in knots all over again.

"So you're writing it off as a shifter thing, huh?"

"You're not?"

Stop, stop, stop. Why do you keep saying all this stupid crap?

There was that crooked smile again and those dimples to frame it. "I mean, it could be. But I've known a lot of shifters, and you're not like them either."

"I blame the plants."

"What?"

His smile didn't disappear as he stopped and looked at her, but now she was sure he'd see her shaking and sweating and acting like a complete idiot.

"Nothing." Amanda shook her head and kept walking, this

time picking up the pace so it forced Matt to hurry after her and catch up. "Forget I even said that."

Great. I can't even talk right, and Fiona's gonna lose it if she finds out I've been blabbing to another shifter about Fatethistle.

They walked in silence for a while along the water's edge. The sounds of dancing, shouting, laughing high school kids faded beneath the chirp of crickets, the drone of insects, and the rustling of nocturnal wildlife moving around through the swamp. Matt's scent was strong in the air around her, and Amanda had to force herself not to look at him.

This isn't a date. Nothing's happening. Why am I even thinking this?

"So." He shot her a sidelong glance. "You're the only shifter here, huh? I mean, besides me."

"Yep." She stared straight ahead with wide eyes.

"That's gotta be pretty weird."

"Not as weird as hiding from girls behind the girls' dorm." Immediately, she cursed herself for being so stupid and bringing *that* up again, but Matt laughed.

"You got me there, I guess. I thought it would let up, but we're halfway through the semester, and nothing's changed. Not something I thought I'd have to deal with again. It's nice to talk to someone who…you know. Can keep it together and have a conversation."

Why would he ever think that's me?

It took her five more seconds to zero in on what he'd said. "Deal with *again*?"

"Yep. New school, same thing. I blame my dad." Matt wrinkled his nose, then shook his head. "Now I'm talking about my parents and making this weird. Sorry."

"No, it's okay." Somehow, his embarrassment had eased hers enough that she could ignore it—or at least more successfully pretend to ignore it. "I'm the last person who'd judge someone about their parent issues."

"Oh, yeah? What did yours do to you?"

Amanda clammed up immediately.

Yeah, right. Like I'm gonna start talking about my murdered family.

Matt seemed to pick up on her instant discomfort and waved off his question. "Sorry. I didn't mean to start—"

"They're dead."

Damnit, Amanda. What is wrong *with you?*

He stopped abruptly and turned to look at her with a sympathetic frown that made her want to step closer and run away from him at the same time. "Whoa. I'm so sorry. I didn't know."

"How could you?" She shrugged and couldn't for the life of her understand how she could feel like a jiggling pile of mush on the inside but still talk and walk like a fully functioning girl. "It happened a few years ago. Right before I came here, actually. I'm…dealing with it."

"Wow." Matt cleared his throat and kept walking at her side—so closely now she could have reached out and touched him if she wanted.

I seriously need to stop thinking about that.

"So you're one of the kids who live here, then."

A sharp laugh escaped her, and she tried to brush that off too. "No. I mean, I've been here since the Academy opened, but I live with my…" Failing to find the right word for Johnny and Lisa made her throat tighten, but then suddenly it wasn't so hard to come right out and say it. "My family. Johnny got me out of a seriously bad situation, and I guess he and Lisa are the closest thing I have to parents now. You wouldn't guess it by looking at them."

"How come?"

Stop gushing your life's story already! What are you doing?

She shrugged and couldn't help a small smile. "I mean, she's a half-Light Elf who used to work for the FBI, and he's a dwarf bounty hunter. Like, *the* dwarf bounty hunter."

"Hold up." Matt turned to face her head-on, his eyes wide and his mouth twitching like he wanted to laugh but couldn't quite remember how. "What's his last name?"

"Uh…Walker."

"No way. You mean the Johnny Walker who built this place?"

"Not really what he's known for, but yeah. That one."

"You're his *kid*?"

Great. Not sure talking about Johnny is any better than talking about my dead parents.

"Yeah, I guess I am now." Amanda kept walking, cursing herself for having brought any of this up in the first place and wondering why she couldn't keep her mouth shut.

"Whoa, whoa. Hey." Matt jogged to catch up with her. "That's awesome."

"Okay."

"I mean…" He let out a nervous laugh and ran a hand over his short auburn hair again. "I mean, I've only thought of him as a pretty scary dude—"

"Ha! Johnny? He's not. Yeah, he wants everyone to *think* he is, but he's…softer on the inside, I guess."

"Doesn't make him any less scary."

Amanda snorted. "Well, it's not like you have to meet my parents or anything."

"Why not?" The crooked smile he shot her blasted a giant Matt-sized hole through the confidence she'd only just gotten under control again. He picked up on that too and started backpedaling himself. "Hey, totally cool if you wanna keep your parents out of it. I know I do."

"Yeah, you said you blame your dad."

Matt wrinkled his nose. "Yeah… I did, didn't I? It's a totally weird thing. And way more complicated now than it was when I was little."

"How come?"

He heaved a massive sigh and scuffed the bottom of his sneaker against the cool grass. "Okay, I'm only telling you this because you told me about *your* family first. Not really something I come out and say to everybody."

"I don't tell everybody either."

Matt's gray eyes shimmered in the moonlight when he met her gaze. "Yeah, I know."

They stared at each other, and the second Amanda realized the scent of this shifter boy standing so close to her was making her dizzy, she shook her head and kept walking. "You don't have to tell me anything. Sorry I—"

"He's different." Matt swallowed. "I mean, my mom's a shifter, right? That's how I got...well, most of what I am. And my dad's...not."

"Not a shifter?"

"Yeah."

"Okay." Amanda shrugged. "That happens a lot. I'm pretty sure half the kids at this school have human parents."

"Yeah, and they have it easy."

"Wait, he's *not* human?"

Wrinkling his nose again, Matt scanned the starry night sky and looked thoroughly confused. Or insanely uncomfortable. "Not even close. My parents didn't ever try to hide it, which is cool, I guess. I had no idea that being his kid and being half-shifter would turn out so...weird."

He blames his dad for being chased down by Matt-crazy girls every-where he goes. What the heck is his dad?

"Actually... Maybe we shouldn't go down that rabbit hole right now." Matt chuckled and shook his head. "I kinda like talking to you like we're only two normal shifters at a magic school, so can we keep doing *that*?"

"Yeah." Despite the mystery of what he'd almost told her and completely yanked away at the last second, Amanda found herself trying to force back a secretive smile. It was impossible. "Yeah, we can keep doing that."

"Cool."

They kept walking along the water's edge, listening to the wildlife and talking. Matt didn't ask her any more questions about Johnny and Lisa or Amanda's life before her new family became a part of it. Instead, he wanted to know about the Academy of Necessary Magic, her favorite parts of being here almost three years, what it was like to come in as part of the school's first-ever freshman class.

She told him about Summer and the soul-stone temple, the wild boar who'd crashed the first Spring Fling dance, having Dark Scream play for Homecoming, the kemana, and her friendship with the kitchen pixies.

What she really wanted to talk to him about was being a shifter—the fact they had magic, that she had fully mature Fatethistle plants in a hidden cellar under the greenhouse, and that if he wanted, Matt could try it out for himself. But that would have meant bringing Fiona into it, and probably the Coalition, and none of that seemed remotely possible.

This is the first time we've talked to each other. Leave the bomb drops at dead parents and bounty hunter guardians. That's enough.

"Okay, okay." When they finished laughing about the debacle with the Dreamscape pollen, Matt drew a deep breath and shoved his hands in his pockets. "That's something I've been wondering about since I got here and heard I wasn't the only shifter."

"What is?"

"The greenhouse."

Crap. I was trying so hard not to bring that up.

"What about it?"

"I mean, I know that's where you go while the rest of us are stuck in Illusions with Calsgrave." He shrugged. "I guess I wonder why they haven't stuck me in there with you too."

"Yeah, you don't wanna be stuck with me in a greenhouse for two and a half hours."

"That's not what I meant."

Smirking, Amanda stepped toward the water's edge and sat right there beside a group of ferns, their huge leaves whispering against each other in the breeze. "I know."

Matt didn't waste a second before sitting down right beside her. She froze when the side of his leg brushed up against hers but didn't pull away again.

It's fine. He doesn't feel it. No big deal. Don't look.

She stared across the glimmering water instead and swallowed.

"So... Are you gonna answer my question?"

"What?"

Matt laughed. "About why Glasket hasn't told me to skip Illusions I can't even actually *do* in class and come help you out with the plants."

"Well..." Amanda frowned. "I had to seriously screw up a lot of things more than once before anyone realized I'd be better off in the greenhouse."

"Oh, I get it. You're saying I haven't caused enough trouble yet."

A shiver raced down her spine, making the hairs on the back of her neck stand completely on end. Slowly, without even thinking, she turned her head to look at him and found that crooked smile aimed her way one more time.

Oh, come on. He's way too close right now.

She didn't pull away.

Neither did he.

"Maybe I need a few pointers from the girl who's been here a while, right?"

She remained frozen in that gray gaze of his, and she could've sworn she saw another flash of silver light behind them. Or maybe that was what she wanted to see.

How the heck did I end up sitting alone by the swamp with Matt Hardy? What am I doing?

"You know, when I got here and heard a few things about

another shifter at this school, I honestly expected things to be a lot different."

Amanda blinked. "Different?"

"Yeah. More...tense, maybe. But you're really easy to be around, Amanda."

Her breath hitched in her throat. "That's like the complete opposite of what I hear regularly."

He huffed out a laugh. "Well, it's true. At least for me."

She couldn't look away from his eyes—except, of course, for when her gaze flickered down to his lips and that crooked smile. Then she knew she'd seriously screwed up.

Oh my God, oh my God. He's leaning closer. What am I supposed to do if he—

The Coalition phone in her back pocket buzzed, and Amanda practically jumped out of her skin with a hiss.

"Whoa." Matt leaned away in surprise, the moment completely broken now, and she couldn't decide if she was disappointed or relieved. "What's wrong?"

"Nothing. I got a—" She clamped her mouth shut and shook her head. "Nothing. Sorry."

I haven't heard a thing from the Coalition in months, and they pick tonight *to start blowing up my phone? Come on.*

"You sure?" He looked her up and down. "Looks like you got bit by something."

"Yeah, maybe." To cover up her tracks, Amanda leaned away again and brushed at the dirt and grass where she'd been sitting. "There's some kind of weird spikey grass here sometimes. I probably sat on it the wrong way or something."

"Okay." After staring at her for a few more seconds, Matt returned his attention to the swamp stretching out in front of them and the rippling surface of the water shimmering under the moonlight streaking through the heavy foliage. He drew a deep breath through his nose and let it all out in one long, slow sigh. "You know, I always had this picture of swamps in my head as, like, a bunch of dead things rotting in gross water. But I like it out here."

"Yeah." She ran her hand through the dirt beside her, closed her fingers around a small pebble, and chucked it into the water. "It grows on you after a while. Honestly, I can't even imagine living anywhere else now. I don't think I'd want to."

She glanced at him sidelong and found the shifter boy sitting there close beside her with his eyes closed as he listened to the nocturnal wildlife and breathed in the cool, salty spring air of the Florida Everglades.

It's true. At least I don't have to lie about that.

CHAPTER TWENTY-THREE

The next morning, Amanda sprang out of bed just after 5:30 a.m., completely awake and humming with a surprising amount of energy. For how late she and Matt had stayed out last night, talking and eventually sitting by the water together without saying or doing anything else, she should have been exhausted. She couldn't figure out why she wasn't.

The rest of the school was still asleep on a Sunday morning, and because she didn't want to be the crazy shifter girl pacing in circles out in the central field before breakfast, she grabbed her shower bag, towel, a fresh change of clothes, and headed for the third-floor showers. The hot water helped, but no matter how vigorously she washed or how hard she thought of the history of magitech essay for Ralthorn or Petrov's bald head or even a chum bucket left out to rot in the sun, she couldn't get Matt's gray eyes and easygoing smile out of her mind.

Only when the water ran completely cold did she realize she wasn't the only one in the dorms who showered, so she hopped out and dressed as quickly as she could.

By the time she finished brushing her hair in her room, the hallway was quickly filling with groggy, bleary-eyed girls shuffling out of their rooms to make their zombie-like exodus to the outdoor cafeteria. Amanda grabbed the Coalition phone from the pocket of yesterday's shorts, shoved it into her loose pedal-pushers instead, and hurried out of her room.

Summer was right there waiting for her in the hall, and Amanda froze.

"Looks like you have some serious explaining to do, shifter girl."

"What? Why would you think that?"

"Because of how stupidly guilty you look right now, for one." The witch snorted and joined Amanda walking down the hall. "Plus the fact that you didn't show up at the dance last night. Like, at all."

"Because I didn't wanna go, okay? That's not weird."

"Yeah, but you being all defensive like this is." Summer nudged her in the arm and grinned. "So spill it, already. What did you break?"

"I didn't break anything, Summer."

"Okay, then what'd you steal?"

Amanda looked pointedly around the hallway, but none of the other girls were remotely awake enough to pay attention to the rainbow-haired witch who couldn't lower her voice even to talk about breaking school rules. "Nothing. I didn't do anything you would do last night, okay? So drop it."

"Uh-huh." They filed after everyone else down the stairwell and across the common room on the main floor. Just before they reached the dorm's front doors, Summer added, "You know, it was *pretty* hard to ignore all the seriously disappointed chicks in dresses and glitter last night. You should've seen it, shifter girl. It was practically a sob fest."

I know where she's going with this, and I won't let her get to me.

"Why?" Amanda growled. "Did someone die?"

"Whoa." Summer barked out a laugh and slapped her hand against the door swinging shut in front of them before they stepped outside. "No one *had* to. They were all freaking out over that Matt guy again, but you know what? I heard he never showed up either."

"Maybe he was tired of the stampede."

"That a hunch, or did you hear it straight from the wolf boy's mouth?"

"Summer!" Amanda whirled on her friend, who only stepped away and laughed. It took everything she had to lower her voice instead of screaming it all in the other girl's face. "Nothing happened, okay? We talked."

"You know what that's code for, right?"

"Stop." No matter how quickly Amanda stormed across the edge of the central field to head for the outdoor cafeteria, Summer kept up with her pace like it was nothing.

"I knew it."

"Summer…"

"Hey, you held out for almost three months, shifter girl. Pretty impressive. But the dude's basically been stalking you since the semester started. Not your fault if you couldn't help it anymore."

"That's not…what happened." Amanda wiped her hands on her pant legs and tried to look anywhere but at her friend. "We're not talking about this."

"Sure. Fine. I get it. Private moment." Summer lifted both hands in surrender and snickered. "But you might wanna tell *someone* before you explode. Which it looks like you're gonna do at any second. And don't expect me to put Humpty Dumpty back together again when Romeo finds out."

"When I find out what?" Jackson said behind them a second before he shoved himself between the girls and slung an arm over each of their shoulders.

"Huh." Summer shrugged out from beneath his arm and looked him up and down. "So you finally embraced the name, huh?"

With only Amanda under his arm now, he quickly withdrew it and fixed her with a grin. "Hey, you feeling okay, Coulier?"

"I'm fine. Why?" Amanda gave Summer a warning glare, and the witch waggled her eyebrows as they headed for the breakfast line.

"Didn't see you at the dance, is all." Jackson shrugged. "You're lookin' a little red. Got a cold or something?" He put more distance between them and grimaced. "Nothing against you. But if you have a cold, I'm gonna…"

"I'm not sick, Jackson. Seriously, everything's fine. I just… needed some space last night."

"Yeah, okay. It's your thing. That's cool. *Man*, I'm starving." He sniffed the air and grinned. "Is that waffles? Yes! Has to be waffles. Hey, Alex! We're over here!"

The Wood Elf jerked his chin up at them and hurried to join them in line, his long brown ponytail swinging across his back.

Amanda hardly heard the conversation as Summer and the guys joked around and went over what they'd seen and done last night at the dance. Most of her focus was on not looking at Summer *or* Jackson and trying to act normal. Yes, a small part of her attention had split off in a casual attempt to scan the outdoor cafeteria for Matt.

Then what? If I ignore him, he'll think I hate him after last night. If I say hi, he'll come over here, and it'll be one giant mess if he says anything about us hanging out last night. Especially with Jackson right here. I can't believe this. I'm totally screwed.

"Hey, you *sure* you're okay?" Jackson asked as he handed her a plate.

"What? Yeah. Totally. I'm fine." She grabbed whatever food was in front of her and jumbled it together on her plate, trying to make herself as small and inconspicuous as possible.

By the time they sat at their usual table to eat, Amanda didn't think she could eat a single bite. Then she saw Matt standing in line with Tommy and Evan, and she knew she couldn't.

"What about those weird tentacle things, though?" Summer asked. "Like, I can't figure out if Glasket was going for underwater palace or torture chamber with all that—whoa, whoa, hey. Where you goin', shifter girl?"

Amanda gave her another warning look and muttered, "I forgot a drink."

She booked it toward the drink station and almost poured orange juice all over the bin full of ice instead of in her cup.

Stupid. I was so stupid last night, and now I have to keep worrying about what my friends will think. Just because some shifter boy shows up and is nice and doesn't get scared off by anything I told him—

"Amanda." Grace joined her at the drink station, her eyes wide. "Where *were* you last night? You said you forgot something in your room."

"Yeah… Then I didn't feel like dancing, so I didn't go. Sorry."

"Okay, well next time, maybe don't disappear again like that. I thought you—"

"Hey, guys."

Amanda jumped when she looked up and saw Matt standing on the other side of the drink station, smiling at her. "Uh…hey."

She tried to smile back, but now she was worried about puking in the ice bin.

"Hi, Matt…" Grace breathed, her eyes wide and glistening now as she stared at him.

His crooked smile flickered, then he scooped ice into his cup. "Heard the dance was pretty awesome last night."

"Yeah. Awesome…"

Amanda wanted to nudge Grace out of her weird goo-goo-eyed stupor but could hardly rip herself out of hers. She finished pouring her juice and stuck the carafe back in the ice. Grace immediately picked it up again and tipped the carafe toward her plastic cup but didn't pour. She was too busy staring at Matt's face.

His gaze flickered from Amanda's face to the carafe and then finally to the blonde witch holding it in a stupor. "Uh, Grace? You gonna use the juice?"

She blinked furiously. "You know my name?"

"Yep. We all have the same classes every day, so... Hey, can I have that?"

"Oh my God, yes." Grace thrust the carafe into his hand and didn't move.

"Thanks." He poured his drink with a chuckle, stuck the carafe back into the ice, then fixed Amanda with another smile. "Got any plans today?"

She cleared her throat. "Not really. Just gonna play it by ear, I guess."

Play it by ear? How stupid can I get?

"Cool." Matt's smile widened, and he nodded slowly. "See you around, then."

"Yep." That one word sounded like it came out as a squeak, but she kept smiling as he turned and headed to the table of junior boys.

Grace let out her breath in one giant burst. "Oh my God. That's...the first time he's ever talked to me."

Amanda snorted. "Aren't you guys partners in Alchemy?"

"I mean outside of class." The witch blinked furiously and shook her head. "Wow. Okay. You know, I'm kind of glad he didn't show up at the dance last night. Probably would've turned into a giant fight with everybody trying to—" She gasped and clutched Amanda's wrist, almost spilling her freshly poured orange juice. "He wasn't at the dance. *You* weren't at the dance."

"So?"

"And you *talked* to him." Grace tightened her grip and lowered her voice into a harsh whisper. "Oh my God, Amanda. You're still *smiling*. Did you two—"

"No and no." She tried to walk away from the drink station, but the other girl wouldn't let her go.

"Hold on a second."

"Grace, seriously, this isn't—"

"No, you know what? Summer's right. You're the worst liar. I mean, except for me, but we're not talking about me right now. You have to tell me everything, Amanda. I'm serious. Like, right now."

"Just stand here in the middle of the cafeteria while everyone's watching? No thanks."

"Nobody's watching…" Grace scanned the students around them and slowly removed her hand from Amanda's wrist. "Oh. Okay, well, only the *girls* are staring."

"That's not making it better. Let's eat, okay? It's nothing."

"It's *nothing*? Look at them. They look like they're about to rip us apart. Or rip *you* apart—Hey!" Grace cocked her head at a group of sophomore girls walking by the drink station and glaring at Amanda. "Hey, you got a problem with orange juice or what?"

The girls shook their heads and hurried to their table, but the dirty looks didn't let up.

Amanda stared at the blonde witch. "Wow. Summer's starting to rub off on you too, huh?"

"Only when it matters. Sophomores. Are you kidding me? They have no idea who they're messing with. Come on."

They walked toward their usual table to join Summer and the guys but stopped when Principal Glasket's voice rose over the drone of breakfast conversation. "Miss Coulier."

Grimacing, Amanda turned toward the front end of the kitchen building and found the principal standing there with none other than Scientist Rick. He wasn't wearing his white lab coat or carrying one of his stupid clipboards, but he scowled at her just the same.

Crap. I can't believe I completely forgot about the text last night!

"Yeah?"

"Would you come with me for a moment, please?" Glasket

waved her forward, ignoring the stares the students shot toward her and the strange man standing stiffly beside her.

With a low growl, Amanda downed her entire glass of orange juice and tossed the plastic cup in the bus bin before making her way to the principal. She glanced over her shoulder at her friends. Grace spread her arms and shook her head. Jackson stared at her, looking completely clueless. Alex was too busy eating. Summer winked at her before miming putting a phone to her ear.

Amanda rolled her eyes.

Yeah, way to be subtle about it, Summer.

When she reached Glasket, she tried to smile and found it almost impossible beneath Rick's glare. "What's up?"

"Follow me, please." After a brief scan of the students—and the entire female population of the Academy's student body still glaring at Amanda's back—Glasket spun and led them not toward the main building but around the corner of the kitchens instead. "All right. Just be sure nobody sees you," she told Rick. "I'm not quite sure I'm prepared to answer those kinds of questions from an entire campus of teenagers. Amanda? Good luck."

"Wait. Dean Glasket—"

The principal was already stalking away from them, her quick footsteps dislodging clumps of grass in her haste.

Rick eyed the shifter girl up and down. "Didn't you get the text?"

"Uh…yeah. Of course, I got it."

He rolled his eyes. "At least this time you can't complain about not being warned."

"Wait, you're talking about packing a bag, right?" Amanda pointed at the girls' dorm. "It's right up in my room. I can get it in like two seconds—"

"Too bad." Rick's hand came down on her shoulder, and the world illuminated in a flash of blue light before Amanda almost stumbled head-first into the wall of the back hallway in Everglades City's Starbucks.

"Oh, come on. You couldn't have waited two more minutes?"

"You couldn't have shown up prepared for once?" He stalked toward the supplies closet and shoved open the door.

"Right, because it's totally normal to show up to breakfast with a fully packed bag in the middle of the semester." With a low growl, she hurried after him and squeezed herself alongside his bulk in the tiny, cramped room. "There's gotta be a better system for this, right?"

"The texting system works fine." Rick cranked down on the elevator handle, and they dropped however far below the Starbucks into the train station.

Amanda gasped when they finally reached the bottom, then the doors to the waiting train car *hissed* open. She stumbled out after the pissed-off shifter sent to collect Dr. Caniss' intern and sat on the empty red velvet cushion as he took his seat across from her.

Her anger grew to the point where she couldn't hold it back any longer. "Look, if you hate this so much, why don't they send someone else to come get me?"

"I've been asking myself the same question," Rick growled. Then he folded his arms and closed his eyes.

Apparently, that's the end of the conversation.

As the Starbucks train filled with the sound of other magical commuters in their cars, Amanda stared at the scientist until she was sure he wouldn't open his eyes again. Then she slipped the Coalition phone out of her pocket as quietly as she could and pulled up the text she'd completely forgotten to read.

Tomorrow morning. 8:30 a.m. Pack for a long trip.

Oh, come on.

Clenching her eyes shut, she pocketed the phone and grimaced.

This is gonna suck so bad. Definitely not packed for a long trip. Probably won't even be that long anyway. Just three days of Caniss listing all the ways I screwed up and ruined their plans before she kicks me out of that lab forever.

CHAPTER TWENTY-FOUR

Amanda couldn't have possibly guessed that Rick was chaperoning her anywhere other than the train station under downtown Denver for another surprise shifter teleport to the valley in the Rockies. When Rick stood at a completely different stop on the Starbuck train's route and waited for the doors to open, she got the immediate impression something was seriously wrong.

"Wait, you can't get off here."

"I don't take orders from you, kid."

"Yeah, I know that but who's gonna teleport me from Denver to the lab?"

"No one. You're coming with me." The doors *hissed* open, and the low murmur of magical voices filtered toward them down the dark hallway beyond.

Crap.

Amanda leapt to her feet and hurried after the angry shifter storming down the hall. The magicals heading toward them to enter the train from this hallway gave Rick as wide a berth as they could in the narrow space, but the shifter girl once more had to duck and weave around them in her struggle to keep up. Then the hallway opened into a much wider, even longer black-walled corridor lined with dozens of small hallways on this side and as many full-sized doors on the other, all of them painted different colors with various symbols above the frames.

He brought me to The Pylon?

"Wait, Rick." She ducked beneath the long ladder clamped under a massive Kilomea's arm and hurried after her guide. "What are we doing here?"

"Looks like you're about to find out."

The central hub for magical business was as busy now as the first time Fiona had brought her here. That, of course, had been for a prearranged meeting with the Coalition board and their chairman, Connor Slate. The discussion that had gone so ridiculously wrong when Summer had decided to crash it with her not-quite-mastered cloaking illusion.

Oh, no. Please let him stop at a different door. Any other door but that one.

Her silent pleading didn't make a bit of difference. Because Rick stopped directly in front of the same door and delivered two swift knocks on the dark wood. Then he turned the handle and opened the door with nothing but an irritated glance at Amanda.

"Okay…" She puffed out a sigh and slowly entered the room.

The door closed instantly behind her, with Rick on the other side and the constant drone of so many other magicals scurrying around to take care of their own business cut off abruptly.

"Amanda." Dr. Caniss glanced at her wristwatch and raised an eyebrow. "Well, at least you're punctual this time."

"I didn't really have a—" Amanda stopped when she saw Fiona leaning back against the edge of the ridiculously long conference table, smirking with her arms folded. Then she saw Connor Slate himself standing at the far head of the table. The Coalition of

Shifters' board director didn't exactly smile at her, but he didn't look nearly as pissed as Rick. "What's going on?"

"I know this doesn't exactly look like the last meeting we had," Connor replied. "But in the interest of time, I thought it was more prudent to waive the presence of the other board members so we could continue."

Amanda swallowed. "With what?"

"Have a seat." He gestured toward the long conference table lined with completely empty chairs.

Fiona winked at her mentee and nodded in encouragement.

Somehow, it didn't make Amanda feel all that encouraged.

But she followed the redhead shifter woman down one side of the long table while Caniss moved down the other side, and when they all sat, there were two empty chairs between them and Connor Slate.

"Dr. Caniss." He nodded at her. "You can take this one if you like."

"Yes." The doctor folded her hands on the tabletop and fixed Amanda with her no-nonsense gaze. "After your most recent operation with Bernard MacMillan and his...team, we've concluded that we must make certain necessary and vital changes within the Coalition's Magical Research and Acquisitions Division."

Great. They had to bring me out here to tell me they're canning me as an intern? Could've sent that in a text.

When the three grown shifters around the table only stared at her expectantly, Amanda cleared her throat. "Okay. I understand."

"Good." Caniss nodded. "After extensive analysis of the scans MacMillan's team managed to gather and return, specifically concerning TS-0513, we believe contracting the services of free-lance units with that...particular skillset is no longer beneficial to our work and therefore no longer required."

Amanda frowned. "I mean, they did try to *kill* that thing instead of study it, so I'd say that's probably a good call."

Why is she telling me this?

Connor narrowed his eyes and leaned slightly forward over the end of the table. "I want to hear your version of events, Amanda. Everything you can remember from the operation with MacMillan's team and TS-0513."

"Everything?" She darted an uncertain glance toward Fiona, who only nodded again with another tiny smile twitching on her lips. "Um...okay. We were supposed to track down the mons—I mean TS-0513 to get the power core back for the evolved mermaids living under the lab."

"Subject UM-43562," Caniss corrected.

"Right. We got out to Elk State Forest in Pennsylvania, and on top of refusing to give me any kind of weapon and laughing in my face about it, MacMillan made me stay back with one of his guys. Wes."

"Which one's that?" Fiona asked.

"The guy covered in tattoos."

"Right."

"Keep going, Amanda," Connor added, sharing a brief look with Fiona that was impossible to read under the circumstances.

Amanda had no choice but to dive into the story she never had a chance to tell during the debriefing in Caniss' strategy room. The wrongness she'd picked up with her magic in the woods. Her decision to investigate with her ghost-wolf instead of as an unarmed shifter girl. What she'd *seen* of the monster and its attempts to protect itself before and after Mac's team had barged in to try taking it out with weapons first.

When she finished, the boardroom was intensely silent.

Connor blinked and cleared his throat. "Dr. Caniss?"

"There's obviously nothing more to discuss." The doctor drummed her fingers on the tabletop.

Here comes the part where they tell me it's over. Bring it. I'm ready.

"I'm not so sure that's entirely the case," Connor added. "There's plenty more." Eyeing Caniss pointedly, he nodded toward Amanda and raised his eyebrows.

She pressed her lips together. "Yes, well, that and the fact that we've come to an understanding regarding the severe lack of awareness, training, and preparation of MacMillan's unit for an operation of this magnitude."

"Which you would have heard from me the first time if anyone had bothered to let me talk," Amanda muttered.

"Be that as it may, we still haven't accomplished our original goal with TS-0513. It still possesses the...artifact the Subject UM-43562 representative asked us to retrieve, and we still require a solution to one crucial problem facing us as we speak."

Amanda's anger flared anew inside her as she had to sit here and listen to Caniss trying to explain away the major flaws in her plan. "The last magical remedy you had me grow mystery plant number one for didn't work."

"No. Our trials with the Godvein yielded less-than-acceptable results."

"Meaning Jenkins is still in a coma," Fiona added.

Caniss nodded curtly. "So we move forward with the rest of our plan to apprehend TS-0513 and retrieve that artifact as soon as possible."

Amanda slapped her hand down on the table and leaned forward toward the doctor. "It took you *two and half months* to get all this figured out?"

"I'll ask you not to raise your voice at me, Amanda. I have impeccable hearing, so it's highly unnecessary."

Fiona snorted.

"What did you guys do? Sit around *talking* about trying out a useless plant on your scientist who didn't get poisoned?"

"No, we discovered the Godvein's inefficacy shortly after your last visit to Omega Industries." Caniss sat back in her chair and held Amanda's gaze without a hint of remorse. "What little data we *do* have took quite some time to analyze fully."

The girl rolled her eyes. "Well, it wouldn't have if you'd listened to me in the first place—"

"Yes, in retrospect, I understand you were closer to the truth in your estimations than I'd expected. Still, we had to exhaust all available options with the safety and wellbeing of a member of my staff as our top priority. Anyone else in my position would have done the same."

"Why, because I'm fifteen?"

"Because I don't enjoy being wrong." The doctor nodded curtly. "Which has clearly been proven now at least twice over, so you'll have to content yourself with that and let it go."

Amanda slumped back into her chair, which spun slowly toward Fiona beneath the impact until Amanda grabbed the edge of the table and turned it briskly forward again. "Fine. Whatever."

"Doctor." Connor gestured toward the shifter girl. "I appreciate your candor in this matter, but we still haven't broached the main point of why we're all *here*. Now. On a Sunday morning."

Caniss' eyebrows did a strange little dance as she studied the man's face as though she didn't quite know how to frown or scowl or show any emotion at all.

Fiona coughed to hide a small chuckle. "I'm happy to tell her if you if you can't handle it—"

"I can handle it, Miss Damascus, and I'd also very much appreciate it if you wiped that incorrigible smirk off your face."

"It's fine." Amanda pushed herself out of the chair and rose to her feet. "Really. You don't have to say anything."

"Amanda, please sit down."

"No, I'll save you both the extra trouble, okay? It's the least I can do." She drew a deep breath and steeled herself as she glanced at each of the adult shifters still sitting and staring at her. "The internship's over. I did my best, though it obviously wasn't enough. That's fine. Monsters and science probably shouldn't

221

ever mix anyway, and I'm not exactly an expert on either of them. Thanks anyway, I guess."

She started to turn toward the door, wondering how the heck she'd get back to school from the Everglades City Starbucks.

Maybe I'll call Johnny. Or Lisa. She won't leave me stranded either, but at least she won't complain the whole drive to campus.

"Amanda," Connor called after her.

The gently commanding firmness of his voice made her instantly freeze before she slowly turned again. Fiona hid a small smile beneath her hand. Dr. Caniss stared expressionlessly at the shifter girl. Amanda shrugged. "I don't know what else there is to talk about."

A small smile broke the thin line of the board director's lips. "Then, please. Join us a moment longer and *listen*. We're not quite finished."

Her legs moved stiffly beneath her as she returned to her chair and sat again. Fiona nudged her arm with a fist and nodded.

"Amanda." Caniss blinked quickly, her gaze stuck like a system glitch on the ceiling as she thought over her next words. "We're sending another team out to Pennsylvania for one more attempt to retrieve the artifact and neutralize TS-0513. *Without* the use of deadly force. Our system has picked up another unknown magical signature in the area. It's almost the same as those we discovered before the first of the year."

"Almost?"

"Yes. You said yourself TS-0513 was capable of restructuring its form and mass. It stands to reason the same applies to its more magical qualities."

"Okay…"

"As such, when we find it—"

"They're sending you back out, kid," Fiona interrupted and broke into a wide grin.

Caniss hissed out a sigh. "Can you not keep your mouth shut for five minutes?"

"Come on, Melody. Cut the girl some slack. You were taking too long."

"Wait." Amanda straightened in her chair. "You want *me* to go back out there looking for that thing?"

Caniss shrugged. "As unlikely as it is, you're the only one qualified enough to make an accurate assessment of TS-0513's physical and magical state. Perhaps even psychological, if applicable."

She couldn't think of anything to say and stared blankly at the doctor until Connor chuckled.

"You don't look especially happy to hear this."

"Happy? I…" Amanda swallowed and brushed her hair away from her face. "Surprised is more like it. I thought…"

"You thought we called this meeting as a private dissolution of your arrangement with Dr. Caniss and Omega Industries." He nodded. "I understand. It's quite the opposite. Though I have to say I'm much more impressed by the way you handled your assumed termination by taking it into your own hands. Shows a lot of initiative."

"Um…thanks?" When she looked at Fiona, her mentor pointed right back at Dr. Caniss a second before the doctor opened her mouth again.

"So you agree to our proposal, then?"

"I mean, I guess, but—"

"Very well. You'll accompany Ms. Damascus back to Omega Industries and put together a team of your choosing. I expect to have a list of your finalized selections in my hand by the end of the day so we can inform all parties involved." Caniss stood and nodded at Connor. "Mr. Slate."

"Doctor." He watched her with a half-smile as she walked briskly across the conference room and through the door. Then he inhaled deeply through his nose. "Well. That went better than I expected."

"What just happened?" Amanda muttered.

"You need some time to process. Perfectly natural." Connor stood, fastened the buttons of his sports jacket, and nodded. "I want to thank you both for the time you've already put into this. And in advance for everything that's yet to come. I'm looking forward to seeing more of your work, Amanda."

"I… Okay."

Fiona chuckled. "Thank you, Connor."

He nodded briskly. "Keep me informed, won't you?"

"That's the plan."

The leader of the entire Coalition smiled at Amanda one more time, then crossed the room with his long strides and disappeared through the door as well.

"You look like you're gonna be sick, kid."

"Probably." Amanda swallowed and turned toward her mentor with wide eyes. "I still don't get what's going on."

"What's not to get?" Laughing, Fiona stood and clapped a hand on the girl's shoulder. "You're moving up in the world. Well, the shifter world, at least. The Coalition has your name now. And your number. Literally."

Amanda only stood again when she was worried Fiona would disappear through that door without looking back and leave her stranded here in the Coalition's conference room at The Pylon. "But Caniss said she wants me to *select a team*. What does that even mean?"

"It means you're going after that monster as the fifteen-year-old kid who gives the orders this time instead of taking them." The woman snorted. "That Mac guy and his crew really screwed the pooch on that one."

"Wait, so I didn't lose the internship. Right?"

Fiona's hand rested on the doorknob, and she gave Amanda another quick wink. "Keep playing your cards right like this, kid, and you can forget the internship altogether. Consider this your first paid mission."

Amanda's mouth opened, but zero sound whatsoever came out.

Paying job? Like, I work for the Coalition of Shifters now?

The chaotic noise of business-magicals racing across The Pylon to their very important meetings overwhelmed her when Fiona stepped into the wide avenue beyond. The only reason Amanda moved at all was that if she didn't, the door would have closed again and smacked her right in the face.

CHAPTER TWENTY-FIVE

They hurried across the central dome at the Canissphere, which was as busy now with scurrying scientists as The Pylon had been with scurrying civilian magicals. "Fiona, how am I supposed to put together a *team* before the end of the day? I don't even know what Caniss is looking for."

"The doc's looking for what *you're* looking for, kid." Fiona snatched two protein bars out of the basket and handed one to her mentee. "If you ask me, she's pretty much given up on making executive decisions on this one. Is it a helluva lot of pressure to put on a kid? Totally. Can you handle it? Come on." She grinned and ripped open the cellophane. "We all know the answer to that one by now."

"I don't even know who to pick!"

"Go with your gut. As far as I can tell, that hasn't steered you wrong once. Not even when it told you to ignore every single warning I gave you and do the exact opposite of what you're supposed to." The woman ripped off a chunk of protein bar and chuckled. "Guess there's something to be said for that kinda willpower, huh?"

"Yeah, but then I have to *go* with them. Like, back out to Pennsylvania to find this thing, and I can't... Oh, no."

"Wha'?" Fiona turned to look at her, chewing on her mouthful.

"I can't do this right now. The junior class is starting *driving lessons* with Shep tomorrow."

"Who's Shep?"

"Mr. Frederick. You seriously don't remember? He's the guy who took me to the kemana all the time when I was doing useless stuff with Adalynn to pay off my—never mind!"

"Oh, yeah..." Fiona tapped the bar against her chin. "Haven't heard from *her* in a while."

"That doesn't matter. I can't do this right now, Fiona."

The redhead shifter smirked and waved her protein bar at Amanda. "Oh, so *now* all of a sudden, getting this creature out there in Pennsylvania isn't at the top of your list?"

"No, but—"

"Not a high priority now that you're leading a team of whoever the hell you want to go nail this thing."

"I'm not—"

"You're right." She patted Amanda's shoulder. "You're not going anywhere."

"Fiona, I don't even have any *clothes*. And if I miss too many days of school..."

"Don't sweat it, kid. It's all taken care of."

Amanda stopped dead in her tracks and stared at her mentor until the woman noticed and turned. "What's that supposed to mean?"

"You'll see. Better get thinking on that list, though. The doc's already fidgety enough as it is handing over this entire operation to a...well, to *you*."

"Oh, yeah. Thanks. That's super helpful."

"Relax. You heard what she said. No one better qualified." Grinning, Fiona strode casually away across the central dome, and Amanda was left there among a sea of scurrying shifter scientists without a single way to vent her frustrations.

"Great. You guys picked the *worst* week to give me a promotion."

She spent the rest of the morning and the first few hours of that afternoon strolling through the maze-like halls of the Canis-sphere and racking her brain for who the heck she was supposed to bring with her on this next "mission."

Let's see. The guy I've had the most contact with lately would be Rick. She snorted. *Yeah, right. He'd kill me first.*

The problem with putting together her team was that she didn't have any kind of list to choose from in the first place. Amanda knew maybe a dozen shifters working at the lab, but that didn't exactly help when she didn't know anything about them other than their names or what they'd taught her during her long weekend days spent shadowing them.

On her third pass through the examination wing, she finally looked up to stare through the wall of glass separating the hallway from the initial observation room on the other side. Most of the creature cages were empty, though someone had brought in what looked like a modified aquarium tank to house a glowing purple glob that sat on the bottom, rhythmically expanding and contracting as if it was breathing.

It probably was.

Then her gaze fell on the white five-gallon bucket on the shelf in the back and a pair of black rubber gloves dangling over the top.

Follow my gut, huh? Fine. I hope nobody resents me for it.

That night, locked up snugly in her private box of a room at the Canissphere, Amanda had a hard time settling her stomach. She'd given her final decision to Dr. Caniss before dinner, and the head biologist hadn't exactly looked all that thrilled when she scanned the very short list of names. Now, Amanda couldn't help but wonder if she'd made the wrong choice.

She'll probably veto the whole thing and tell me to start over from scratch.

That would make the fact that Fiona had somehow packed a week's worth of Amanda's clothes—plus her backpack and schoolbooks—in Amanda's duffle bag from her dorm room all the more useless. Not to mention impossible to figure out how her mentor had managed to get it done.

With a sigh, she stopped pacing and plopped down onto the chair in front of the built-in desk. The Coalition phone dug painfully into her backside, and she pulled it out with a snarl.

Oh, crap. She's gonna be so pissed.

It was incredibly weird to type her cell number—her first one, anyway—but she'd made a promise.

Can you talk?

The reply came almost immediately.

Does a shifter girl shit in the woods?

"Oh, Jeeze." Amanda rolled her eyes. Then another text came through right away.

Ha! Just kidding. Of course, you do. Let's do this.

She immediately sent the call and couldn't believe Summer would make her wait through four rings if she was sitting in her room on campus with that phone literally in her hand. Then the witch finally picked up.

"Well, look who decided to call!"

"Okay, it's not like I've had all day to whip out the phone I'm *not* supposed to be using for anything but Coalition stuff."

Totally a lie, but she doesn't know that.

"Yeah, yeah, whatever." Summer crunched on some kind of snack and spoke through a full mouth. "So what's up in super-secret-science land, huh?"

"Crazy stuff, actually. I mean, I'm okay. I just don't think I'll be coming back to school for…a while."

"Oh, yeah?" The witch's swallow was so loud, Amanda jerked the phone away from her ear. "What, they got you busy teaching all the freaky animals how to talk or something?"

Amanda rolled her eyes. "I should've known it was a bad idea to give you that phone."

"Are you kidding? No way. This is the only thing keeping me from sneaking back into the west wing to see what else I can steal from the—"

"Not over the *phone*, Summer. Come on."

"Fine. Whatever. So let's hear it. Why's your internship so much more important than school *this* time?"

Amanda briefly considered telling her friend that the internship had actually turned into a paying job—as far as she knew—but that would only open a whole new set of questions she'd rather avoid from her incredibly nosy friend. So she gave Summer a brief rundown of what was happening at the Canis-sphere and her impending "mission" with her team. "So tell Grace and the guys for me, okay?"

Summer snorted. "Jesus, shifter girl. If I knew I'd have to repeat your crazy-ass story, I would've pressed record when you called."

"Fine. It doesn't have to be verbatim or anything. Just let them know. That was the whole point of me giving you that phone—"

"Yeah, yeah. I know. Don't wanna make Blondie pull out all her hair. Hey, what about The Matt?"

Staring at the wall in front of her, Amanda cocked her head.

That's the best nickname she could come up with?

"What about him?"

"Want me to tell him too?"

"What? Summer, no. That's insane."

"I don't know, shifter girl. He's been asking about you. Looked pretty torn up when I told him I hadn't seen you since breakfast, so…"

"Don't tell Matt. Don't even talk to him, okay?"

"Ooh… Getting a little territorial, huh?"

"Summer, I'm serious—"

"Relax." Summer crunched down on another handful of chips or crackers or whatever she'd pilfered into her room. "I'm not trying to step on your shifter-romance toes, okay? Just don't forget to let me know you're still alive when you're done monster-hunting, yeah?"

"Yeah, if I don't die, I'm pretty sure you'll know." Amanda huffed out a laugh. "Thanks."

"Yup." More loud chewing. "That it?"

"I guess so—"

Summer hung up abruptly, and Amanda stared at her phone.

Didn't know there were people in this world who shouldn't have cell phones until literally right now.

Now that she'd made the call, she had one less thing to worry about. The relief probably would last through the night if she were lucky.

Definitely won't feel this great in the morning. I know that. Ten hours 'til I'm out there leading a team who may or may not hate me for dragging them into this. If Caniss is paying me, it better be a lot.

She didn't need any kind of alarm the next morning and woke up just before 5:00 a.m. on her own. The mess hall dome already buzzed with Omega Industries staff getting ready for their morning shifts or coming off the night shift. Dominique greeted her with a warm smile in the order window. "Good to see you back here again, girl. It's been a while."

"Thanks, Dominique."

"Here you go. Fresh off the griddle." The woman handed over a paper plate piled high with steaming pancakes. "Syrup and butter on the condiment table. Hey, does this mean we'll see a lot more of you now?"

Amanda tried to smile, her mouth watering at the smell of pancakes and simultaneously turning over at the prospect of what she was about to do after breakfast. "Maybe. I guess we'll see."

"Well, good luck, Amanda. Eat those while they're hot, huh?"

She practically inhaled her breakfast without tasting any of it, though she was sure she could have told Dominique they were the best pancakes she'd had in years. Then she got another text on her Coalition phone and didn't have to worry about anyone seeing her check it here.

Strategy Room. Five minutes.

Oh, boy.

She tossed her trash and headed down the winding corridors to the room that had become her least-favorite in the Canissphere. The door was already open, and when she stepped inside, she found her entire team assembled right there in front of her around the holographic battle-plan table. Dr. Caniss stood behind it and swiped a finger across the panel in front of her. The door *hissed* shut, and only the soft, whispering hum of all the gadgets and constantly running tech in the room filled the air.

"Now that we're all here," Caniss said, "let's begin."

"Wait a second." Fiona turned in the spinning chair bolted to the floor by the table, and propped an elbow up on the display screen. Caniss flared her nostrils but didn't say anything. "This is it, kid? Your entire team?"

Amanda shrugged and glanced from face to face in the room —Fiona, Dr. Caniss, and Bill Chamberlain. "Yep. This is it."

"Maybe I should've waited 'til you were hungry before telling you to follow your gut. I'm not so sure the four of us are gonna have much more success than the last failure of a team."

"Three of us." The girl swallowed and tried to plaster on a weak smile. "Dr. Caniss is here to, um…"

"To oversee the briefing before you begin." The doctor nodded and started to type away on the control panel in front of her. She stopped with an aggravated chuff when Bill cleared his throat.

"Sorry. I'm not trying to put a wrench in things here, but…" A self-conscious chuckle escaped him. "I'm not exactly sure what *this* even is, honestly."

"Amanda's latest assignment was to put together a team of her choosing to help track down TS-0513 and get the giant egg thing those mermaids want so badly. Yeah, yeah, I know, Doc. Subject UM-43562. My bad." Fiona grinned at the confused creature-caretaker and spread her arms. "Apparently, that's us."

"Wait, you mean out in the field?" Bill fell into a fit of snorting laughter. "That's… I mean, that's a little outside my area of expertise."

"No, it's not," Amanda countered.

Everyone looked up at her, and Dr. Caniss slowly removed her hand from the control panel. "I can't say I enjoy delaying this briefing in the slightest, but I have to admit I'm curious as to your reasoning. It honestly defies rational thought."

"Okay, look." Amanda sat in the empty chair between Bill and Fiona and sighed. "The last team that tried to go after this thing had no idea what they were doing. I mean, if they were supposed to go out there after some kind of rampaging, bloodthirsty predator knocking down buildings and killing innocent people, then yeah. They'd probably be the right guys for the job. That's not what this is."

Fiona stroked her chin and gazed at Amanda with hooded eyelids. "Interesting…"

"I got the creature's attention when I was out there with my ghost-wolf. I don't think it felt threatened. Not until Mac and his guns showed up. There's a much bigger chance now that it'll recognize me and probably get scared again if it thinks I'm with the same team. Or any weapons at all."

Caniss snorted. "Scared."

"I'm serious. The creature's smart enough for that. Bill, you're the only one here who's had as much experience and time working with the…divergent species that come through here. You take care of them, and they like you."

"That's absurd," Dr. Caniss interjected.

"Hold on." Fiona lifted a finger to shush the doctor. "I think she's onto something."

"Yeah, me too." Bill ruffled a hand through his hair and sat back in his seat. "As weird as this is."

"That…TS-0513, I guess," Amanda continued, "isn't trying to hurt anybody. Like I told you guys yesterday, I think it took the mermaids' power core without knowing what it was. Maybe thinking the thing would power its magic, or perhaps because it couldn't help itself. Like, it acted on instinct or something. I don't know. But I'm pretty sure the power core is making it stronger *and* sicker at the same time."

"Kid, from the scans I've seen," Fiona added, "I'd say calling that thing *sick* is a hell of an understatement."

"Probably. But it wasn't dying." Amanda scanned the surface of the table but didn't see it. She was too busy trying to pull up the memory of what she'd seen that day in the forest. "It fought back when Mac's guys attacked it. It had enough strength to get away like that." She snapped her fingers. "So I think when we find it, we need to figure out how attached it is to that giant egg before we get in there to take it away again."

"It's obviously attached," Caniss said. "If you can even apply such sentimentality to a creature's instinctual nature. It's been guarding that artifact for months."

"Yeah, I meant literally."

"What?" Bill looked ready to jump out of his chair and run out of the room.

"I think..." Amanda wrinkled her nose. "I think the artifact's, like, melding itself to the creature. Because obviously, they don't belong together. It's another species' magic. So if we can figure out how to detach the egg, I guess, then we have a pretty good chance of saving TS-0513 too. Maybe even bringing it back here, if we can."

"I have no idea how you've come to that conclusion." Caniss folded her arms. "It's nothing but pure conjecture without any basis in—"

"Ah-ah-ah." Fiona lifted a finger toward the doctor again, who looked like she was ready to bite it off. "You don't really need a reminder of how many times she's been right, but you just wrote off everything she told you based on your *personal* opinions, right?"

"I based my decision on the evidence. Or lack thereof, in this case." Caniss tilted her head in admission. "Perhaps slightly colored by my subjective judgments. Slightly."

"I like the plan, Amanda." Bill folded his arms and nodded. "Really, I do. But if that artifact is attached to TS-0513 like you said, creating this influx of both heightened strength and severe injury, I'm not sure the creature will survive an extraction like that."

Fiona shot him a crooked smile. "You mind repeating that in layman's terms, Bill? You know, for the non-scientists among us."

"Sure. It's, um... It would be like performing surgery out in the woods to remove a major organ. No anesthesia and we don't have enough data to support even an educated guess about what would anesthetize something like TS-0513. We'd be killing it right then and there."

"You guys have tons of medical supplies here," Amanda said. "For magical species, I mean. You don't know what will and won't work on them before you do a little trial and error, right? Same thing. We go in and trade the egg for Oriceran-monster medicine."

Bill scratched his chin. "In theory, sure. I worry about what kind of damage we *wouldn't* be able to mend in time."

Fiona drummed her fingers on the table. "Huh. You really are the creature guy, aren't you?"

"Thanks." He was too distracted to think anything else of the comment and kept frowning at Amanda. "The medical inventory we have here is meant for much smaller wounds. Not the life-threatening kind one finds after removing a power source that's literally melded into the subject's flesh. That may be the only thing sustaining it at this point, and nothing we have works *that* instantaneously."

Amanda bit her bottom lip, then practically jumped out of her seat when the idea hit her. "Then we'll have to make it work faster."

He let out a humorless chuckle. "I like your optimism, but I don't think that's even possible—"

"Hold up." Fiona pointed at her mentee. "You have a point."

"I know." Amanda grinned. "And I know exactly where to get more."

"I severely dislike the vague turn this conversation has taken," Caniss muttered. "Explain."

"The accelerant." Amanda gripped the edge of the table in her excitement. "That would work. Mix it with all the healing stuff you have here, get close enough to use it, and everybody comes out this alive. Including the… Jeeze, we need a better name than TS-0513."

"Has to be strong enough, though," Fiona added. "That a possibility?"

"Definitely."

"Someone please elaborate on this *accelerant*," Caniss growled.

"Amanda's secret weapon when it comes to growing all your plants in record time, Doc."

"I see." Realization dawned on the doctor's face now too. "You have more of this…accelerant?"

"No, but I know how to—"

"Then I suggest you get to work, Amanda. We're running out of time with this one, and I haven't the slightest interest in testing how long Jenkins will survive in his current state. Whatever you did to accelerate the growth of those plants, I recommend you repeat the process this time with much more haste." Caniss nodded curtly and headed for the door. "We'll reconvene when it's finished—"

"No." Amanda stood, her fists clenched at her sides until the doctor turned slowly around and cocked her head. "I'm not making anything else."

"It was *your* idea."

"Yeah, and I made a promise it was a one-time thing. You have no idea what I had to do to get that plant ready for you in time. Even though it didn't even work."

Caniss looked at Fiona, one eyelid twitching now. "What is she talking about?"

Fiona shrugged. "Don't look at me, Doc. I'm only the hired help on this one."

Amanda pulled her phone from her back pocket and scrolled through the very short list of recently called numbers. She stopped at Wallace's, then looked up at Caniss with a smirk. "Who knows? Maybe he'll give me a future discount for referrals."

CHAPTER TWENTY-SIX

Wallace came through on the rather large order of accelerant Dr. Caniss ordered from him. It paid to have Coalition funds to back up her request for immediate production and delivery.

Amanda knew her brokered deal had gone through even before the shipment arrived. That night, after she'd sent another text to Summer to keep her updated that she was *still alive*, she got an incoming message from Wallace's number.

Good to know you're a woman of your word. If you need anything, you know how to get hold of me.

She grinned and didn't bother sending a reply.
Yeah. I'm cutting out the middleman.

The shipment arrived early the next morning, and Caniss ordered a team of half a dozen shifters to help Amanda, Bill, and Fiona pack their gear and get ready to head back out to Pennsylvania—this time with a lot fewer guns and a much better game plan. Plus, since the entire team was essentially in-house and not exactly contracted work, Caniss thought it was appropriate to offer the use of the weird military-looking jet that had picked Amanda up outside the lab last time. Only now, the pilot would take them a lot farther than down out of the mountains and into Denver.

Amanda and her team got to ride in the bouncy flight seats to Saint Mary's.

They had hotel rooms waiting for them too, though Amanda and Fiona had to share one while Bill got his own. When they arrived and settled in for their first night on the road before they'd head out the next morning, Amanda flopped down on one of the queen-sized beds and sighed. "I don't get it. She trusts me to lead a literal *mission*, but she doesn't trust me to have a hotel room?"

Fiona snorted as she hung her light denim jacket on the hook by the door. "It's not about the doc's trust, kid. Though I'll go ahead and say right now that if she tells you straight up that she *trusts* you, I'd run for the hills. What's the big deal, anyway? You don't like me?"

"No." Amanda playfully rolled her eyes. "Just doesn't make sense."

"You know, if there's one thing you can expect from Dr. Melody Caniss, it's the truth. The woman doesn't play in guesses or feelings or opinions. Just the facts."

"What does that have to do with anything?"

Fiona laughed. "Well, she's not going to lie about your age to book you a separate room. I don't think fifteen-year-olds are allowed to have their own. Legally speaking. Even fifteen-year-old super shifters with all the Coalition's resources at their disposal."

Amanda shook her head and stared at the ceiling. "Well, if that's the only thing affected by my age right now, I guess it's fine."

"Sure doesn't bother *me*." Fiona sat on the other bed and sucked in a sharp breath. "I gotta ask, kid. Why me?"

"Why you what?" The girl pushed herself up onto her elbows and frowned at her mentor.

"Why'd you put my name down for your monster-hunter team? I mean, other than how many sane magicals might frown at you and Bill going off on this insane mission with only the two of you."

"What? No. Bill's awesome. I was alone with him, like, every weekend when I was still training with the creatures at the lab."

"Okay… Then why am I suddenly so qualified to be on the job with you?" Fiona wrinkled her nose. "Wait. This isn't you trying to let me down easy, is it? Bring me along for one last hurrah before you kick my ass to the curb and tell me you don't need me anymore?"

Amanda burst out laughing. "I can't believe you're worried about that."

Her infectious laughter quickly caught on, and they both keeled over on their separate beds in fits of hilarity. Finally, Fiona wiped her eyes and sighed. "Don't get the wrong impression, kid. I'm not even a little worried about either of us. Just curious."

"I don't know." Amanda brushed her hair away from her face and managed to catch her breath again. "I guess there are a few reasons."

"Oh, do tell."

"I mean, you're not exactly the best with animals. I've never seen you with a gun or out in the field, let alone doing any kind of research at the lab. You know what? I don't think I've ever actually seen you do *anything* besides sit in on meetings and show up at the worst possible times to grab me and haul me off somewhere."

Fiona pulled off her boots and let them thump to the ground beside the bed. "Okay, I didn't ask you for all the reasons I *shouldn't* be doing this with you."

Amanda grinned. "I know. But out of all the shifters I know even a little, you're the only one I really trust. You know, with the important stuff. I already know you haven't figured out how to answer your phone yet."

"Aw, that's sweet." The woman winked. "Only with you, kid."

"And…you're the only shifter I know who can teleport and who doesn't hate my guts at the same time."

"Well, that's interesting." Fiona cocked her head. "Why would that make a difference…wait. No."

"Yep." Amanda kicked off her own shoes and climbed up to the head of the bed before wiggling down under the covers. Then she met her mentor's gaze and gave her one of those mischievous grins Fiona had been giving her for almost two years now. "I'm gonna need you to teleport Bill right on up to that thing when it's time."

"Oh, come on. What about you?"

"I don't need to get as close as either of you. Not physically, at least."

"Okay… Feel like letting the one shifter you trust in on this plan that sounds a hell of a lot like suicide?"

"Nope. Goodnight."

Amanda clicked off the light beside her bed and rolled over, grinning when she heard Fiona scoff and mutter under her breath, "Teenagers."

Finding TS-0513 was easy enough. Fiona teleported all three of them and their gear out to Elk State Forest, and they tracked the creature's magical signature with prototype devices someone at the Canissphere had cobbled together for this purpose. Amanda's ability to sense the creature's discomfort the closer they approached helped.

The hard part was getting the creature to stay in one place

long enough for Amanda to try out her plan. Every time she and her ghost-wolf got close enough to get a good look at the amorphous mountain of scales, feather, and fur—although the thing's face hadn't changed much and still looked like a purple, somewhat scaly bear—TS-0513 zipped out of the area like it had the first time they'd met.

It still left that zigzagging trail of magical energy behind it, though, which gave Amanda multiple opportunities to track the creature down one more time and try again. But the outcome was always the same.

Every day for three weeks, she and her team returned to the creature's general stomping grounds in the woods to reproduce the same outcome over and over again. They returned to the hotel before the sun went down. Amanda checked her email for the day's assignments sent by Principal Glasket—courtesy of Fiona having "set everything up" for her ahead of time—and she got through as much work as she could before her eyes couldn't take the strain anymore. Then she'd dial her phone number and hopefully talk to Summer.

Sometimes, she called so late that her friend didn't answer. So she sent a text instead, basically repeating what she'd said or texted the night before—she was fine, still chasing monsters, still alive.

The most frustrating part of the whole thing wasn't that she was still out here, missing school and her friends, not to mention the driving lessons from Shep. Yeah, she cringed every time she thought of Matt and what he probably thought of her after she'd disappeared, and no one would tell him where she'd gone or why.

Amanda liked being out here, *in the field*, heading out every day not to the outdoor cafeteria and a stuffy classroom but into the Pennsylvania forest with two adult shifters who were willing to try any suggestions she offered.

The worst part was that they had everything they needed to get this done—to remove the mermaids' power-core egg and *heal* the terrified and wounded creature—but the thing wouldn't stay still long enough for them to try. If the thing would *cooperate*, Amanda knew they could do this.

At the end of the third week, Amanda had chased TS-0513 around the forest six different times as her ghost-wolf, and she was exhausted. Fiona and Bill caught up to her like they always did once her awareness returned to her body, and she muttered into the fancy comm headsets from Caniss that it was another failure.

"This isn't working." She pushed herself to her feet and stumbled a little, her head reeling.

"Hey, kid." Fiona reached out to help steady the girl, frowning in concern. "You eat any of those protein bars I stuffed in your pack?"

"No."

"Why the hell not?"

"Because I'm trying to get this done!" Amanda drew a deep breath and forced herself to calm down. "Sorry. I'm just... I don't want to be out here any longer than we have to be, you know?"

"We can always go back. Try a different tactic—"

"No. We can't. I *know* this will work. I just have to figure out how to convince this thing that I'm not here to blast it with magical bullet holes."

"I can reach out to some of my contacts if you want," Fiona suggested. "Got a few other friends who can do what you do. Ghost-wolf and everything. Maybe it's that this thing's already seen you and can't separate your magic from knowing it's about to get shot at."

"Right. Who's gonna take you up on *that* offer, huh?"

Fiona smirked and scratched the side of her head. "Yeah, they're crazy but not *that* crazy."

"I know we can do this." Amanda ripped a protein bar out of her pack and tore open the wrapper before chowing down. "Dr. Caniss was right, though. We don't know how much longer

Jenkins is gonna last under the mermaids' sleeping spell. And I'm not about to try the easy way and go right for this creature's throat. Not if we don't have a good reason for it."

"Not that I can see," Bill added. "As far as I'm concerned, you're making all the right calls. For what it's worth."

"A lot, actually." She stuffed the wrapper into her pocket and ran a hand through her hair, sighing as she scanned the thick woodland around them. "Thanks."

"We can come back tomorrow if you want. Call it a day earlier than usual."

"No. Let's try one more time." Amanda nodded at the tracking devices. "Can you get another read on it?"

Bill tapped around on the device and nodded. "A few miles north this time. We'll go wide. Let you know when we have a visual."

"Yeah, okay."

Fiona slapped a hand on her mentee's back, which she probably meant to be reassuring. "You got this, kid. No doubt in my mind."

"Thanks." She tried to smile at her team as they trudged off through the trees to get barely within visual range of the injured, elusive, and impossible-to-miss TS-0531.

What are we missing here? That thing has to know I wasn't trying to hurt it. I mean, yeah, the mermaids sent me after it to get back their egg, but they didn't say anything about...

Amanda froze where she stood and stared blankly ahead through the woods.

They didn't have to say anything. The mutated mermaids want me to kill that thing. That wasn't part of the deal, obviously, but if the monster can tell I'm not here to hurt it, what else does it know?

Anyone else would have called her crazy for entertaining the new plan quickly coming together in her mind. But magicals had called her crazy for a while now—and too spirited, too stubborn, too curious, too young.

It needs to see I'm different. Worth a shot, right?

She slung her pack over her shoulder and marched north through the trees, completely changing her team's procedure. For three weeks, she'd stayed where she was until she'd heard Fiona and Bill in her headset telling her they were in range. Then she'd let out her ghost-wolf and gone to meet up with them that way. This time, she wasn't waiting at all.

Almost forty-five minutes later, Fiona's voice buzzed in her ear. "All right. Attempt number bajillion, kid. TS-0513 spotted and hanging out in its usual gross bloodbath right outside a cave."

"Ready when you are, Amanda," Bill added.

"Thanks." She didn't need them to tell her where the thing was despite not having a tracking device of her own. Her magic picked up on the wrongness emanating from the giant creature all by itself, and she used that as a guide to bring her as close as she could get.

When she finally saw the heaving mound of divergent…whatever it was, Fiona and Bill saw too.

"What are you doing, kid?" Fiona whispered. "You're supposed to leave your body back there where *we* left you."

"Don't say stuff like that," Amanda muttered. "You sound like Mac."

"Ew."

"Amanda, this isn't part of the plan," Bill added. "You're safe when you…project, I guess. If you get physically hurt, there's no coming back from that."

"Good thing we have a buttload of accelerant-laced healing potions then, huh?"

"That's not what I meant—"

"Listen. I had an idea, and I'm already here, so there's not much time to explain. Trust me."

"You know what we *should* do," Fiona hissed. "We should call this whole thing off and haul your ass back into the woods."

"Hey. Who's leading this stupid mission, huh?"

Her team fell silent, and it brought a small smile to Amanda's lips.

"Be ready with that giant container, okay? And the teleporting."

"Copy that, kid." Fiona didn't sound in the least bit happy about taking *these* orders from a teenager shifter, but she would have to deal with it.

Amanda slowed her pace and walked silently across the underbrush. The snow had melted, replaced by new sprouts of green grass and wild plant life, and it made movement a lot quieter.

It still wasn't silent enough to fool the heaving beast in front of that cave that now looked stuck halfway between a double-sized rhino and a multi-colored ostrich with the unchanging bear's face. The creature noticed her presence and grunted, shifting its massive bulk with many wet crunching noises and sickening squelches. Two giant blue bird legs had newly sprouted from the monster's side and flopped against the rest of its amorphous form as it turned to fix Amanda with those swirling silver and gold eyes.

"Ugh," Fiona whispered. "That's disgusting."

Amanda ignored her and stopped where she was, holding the giant monster's gaze.

This is me. Not my magic. Not a wolf. Just me.

She slowly slid her pack off her shoulder and set it gently in the grass at her feet without looking away. Then she lowered herself to her knees at the same agonizing speed and let out a long, slow breath.

I seriously hope this thing puts the pieces together on its own. 'Cause this is the last option.

The creature chuffed and lowered its head to the ground, looking like a second giant monster had swallowed the colorful bear whole but hadn't yet gotten to the head. A low, warbling groan rose from its throat, and after thirty seconds of staring at the shifter girl kneeling in the new spring grass, TS-0513 lifted what had probably at some point been a foreleg to expose the giant turquoise pulsing egg.

There we go. Holy crap, I can't believe this worked.

"You get down here the second I'm out," she whispered.

"Yeah, you better get out," Fiona muttered in her earpiece. "Jesus, kid..."

"Shh." That was all Bill had to say on the matter.

He's probably burning this whole thing into his memory at this point. Pretty sure I will too.

Still gazing at the grotesquely malformed creature's eyes, Amanda did something she'd never done before.

She purposefully called out her ghost-wolf without closing her eyes, without propping herself up against something first, and without much more of a plan than that.

The change happened as quickly as it always did. One second, she was on her knees, staring at the creature who'd caused all this trouble for everyone else and itself. The next, she was still staring into those eyes of swirling silver and gold, but now she was moving forward, gliding across the air without having to set a single ghostly-white paw of her magic on the ground.

The sound of her body slumping backward and hitting the ground barely registered as she and her ghost-wolf sailed toward the creature.

With another low, whining grunt, TS-0513 sniffed at the air but didn't move. It watched intently as the white wolf finally settled onto the forest floor and padded completely silently into the ring of blood-soaked earth and dismembered creature parts.

I knew it. Yes. Okay, Bear. Just...hold out a little longer for me, okay?

When Amanda reached the exposed turquoise egg larger than her body curled up in the same shape, the creature didn't pull away or disappear again. It only watched her, grunting and letting out low and wary warbling sounds.

She stopped only briefly in front of the egg, seeing exactly how right she'd been about the mermaids' power-core having embedded itself in this new monster's flesh. Blood oozed around the site, joined by some other thick silver substance that pulsed faintly. Probably with the creature's heartbeat.

At least I won't have to take a bath after this. Fiona and Bill better be ready.

Slowly, not wanting to scare the giant wounded beast any more than this next part would, Amanda and her ghost-wolf stepped forward and *through* TS-0513's flesh. Despite having no body to feel anything, she felt the pulsing rush of tingling energy racing all around her and her ghost-wolf as they padded around the outside of the turquoise egg. She'd expected the smell alone to shove her back into her body, but there was nothing. No scent at all. Only wave after rippling wave of magic so intense, it almost felt hot.

Okay. Like with the gloves, right? Back to the basics.

She focused on the egg and only the egg, which was surprisingly easy to see from *inside* the giant creature holding perfectly still around her. Then she and her ghost-wolf leapt up, placed their forepaws against the egg's side, and pushed.

The creature let out a startled grunt, and at first, Amanda thought she'd miscalculated. Maybe she'd assumed her magic was strong enough to separate the artifact from the beast who'd gotten itself wrapped around it.

When she pushed a second time, the most horrendous sucking noise filled her ears, followed by TS-0513's massive bellow of agony. She shoved with all the force she could muster behind her magic, and the egg came free.

Amanda hadn't thought about how it would all play out after that, but now she moved on instinct. She leapt after the artifact and pushed it across the grass with her ghostly paws, and kept doing it fast enough that the screaming monster didn't roll over and crush the thing. She went in the complete opposite direction of her body so *that* didn't get crushed either.

"Now, now, now!" Bill shouted.

A brilliant burst of blue light came from the top of the hillside above the cave's entrance. The same flash immediately followed right in front of the roaring beast's exposed underbelly with a massive egg-shaped hole in the middle of all the fur and scales. Fiona and Bill appeared there together. The redhead woman stumbled backward, pinwheeling her arms to keep from tripping over the creature's grotesque limbs and the body parts it had already shed. Bill was already fully prepared to get right to work.

The massive glass cylinder of accelerant-laced healing potion glowed a brilliant green in his hand. He quickly twisted off the cap by its sturdy steel handle, then knelt beside the gaping hole in TS-0513's flesh to pour the entire mixture into the wound. Thick green steam billowed up from the monster's hide, and the nauseating scent of singed hair and cooked meat filled the air.

The creature let out another agonized groan and tried to thrash around, but it didn't exactly have the right limbs in the right places to move its giant bulk.

"Get out of there, Bill! Are you crazy?" Fiona shouted.

He stepped quickly backward, almost tripped over a bloody piece of discarded monster, but caught himself in time to leap away before dropping to his knees. The empty canister toppled to the grass, and he spread his arms as he tried to catch his breath. "There. There, that's it. All done."

TS-0513 groaned and shuddered as the green smoke and charred-meat smell kept rising into the air.

"Okay, we're outta here." Fiona grabbed his arm and tried to haul him backward, but the creature caretaker was too enraptured by what was happening to notice.

"I don't believe it."

"Yeah, me neither, pal. So let's split before we can't believe we're dead—"

"Fiona, look."

"I don't want to—" She stopped when she did look back up at the monster, and her mouth fell open. "Would you look at that…"

Amanda watched all this from behind the first line of trees surrounding the clearing in front of the cave. The turquoise egg lay on its side in the grass, but now that she'd freed it, she had all the time in the world to watch through her ghost-wolf's eyes as the accelerant potion did exactly what she intended it to do.

The wound big enough to crawl into was closing. Bone, muscle, fat, and fur knitted themselves together with surprising speed, and the monster's heaving sides slowed now as it realized what was happening too.

Then the change was impossible to ignore.

As soon as the wound stitched itself back up, TS-0513 lit up in a brilliant flash of silver light. The hulking mass of indiscernible flesh shrank into itself, pulsing with so much magic emanating from its fully healed form. Four brilliant wings lurched from its back and spread to their full expanse. A tail of shimmering golden scales whipped through the air and thumped against the ground, sending up a spray of disturbed dirt and, yes, a few bloody abandoned parts. Claws and paws dug across the grass as three horns of purest cobalt-blue flashed in the sunlight when the creature tossed its head and snorted.

Later, Amanda, Fiona, and Bill would argue good-naturedly about how many legs the new Oriceran species actually had and exactly what it looked like. Now, though, all three of them were caught in the spell of this incredible creature fully pulling itself back together into its true form—or at least one of them—and the sound of a thousand tinkling chimes ringing together in glorious tones.

Fiona's breath escaped her in a rush, and she set her hand on Bill's shoulder to reassure herself they were both there.

Then the creature lifted its bearlike head and let out a fierce cry that sounded like nothing else. It beat its four wings once, sending up a flurry of dirt and dead grass and buffeting its three witnesses with a gust of air.

The next second, it was gone.

The woods were completely silent. After several seconds, Fiona sucked in a sharp breath and hastily wiped away the tears that had snuck from the corners of her eyes. Then she spun to see the giant turquoise egg and the small wolf of white mist sitting beside it. "Well, hell. Guess we still get points for *that* thing."

The second Bill spun to look, Amanda gasped on the other side of the clearing and pushed herself off her pack digging painfully into her ribs. "Jesus, that was weird."

"Amanda." He wiped the sweat from his forehead and uttered a sharp laugh. "You're crazy enough to be brilliant. You know that?"

"Yeah. I've heard that a few times." She rose on shaky legs, though she felt more energized and awake now than she had over the last three weeks. "Got the egg."

"Yes, you did." Fiona threw her head back and cackled. "Damn, what a day, huh? Let's get this thing strapped up. Who wants the first haul?"

Bill turned to scan the empty clearing. "Would've been nice to get a better look at that thing."

"Yeah, but it's better now." The redhead shifter waved him off. "We freed Willy, okay? Man, am I ready to get this thing back in the right hands so Caniss will quit *harping* to me about her failure to bring Jenkins out of a coma."

Amanda and Bill locked gazes, and the caretaker smirked. "I think we fixed that little problem, don't you?"

She rolled her eyes and huffed out a laugh. "I seriously hope so."

CHAPTER TWENTY-SEVEN

True to their word, the divergent mermaids—otherwise known as Subject UM-43562—released the incapacitated scientist from their magical hold over him the second their power-core egg hit the water of the lake beneath the Canissphere. And once again, Amanda was proven right.

Amanda stayed at the lab another two days, sitting in on one debriefing after another because apparently, Dr. Caniss couldn't fit the pieces together in her head the first time. Or the second. Or the third. By the time she'd finally given up trying to find holes in their story and new ways to find the TS-0513 for *observation*, word of Amanda's first successful mission had already spread to every corner of the facility. Now, the scientists had taken to calling TS-0513 by its newest moniker—the Coulier Bear.

She thought it was ridiculous, but there was nothing she could do to make dozens of scientists drop the name after it had already caught on so well. Then Fiona told her to pack up her things because it was time to get back to school.

"Right. School. Seems kinda pointless now, don't you think?"

The shifter woman snorted and clapped a hand on her

mentee's back. "Always stay in school, kid. Monster-hunter rule number one, I'm pretty sure."

Even after three weeks spent keeping up with her school assignments as best she could while hunting "the Coulier Bear," Amanda didn't have any problem getting right back into the swing of things with her classes. Of course, she'd missed the week of driving school with Shep, but other than that, she still got to take part in everything else. That included the last Louper game of the season, which she went to, and the graduation ceremony for this year's seniors. All of them had fortunately found themselves starter jobs with the various headhunters who now came to the school every spring semester to take their pick of the Academy of Necessary Magic's newest graduates.

Passing her classes was a walk in the park. Apparently, Calsgrave figured the shifter girl had done enough with the ridiculous number of plants she'd cultivated that a passing grade was pretty much a given. Zimmer held to her word and didn't mark down Amanda's final score out of spite, so she evidently didn't hold anything against her shifter student for breaking into her storeroom and stealing alchemy supplies—even the returned ones.

When it came time for Combat Training finals, Amanda couldn't believe her ears when Petrov barked at her to get lost. "Your team got the most points for Bag the Bounty this semester, Coulier. Get out of my training room and don't come back 'til next year."

We won the most points?

She found Corey Baker shuffling around outside the training building and couldn't keep from asking. "Hey, Corey. You guys brought in the most points this semester? For real?"

The half-Kilomea looked up at her and shrugged. "Yeah."

"But you guys were down a player."

"Nope."

"Yeah, it was me. I was gone a *lot*. You guys didn't have any problem 'chasing the bounty' on your own, huh? That's awesome."

He raised an eyebrow at her and shook his head. "We weren't down a player. We got Matt when he joined at the beginning of the semester. You been living under a rock this whole time or something?"

"Oh." She scrunched up her face and laughed. "Right. Of course. Trade out one shifter for another. I get it. Well, uh…good job. Thanks for that."

"Whatever. Have a good summer, Amanda."

"Yeah, you too."

As if he could hear them talking about him from a mile away —and he probably could, honestly—Matt Hardy strolled across the training field toward her with a huge grin. "Look at that. Pretty neat showing up at the end and not having to take finals, right?"

"Ha. Yeah. I guess I should thank you for that too, right?"

He shrugged. "It was pretty fun. I heard you, uh…had a lot more fun somewhere else, though. You know, wherever you disappeared to for almost a month without telling anyone anything."

Amanda glanced at him sidelong and squinted. "What did Summer tell you?"

"Nothing." Matt lifted both hands in surrender. "Absolutely nothing. At least, not with any details that made sense."

"Oh, man. I'm gonna kill her."

They both laughed, and he stuck his hands into his pockets as they ambled across the field together. "Listen, I know you have a lot going on right now with your…secret whatever. Like, a *lot*."

"Yeah. You have no idea."

"I'm not trying to get caught up in the middle of anything or make things harder for you, so you don't have to worry about that."

"I wasn't."

"Yeah, I know. I mean, I'm just putting it out there." He puffed out an uncertain laugh and ran a hand over his short hair. "What I'm trying to say is I still like talking to you. And when things aren't so weirdly complicated for you anymore, maybe we can keep talking. I'll be around another year."

"Oh, um..." She wiped her hands on her pant legs and shrugged, her mouth opening and closing soundlessly before she finally settled on, "Yeah, I wouldn't hold your breath waiting for things to get *un*complicated. That's kind of my thing. So, you know, some people can handle it, some people can't."

"Yeah, I've noticed. Your friends can handle it. Must be pretty good friends to stick around for so long."

"I mean, yeah. They put up with a lot from me."

Matt fixed that winning smile on her that made her seriously grateful for the Florida heat at this time of year, nodded, then broke away from her to head for the boys' dorm. "Still. I can wait."

"Okay..."

He turned back to look at her one more time before disappearing into the dorm, and she puffed out a sigh, blinking furiously.

I have no idea what that's supposed to mean, and I don't even have it in me to try figuring it out. I guess we'll just...see how it goes next year?

After packing all her things and saying her goodbyes to her friends, Amanda headed out to the edge of the gravel drive at the Academy's entrance to wait for Johnny. Then she heard Summer shouting at her and turned to see her friend jogging across the central field toward her, looking seriously freaked out.

"Whoa. What's going on?"

"You're not leaving, are you? I mean, already. Not right now…" Summer puffed out a sigh and shuffled back and forth, her gaze darting all over the place as if she was trying to hide from someone.

"No, I'm still waiting for Johnny." Amanda frowned. "What'd you do?"

"What? What is it with the constant accusations, shifter girl? I don't have to *do* something to be…this." Summer gestured at her face with both hands, then quickly folded her arms. "Shit. This sucks."

"What's going on?"

"I mean…" Summer sidled closer and lowered her voice, scanning the field to make sure no one was listening. "I told you about all the bullshit with my—with Marianne, right?"

"Yeah."

Her mom kicked her out and moved without telling her where she was going. She's right. That definitely sucks.

"I just… I mean, Glasket told me I could stay over the summer, but who the hell *chooses* that, you know? I can't stay here, Amanda. I'm already freaking out. Hell, we're in the middle of the swamp, and I'm *still* gonna die of cabin fever or something."

"Okay, chill out for a second." Amanda grabbed her friend's shoulder until the other girl finally looked at her. "You'll be fine, Summer. Whatever you do, wherever you are, you're unstoppable."

"Ha. Says the shifter girl who gets to leave whenever she wants." Summer nodded at the dust cloud rising along the drive toward them at the school's entrance. "Speaking of which…"

"Yeah. Here's Johnny." Amanda readjusted the strap of her duffel bag over her shoulder and smiled as the bright red fender of the dwarf's Jeep came into view, hurtling rapidly through the dust.

Johnny slammed on the brakes with a roar of tires skidding across gravel and a spray of even more dirt, then hopped down out of the driver's seat. When he slammed the door shut, Amanda knew he was pissed even before he stomped toward the girls, scowling beneath his black sunglasses.

"I wanna know what the hell happened here."

"Hi, Johnny." Amanda's smile faded. "Good to see you too."

"I spent damn near four months wonderin' why you'd figure a change of attitude was the best way to handle it. Then I finally reckoned what it was. Ain't you spittin' that crap back at me, kid. So who was it, huh?"

Amanda gave Summer an apologetic look, and the witch raised her eyebrows, scanning the rows of trees lining the drive instead. "I have no idea what you're talking about—"

"Who stole your damn cell phone, Amanda? *That's* what I'm talkin' 'bout. You cough up a name, and I'll beat the livin'—"

"Whoa, whoa. Hold on. Nobody stole my cell phone."

"Well, it damn sure wasn't *you* talkin' to me like that. Might be I know you better'n you think."

"I don't remember talking to you at all."

"Uh-huh. Fine. I'll figure it out my damn self." Johnny jerked his phone from his back pocket, flipped it open, and punched the buttons before practically slamming the phone against his ear. He stood there fuming at his ward until a low buzz came not from Amanda's pockets or her bag but from Summer instead.

With a sheepish smile, the witch chuckled, pulled out the cell phone that looked very much like Johnny's, and answered the call. "Hello?"

The dwarf slapped his phone shut and wagged it at the girls. "What the hell is this?"

"Oh, no." Amanda leaned toward her friend and whispered harshly, "What did you *do*?"

"What? It's not a big deal."

"Summer, I told you not to—Give me that." She snatched the phone away and quickly opened the text history. No, she hadn't saved Johnny's number in her phone, but she knew it by heart. Summer, obviously, did not. "Oh my God. 'Leave me alone?' 'Back off, creep?' 'I will hunt you down and rip your face off if you don't stop bothering me?' Summer!"

"See?" Johnny folded his arms and sniffed. "I knew it wasn't you."

"Oh, shit." Summer barked a laugh. "This is your… All those texts from… Damn, Johnny. I had no idea. You should start saving numbers in your phone, shifter girl. You know that, right?"

"That's…not even relevant."

"What?" The witch spread her arms as Amanda rolled her eyes and pocketed that cell phone too. "Come on. He would've thought something was seriously wrong if I *didn't* answer, right? See? Day saved."

"Seriously wrong, huh?" Johnny pulled his sunglasses down over the bridge of his nose and stared at his ward. "Got somethin' to say?"

"Uh-oh." Summer exaggerated a grimace. "Guess you forgot to tell him, huh?"

"Summer, shut up."

"Tell me what, kid?"

Amanda wrinkled her nose. "Yeah…that's a pretty long story."

"Then you can start talkin' on the ride. Maybe I'll do a few laps to give you enough time." Johnny spun and stormed across the gravel toward his Jeep.

"Johnny, hold on a sec!" Amanda dropped her duffel bag and darted after him.

"Seriously?" Summer glanced at the bag, then shouted, "Screw the witch standing here without a goodbye. Pretty sure you left all your stuff too."

"Wait." Amanda gave her friend a warning look but softened it with a coy smile that made Summer narrow her eyes. "Johnny. Wait."

"I'm waitin' as long as it takes you to get in the damn Jeep, kid. Let's go."

She folded her arms on the driver's-side paneless window frame and waited until the bounty hunter's angry revving of Sheila's engine subsided. "I have a favor to ask."

"Great. Ask someone else."

Amanda plastered on the sweetest smile she could muster and leaned forward to catch his gaze. "It's a big favor, Johnny."

He slumped back against his seat, then whipped off his sunglasses to stare at her. "How big?"

"Like, *big*-big."

"Well? I ain't got all day, kid. Better speak your mind before I change my mind and tell you to walk home."

Wow. He really doesn't like the idea of someone stealing my phone.

Forcing herself not to laugh, Amanda turned back toward Summer and pointed at her. "Summer's mom kicked her out of the house."

"Huh. Probably deserved it if you ask me."

"And she moved without telling her daughter *where* she was moving. So my friend—my *best* friend—doesn't have anywhere to stay for the next three months."

"Kid, you said you had a—" Johnny's eyes bulged, and he looked back and forth between his ward and the teenage witch with a serious attitude standing at the end of the drive. "No. Aw, hell no. I ain't a youth shelter."

"Please, Johnny?" She leaned forward to mutter in his ear, "I'm pretty sure she might blow up the entire school if she has to stay here any longer."

"Blow up the—" He cocked his head and lifted a finger from the steering wheel to point at Summer. "That the witch who blasted a hole in the ground and found that temple with you your first year?"

"Yes."

He slapped a hand to his mouth, rubbed it vigorously, then slammed his palm against the steering wheel again. "You're killin' me, kid."

"Really?"

"Yeah, fine. But I ain't sleepin' on the couch 'cause your friend wants her own room."

"Totally fine. Summer!"

"That's my name!"

Amanda waved at her friend, then thumped the side of the Jeep. "Come on."

"Don't screw with me, shifter girl."

Johnny stuck two fingers in his mouth and let out a piercing whistle that made Amanda duck away. "You don't quit screwin' with *me*, witch, you can stay here!"

Summer's mouth popped open, then she threw her head back for a special brand of Summer cackling and snatched Amanda's duffel bag off the ground. Then she darted toward the Jeep, grinning like a lunatic. "Holy shit! This is great!"

"Don't count your chickens," Johnny grumbled.

Summer dumped the bag into the back and launched herself into the back seat without even opening the door. "What does that even mean?"

Amanda got into the front passenger seat and immediately strapped on her seatbelt. "We used to *have* chickens."

"Man, magicals are *insane* down here."

"Don't push it." With a grunt, Johnny shifted into reverse and peeled away from the Academy at breakneck speed, smirking when the howling laughter and joyous whoops of two teenage girls rose over Sheila's roaring engine.

Get sneak peeks, exclusive giveaways, behind the scenes content, and more. PLUS you'll be notified of special **one day only fan pricing** on new releases.

Sign up today to get free stories.

JINX IN THE HINTERLANDS

JINX IN THE HINTERLANDS

MARTHA CARR & MICHAEL ANDERLE

MARTHA CARR & MICHAEL ANDERLE

MARTHA CARR & MICHAEL ANDERLE

MARTHA CARR & MICHAEL ANDERLE

Visit: https://marthacarr.com/read-free-stories/

AUTHOR NOTES - MARTHA CARR

Summer officially started today.

By the way, I'm in an anthology, Summer Solstice Anthology with a short story, The Origin Story of Monsters, that came out today. Just saying, if you're looking for something good to read. And if there's a lot of enthusiasm for it, that could be a new series. It was kind of fun.

Anyway, back to the point. The official start of the season. Of course, I'm in Texas so it's been hot for a while, and it will be till September. The indoor pool at the Y seems like a refuge to me during the dog days. I'll be headed there in an hour, and I'll sink under the cool water and do my best to meditate as I cross back and forth, following the thick, black line.

It's a good way to destress and I've needed plenty of that lately. Third stage melanoma, lots of surgery, a massive garden being installed during record rainstorms and then all the usual things to pay attention to in an ordinary life.

But life goes on and I'm going to go with it. There are a lot of things I don't have control over. How I choose to approach any given day is still mine.

There was a moment during the PET scans and surgery and a

backyard full of mud with a moat that curved around one side that I could feel the anxiety creeping up to my neckline. Things that weren't even a problem were beginning to bother me. It was like I was carefully building a wall of exhausted resentment, brick by brick.

That's not me, no matter the circumstances. It was time to turn things around, or better yet, let go of what I had no control over, do what I could for the rest, and get on with things in general.

The cancer was first on the list. Something about that word makes people sit up and take notice. I found a great doctor at MD Anderson, learned what I could and made peace with the idea that my timeline may not be as long as I'd like. I have an 80% chance of survival, so I'm probably going to be around for a while to bother Anderle, write more stories, be there for the Offspring and finally get to a little house in Italy – or maybe Scotland. We'll see.

On the off chance that I'm not, I've been taking a good, long look at my life and asking myself – am I doing what I want to be doing? The answer for 99% of it is yet. That's amazing. But there are things I could tweak to make it even better and I'm doing that.

I'm also making a series of short videos for the Offspring to have for big life events, just in case. By the way, he never reads these author notes, so he still won't know. I figure if I live to be a very old lady, they will still be fun to have to see who I was, way back when.

I've also booked a few trips this year to a few spas with a few old friends. I've never been to a spa resort before, and it was time to change that. Started eating healthier, going to yoga, meditating, swimming and boxing. All things I like to do. No more exercising where I dread every minute of it. Only fun.

That's pretty much my new motto. Only fun whenever possible, and it's always possible. It's all attitude, anyway. Something isn't innately fun. It's fun because I perceive it that way. My friend, Marissa loves roller coasters. I hate the kiddie-sized ones. Not fun.

As for the garden. It called for patience and communication. The rain stopped, the ground dried, I asked lots of questions, things got fixed and at last it's starting to look like a garden and a refuge. The port-a-potty in my front yard will disappear some time this week. The pile of mulch is dwindling in my driveway and a day is near when I will be able to park there again.

Tomorrow, I start my first infusion of immunotherapy and I will even get used to that and look for the blessing in moving slower, sitting on the back deck and noticing things in more detail. I'm over spending time wondering how to get to any particular place. Instead, I'm going to let the river carry me and trust that the distant shore holds something fun. More adventures to follow.

AUTHOR NOTES - MICHAEL ANDERLE

JUNE 21, 2021

Thank you for not only reading this story but these author notes in the back as well!

With COVID, we (along with the rest of the world) have not been traveling. Therefore, one of the situations that occurred fairly often in the past when we traveled for business six or more times a year was the desire for *American* food.

I don't mean burgers; you can practically get those anywhere I've ever traveled. Although, you might be surprised (I certainly was) that the burgers in the UK might not be what you are expecting.

Forewarned is forearmed.

One of the burgers I had while there was very American, one was more a burger-crumble with a LOT of onion mixed in.

Right now, I am in Cabo San Lucas (vaccinated about three months ago) and will be taking the COVID test before coming back in a couple of days. If there is ANYTHING that makes me pause about travel, it's the test.

I hate it.

This will be my second time, and unfortunately, I know what is awaiting me in a couple of hours. Pain and discomfort. Yuck.

My wife and I live in Henderson, NV, about twenty-five minutes from the Las Vegas Strip. One of the things I love about where we live is the huge selection of restaurants. It is rare when I can't find something I want to eat in town.

In Cabo, you can eat steak, seafood, Mexican, and Italian all day long and never miss a beat. There are two (2) passable Chinese restaurants, but they are pretty far apart, so unless you are either in the Pueblo Bonito (Sunset Beach) or near Palmilla, you are out of luck.

If you know of something other than Chin's (Palmilla), please let me know. While I can cook, I haven't figured out how to cook fried rice the way I enjoy it.

The only BBQ place shut down during COVID, I think.

So, until we acquire our house here in Cabo, I can't make some of the food I'm familiar with down here, including chili, chicken-fried steak, and other goodies I miss.

While I don't write Westerns, I completely understand the old adage "the way to a man's heart is through his stomach."

Now, I just need to get my wife to stop HATING the smell of chili and help me figure out my mom's recipe.

Nah, she already has my heart…and hates the smell. ;-)

Take care of yourself, enjoy your week or weekend, and talk to you in the next book!

Ad Aeternitatem,

Michael Anderle

WAKING MAGIC

Solve a murder, save her mother, and stop the apocalypse?

What would you do when elves ask you to investigate a prince's murder and you didn't even know elves, or magic, was real?

Meet Leira Berens, Austin homicide detective who's good at what she does – track down the bad guys and lock them away.

Which is why the elves want her to solve this murder – fast. It's not just about tracking down the killer and bringing them to justice. It's about saving the world!

If you're looking for a heroine who prefers fighting to flirting, check out The Leira Chronicles today!

<u>**AVAILABLE ON AMAZON AND IN KINDLE UNLIMITED!**</u>

OTHER SERIES IN THE ORICERAN UNIVERSE

JOIN THE ORICERAN UNIVERSE FAN GROUP ON FACEBOOK!

BOOKS BY MICHAEL ANDERLE

Sign up for the LMBPN email list to be notified of new releases and special deals!

https://lmbpn.com/email/

For a complete list of books by Michael Anderle, please visit:

www.lmbpn.com/ma-books/

CONNECT WITH THE AUTHORS

Martha Carr Social

Website: http://www.marthacarr.com

Facebook: https://www.facebook.com/groups/MarthaCarrFans/

Michael Anderle Social

Website: http://lmbpn.com

Email List: http://lmbpn.com/email/

Social Media:

https://www.facebook.com/LMBPNPublishing

https://twitter.com/MichaelAnderle

https://www.instagram.com/lmbpn_publishing/

https://www.bookbub.com/authors/michael-anderle